The Young Widow's Courage

a Victorian romance saga

HOPE DAWSON

Copyright © 2024, Hope Dawson
All rights reserved.

First published worldwide
on Amazon Kindle,
in April 2024.

This paperback edition first published
in Great Britain in 2024.

ISBN: 9798323197613

This novel is a work of fiction. The characters, names, places, events and incidents in it are entirely the work of the author's imagination or used in a fictitious manner. Any resemblance or similarity to actual persons, living or dead, events or places is entirely coincidental.

No part of this work may be reproduced, stored in a retrieval system, or transmitted, in any form or by any means, without the prior permission of the author and the publisher.

www.hopedawson.com

This story is part of
The Victorian Orphans Trilogy

Book 1
The Courtesan's Maid

Book 2
The Ragged Slum Princess

Book 3
An English Governess in Paris

Book 4
The Young Widow's Courage

Chapter One

Madeleine was pulled out of her dark and dreamless sleep by the hushed sounds of curtains being drawn. Pale morning light filtered through her still-closed eyelids as her maid Mary moved quietly around the bedroom.

"Good morning, ma'am," the young girl said softly. "Would you like me to help you get dressed or brush your hair this morning?"

With a resigned sigh, Madeleine forced her eyes open, squinting against the brightness. "No, thank you, Mary. I can manage."

"Very well, ma'am. Breakfast will be ready for you downstairs."

The maid bobbed a quick curtsy and left the room as Madeleine sat up, the last wisps of sleep leaving her. She looked at the portrait of her late husband that hung on the far wall.

"Good morning, my dear Benjamin," she whispered.

Six months it had been since a sudden illness had stolen him from her. Madeleine didn't think she would ever get used to waking up alone. She missed his comforting presence beside her in bed, as well as the warm smile he always greeted her with each morning, from the moment he laid eyes on her.

Now, all she had left was his image on the wall. It was a poor substitute for the man himself, but it was better than nothing.

After heaving herself out of the empty bed, she washed her face and hands at the washbasin in the room. Then, she dressed methodically, donning each piece of her mourning clothes slowly.

She hadn't worn anything but black since the day Ben had died. Her old colourful gowns hung abandoned at the back of her wardrobe. Looking at them always sent a pang of raw pain through her heart. Because those dresses reminded her of happier times.

Times that would never come again.

Perhaps I ought to give them away, she thought not for the first time. Closing the wardrobe and the memories it held, she sat down in front of the mirror on her dressing table to brush her hair. Her movements were effortless and mechanical, but she tried her hardest to focus on what she was doing nonetheless.

Because she knew that if she let her mind wander, she would imagine seeing Benjamin behind her in the mirror – admiring her and telling her how beautiful she was.

With a final glance at her own reflection, Madeleine set the brush down and smoothed back any stray wisps from her simple chignon. She stood, straightened her dress and braced herself for the day ahead.

No use in dwelling on the past, she told herself. Not when so many other people depended upon her.

Squaring her shoulders, she left the bedroom and made her way down the grand staircase, running her hand along the smooth mahogany bannister.

As she approached the door to the dining room, Madeleine dreaded setting foot in the place that was filled with so many memories of festive meals and happy moments with her dear Benjamin. But then she heard the soft clatter of dishes being set out, accompanied by her cousin Charlotte's lively hum.

Dear Charlotte, unfailingly the first to rise and greet each new day with cheerful vigour. Nothing in the world could get between Charlotte and a good breakfast. Or any other meal for that matter.

"Good morning, Maddie," her cousin smiled when Madeleine entered the room. "Did you sleep well?"

"As well as can be expected," Madeleine shrugged. "Although no matter how much time I spend in bed, I keep feeling utterly drained."

The two women took their seat at the table. "That's only normal, dear," Charlotte spoke, placing a soothing hand over Madeleine's. "These things take time."

Charlotte unfolded her napkin and eyed the various dishes on the table. "But it's important that you keep your strength up. You really ought to eat more at breakfast."

While her cousin helped herself to a decent serving of bacon and eggs, Madeleine limited herself to some porridge. Charlotte was right, she supposed. But most mornings she could hardly stand the idea of food.

"Where's Ellie?" she asked.

At that moment, heavy footsteps could be heard stomping down the stairs. Seconds later, Madeleine's seventeen-year-old daughter came whirling into the dining room, wearing the usual moody scowl on her face.

"Morning, Mother," the girl mumbled before dropping unceremoniously onto her chair. "Morning, Charlotte."

"Good morning, my sweet angel," Charlotte replied brightly. "You're looking lovely again today. Sleep well last night?"

"Like the dead," Ellie replied grimly.

Madeleine winced. "I wish you wouldn't say such things, Ellie. Sometimes I wonder if you do it on purpose."

"Sorry, Mother." She ladled some porridge into her breakfast bowl and pulled a face. "Disgusting. Much too lumpy."

Madeleine made a bristling noise. But before she could say anything, Charlotte chuckled. "Why, Ellie dearest. Only yesterday you were complaining that Mrs Dobbs makes the porridge too thin and watery."

"Don't waste your breath, cousin," Madeleine said. "Ellie's merely being contrarian."

"I am not," the girl shot back angrily. "I just don't happen to like this porridge, that's all."

"Try the shirred eggs instead," Charlotte said quickly in an obvious attempt to defuse the situation. "They're rather divine with some buttered toast."

Madeleine pressed a hand to her temple, feeling the beginnings of a headache. Their breakfasts often proceeded this way lately, with Ellie finding fault in everything and Madeleine losing her patience. She missed the days when her daughter was still her sweet, cheerful girl. Now, it seemed they could barely hold a civil conversation.

"Maddie," Charlotte chirped happily. "Do tell us what your day will look like. Any interesting business at the factory?"

"Much the same as always, I'm afraid. More paperwork, more ledgers to balance. I confess I don't look forward to it." She hesitated, staring down at the food she had barely touched. "I know so little of how to run the business. I still feel quite adrift."

Charlotte reached over and gave her hand an encouraging squeeze. "Nonsense. You're doing wonderfully for having been thrown into these circumstances. Benjamin would have been proud."

Would he, Madeleine wondered? Or would he be disappointed in how she was struggling to fill his shoes? She managed a thin smile and pushed her porridge around with her spoon.

"And what about you two?" she sighed. "What are your plans for the day?"

"French lessons this morning," Charlotte replied. "And then some time at the piano in the afternoon."

"I hate French," Ellie grumbled. "And I despise the piano. I'd sooner set fire to that infernal instrument than be forced to practise more scales again."

"Eleanor Fletcher," Madeleine admonished. "Mind your tongue, young lady."

Ellie rolled her eyes. "Yes, Mother. Sorry, Mother. May I be excused?" Without waiting for an answer, she shoved back from the table and flounced out of the room.

"I swear that girl's become impossible," Madeleine seethed.

"She's still sad about Benjamin, dear. Just like you," Charlotte soothed. "We must be patient."

"I try, Charlotte, I do. But she is so stubborn, so angry all the time. I feel I hardly know her anymore."

Madeleine exhaled, feeling exhausted even though the day had barely begun. She dabbed her mouth with her napkin and stood.

"I should be off. The carriage will be waiting."

Charlotte rose to her feet as well and gave Madeleine a fond hug. "Try not to worry too much, dear. Time heals all wounds, they say."

"Let's hope so." Madeleine sighed, suppressing a sudden urge to burst out in tears. "I will see you this evening."

She hurried from the dining room before she lost her composure entirely. In the foyer she paused to collect herself as she took a few deep breaths. Crying wouldn't change anything. She had to be strong.

Once the threat of tears had passed, she stepped outside.

"Morning, Mrs Fletcher," their broad-shouldered coachman nodded.

"Good morning, Bill."

She let him help her into the carriage and then settled onto the leather seat, arranging her skirts around her.

After Bill had climbed onto his box and expertly guided his trusted old mare forward, Madeleine gazed out at the passing city scenery.

She wished she knew how to reach Ellie, how to bridge the painful gap that had formed between them. Her daughter was so quick to take offence these days, rejecting any attempts at polite conversation.

Madeleine missed the playful, affectionate child Ellie used to be. But she was nearly a woman now, and one whom Madeleine understood less with each passing day.

If only Benjamin were here.

He'd always had a knack for getting through to Ellie, for making her laugh and letting her see reason when she was being stubborn or difficult. Without him, Madeleine felt lost.

When the carriage rounded a bend, Madeleine's thoughts shifted to her other pressing worry: the factory. Its tall brick chimneys came into view, reaching up to the sky like giant smudged fingers.

This was her late husband's legacy, now hers to manage. But she still felt like an imposter in Benjamin's office.

As they pulled up to the tall iron gates, Madeleine took a deep breath to steady her nerves. She had to at least pretend to feel confident in front of the workers.

"Come back for me at lunchtime if you would, Bill," she said as the coachman handed her down.

"Of course, ma'am."

Bravely, Madeleine lifted her chin and strode towards the entrance gate. Despite her outward assurance, she trembled inside.

She prayed that she would succeed in getting through another day without embarrassing either herself or Benjamin's memory too badly. With her limited knowledge, she never felt more out of her depth than when she was immersed in the endless numbers and minute details that were now her responsibility.

Chapter Two

Stepping through the iron gates of the Fletcher & Redhurst Steam Engine Works, Madeleine's low heels clicked on the cobblestones. The familiar cacophony of machinery and men's voices washed over her as she made her way across the factory yard.

Though she had been here nearly every day for the past six months, she still felt like an uninvited guest in this masculine domain that had once been her husband's territory.

Benjamin had loved this place and he had devoted his entire life to it. Madeleine wished she shared even a fraction of his knowledge and competence.

As she walked by, workers tipped their caps or nodded at her. "Mornin', ma'am," several of them mumbled politely. She returned their greetings, hoping her smile concealed her discomfort.

She knew how uncommon her situation was: a woman running the largest steam engine factory in Sheffield. Her status as co-owner and manager had become the talk of the town over the past months.

So far her own workers had treated her with respect, but she sensed their curiosity and uncertainty. Did they doubt her abilities? Were they questioning if she deserved her position?

She couldn't blame them for wondering if a grieving widow was fit to lead. Their livelihoods depended on the factory's success.

How I wish I could read their minds sometimes.

But then again, she realised all too well that she might not like what she found there. For now, all she could do was prove herself worthy of her late husband's legacy, one day at a time.

Upon entering the main factory building, Madeleine was met with a blast of oppressive heat. The furnaces roared, while the tang of hot metal assaulted her senses. Men in aprons and rolled up sleeves operated complicated machinery that hissed, clattered and groaned with purposeful rhythm.

Madeleine watched and admired how the men all seemed to move with practised expertise, confident in their various tasks as they crafted the intricate parts that made up the steam engines produced on this very site.

In contrast, she felt utterly out of place.

The strange sights and smells baffled her mind and the din made her want to cover her ears. She was like a trespasser wandering around in a foreign world. Her dark gown and feminine gloves marked her as an intruder in an industrial beehive that seemed a universe away from her own refined upbringing.

"Madeleine," someone called out to her. Even without looking she knew who it was. Only one man was brazen enough to call her by her first name in front of everyone in the factory: Ashton Redhurst.

The Chief Engineer and co-owner of the Fletcher & Redhurst Steam Engine Works had been the bane of Madeleine's existence over the past few months.

"I'm so glad you chose to grace us with your presence today," he smirked. A small group of engineers stood around him. Some of them grinned along with him, while others stared at their feet, seemingly embarrassed.

"I fail to see what's so special about my presence," Madeleine replied as she approached the group of men. "After all, I've been coming to work nearly every day of the week since Mr Fletcher passed away."

"Indeed you have, my dear," Ashton smiled. "And a very brave thing it is, too. Most women in your position would resign themselves to quietly mourning the loss of their husband from the comfort of their home."

"My decision is my own, Mr Redhurst. And I don't care whether you approve of it or not. Now, if you will excuse me, there's probably a pile of paperwork waiting for me at the office.

Gentlemen." She nodded at the engineers and continued on her way.

Ashton rolled up the blueprints he had been holding and hurried after her. "Can you spare a moment for your business partner, Madeleine?"

"Of course," she said, trying not to let his condescending tone irritate her. "Though if it's about that steam turbine of yours, then I'm afraid my answer remains the same."

Grumbling a muttered curse, he placed a hand on her arm, forcing her to stop. "Why do you refuse to invest in the future of this company?" he demanded gruffly.

"We've had this conversation before, Ashton," she replied as she shook her arm free. "I'm not convinced this wild idea of yours is where we should focus our resources. Not when our piston engines have been serving us so well for many years."

Wishing he would drop the matter, she started walking towards her office again. But like a stubborn bulldog, he was right on her heels.

"We need to look to the future, Madeleine. Steam turbines will be more powerful and more efficient. Not that I'd expect a woman to understand such complexities."

"Even my feeble female brain can see the advantages," she bit back. "But the truth is we can't afford to bear the risk at the moment."

"Then find us more money. Look for investors. Sway them with your feminine wiles."

Madeleine entered her office, resisting the urge to slam the door in Ashton's face. "How am I supposed to persuade any potential investors when you don't have a working prototype yet?"

"That's merely a matter of time," he said, brandishing his rolled-up blueprints at her. "Honestly, Madeleine, I'm deeply disappointed you're being so close-minded about this."

"Ashton—"

"If you insist on clinging to the past, then this company will crumble. Fletcher & Redhurst will be left behind, while our competitors surge ahead."

Madeleine opened her mouth to issue a scalding retort when her assistant Robert Adams knocked and popped his head round the door.

"Pardon the interruption, Mrs Fletcher, Mr Redhurst," the young clerk said with blushing cheeks. "But Mr Wainwright is waiting just outside. He says he would like to have a quick word with you, ma'am."

"Very well, send him in," Madeleine nodded. She was rather fond of Jack Wainwright, one of their veteran foremen. He was a plainspoken Yorkshireman and a doting father to his son, Stuart. The young man had just secured an engineering apprenticeship last month and Jack was terribly proud.

The foreman entered, turning and twisting his cap in his rough hands. "Ma'am. Sir. Apologies for disturbing you unannounced like this."

"No need to apologise, Mr Wainwright," Madeleine said gently. "What seems to be the trouble?"

The stout man shifted on his feet. "Well now, it's a bit awkward, you see. The lads... that is, some of the men on the factory floor... They've got concerns, and they asked me to have a word with you about it."

"Concerns?" Ashton snapped impatiently. "What sort of concerns? Out with it, man. We haven't got all day."

Jack's weathered face flushed red. "Yes, well... Begging your pardon, Mrs Fletcher, but there's been some talk going round. Worried whispers and the like. The men are concerned that with Mr Fletcher gone, God rest him, the business may soon run into hardship. There's fears about wages not being paid if money gets scarce."

Madeleine's chest tightened. Rumours like this were dangerous. If left unchecked, they could spread like wildfire.

"Please assure the men they have no cause for concern, Mr Wainwright," she replied, trying to put as much confidence in her voice as possible. "My husband left the finances in excellent shape. No wages will go unpaid on my watch."

Jack nodded, relief evident on his open face. "That's good to hear, ma'am. I'll let the lads know there's naught to worry about."

Ashton, however, was not appeased. "This is preposterous," he fumed. "Who's been spreading this disgraceful gossip? I want their names."

"No one in particular, Mr Redhurst, sir," Jack said, nervously fiddling with his cap. "You know how these things go. It's just talk, that's all."

"Just talk, eh?" Ashton grumbled. "Perhaps it was you who started it. Ungrateful wretches, the lot of you."

"Ashton," Madeleine said sharply. "There's no need for such language. Mr Wainwright is merely the messenger."

"That's right, ma'am," the foreman nodded, shifting his weight. "The men are worried. We all have families to support and mouths to feed. Some a few more than others. And they chose me to talk to you about it."

"Well, you've had your say," Ashton barked. "And you've been given reassurances. Now get back to your station, man."

"Yes, sir. Thank you, sir." Putting his cap back on, Jack turned to leave the office.

"And tell your men," Ashton added darkly, "that if I catch anyone causing trouble, I will personally give them the boot."

"You will do no such thing, Ashton," Madeleine replied hotly. "People are afraid for the welfare of their family. Making idle threats won't improve the situation."

"There was nothing idle about my threat," Ashton muttered.

"That's enough," Madeleine said fiercely. "Mr Wainwright, please ignore Mr Redhurst's remarks. As long as I control half of this company, no one will lose their position simply because of some unfounded gossip."

The foreman smiled awkwardly, clearly uncomfortable about being caught in the middle of an argument between his two employers. "Thank you, ma'am. Good day to you both."

The foreman was barely out of earshot when Ashton rounded on Madeleine. "You're far too soft with them. Weakness will undermine your authority – mark my words. A woman in your position must be firm and uncompromising."

Madeleine bristled, stung by the contempt in his tone. "Benjamin never treated our employees so callously, Ashton. And yet, he had their utmost respect. A little compassion often yields better results than an iron fist."

"Soft hearts don't build steam engines, my dear," he scoffed. "Even your husband knew that. It's a pity Benjamin didn't pass on some of his business talents when he left you half of the company."

Madeleine reeled, feeling as if he had struck her across the face. She longed to give him a piece of her mind, and unleash the torrent of words boiling up inside her. But she bit her tongue until the urge passed.

"If that'll be all, Ashton," she said icily. "I have work to attend to. Do let me know when you've made any progress on your prototype."

"Of course," he replied starchily before leaving.

Alone in the quiet of her office, Madeleine let out a long, shaky breath. Their confrontation had left her rattled.

She knew that Ashton would never accept her as an equal partner. At every turn, he seemed determined to undermine her and remind her this wasn't a woman's place. But his hostility also added to her own nagging self-doubts.

Could she really do this? Could she fill her late husband's shoes and earn the respect of the workers? Ashton clearly thought her unfit for the task.

Shaking her head, Madeleine straightened her shoulders. She refused to let Ashton intimidate her into giving up. Too many livelihoods depended on the company's success.

Chapter Three

Madeleine sat at the large oak desk in her husband's old office. A bright shaft of sunlight came streaming in through the windows, illuminating the columns of numbers in the ledgers spread out before her.

Across from her was Mr Underwood, the factory's senior accountant. His spectacles were perched on the tip of his nose as he pointed out various figures and totals, his voice low and apologetic.

"As you can see, Mrs Fletcher, profits from the previous quarter are down nearly fifteen percent from this time last year. And I'm afraid our operating costs have continued to rise, what with the repairs needed for the new equipment and the increased wages after we took on more workers for the second shift."

Madeleine nodded, trying to keep her expression neutral as a growing sense of disappointment began to take hold of her.

"I'm surprised by that big drop in our profits, Mr Underwood," she said. "I was under the impression we weren't doing too badly."

The grey-haired accountant nervously wrung his hands. "Our finances are still relatively sound, ma'am... For now anyway. But there appears to be a downward trend that – in my personal opinion at least – would merit some concern."

Leaning closer, he pointed a scrawny finger at one of the columns in the ledger. "For instance, if you were to direct your attention to these numbers here–"

"Yes, I've seen them, Mr Underwood. And I must say they make for unpleasant reading."

"Of course, ma'am." He hastily pulled back his hand from the ledger, seemingly afraid to cause offence. "Unfortunately, numbers don't lie."

Madeleine let her eyes dwell over the full length of the column and shook her head. When Benjamin was alive, he had made running the factory look so effortless. He understood the complex world of business and finance. Without him, she was floundering and struggling to keep things afloat.

"Do you have any suggestions, Mr Underwood?" she asked, hoping the experienced bookkeeper might provide the guidance she desperately needed.

The accountant frowned and licked his thin, dry lips. "I fear the only solution is to increase our capital, Mrs Fletcher. Attract new investors, take out further loans from the bank. It is the only way to purchase the raw materials and equipment needed to increase production."

Madeleine sighed, the figures in the ledgers blurring before her eyes. Benjamin had warned her about becoming overextended with loans and credit. But what other choice did she have?

And despite her personal feelings about Ashton and his odiously rude manners, she knew her business partner had a point: Fletcher & Redhurst needed to innovate in order to secure their future.

But innovation came at a price. A price they were currently unable to pay, according to what Mr Underwood had been telling her.

Madeleine's head was beginning to ache. She closed the ledger, hiding the numbers that seemed to accuse her. Surely, those figures bore evidence of her own inadequacy? What had made Benjamin think she would be able to handle this?

"Thank you for the report, Mr Underwood," she said wearily. "I shall reflect on what must be done."

"Of course, Mrs Fletcher." The accountant seemed relieved to be dismissed from the unsettling task of informing her about the company's financial troubles. He gathered his papers and showed himself out.

Alone again, Madeleine pressed her fingers to her temples, trying to massage away the tension behind her eyes. She glanced at the small portrait of Benjamin on the corner of the desk, his handsome features and warm brown eyes so achingly familiar.

"Oh, Benjamin," she murmured. "I wish you were here to advise me. I feel so lost without you."

She gazed out the window, watching the smoke rise from the towering chimney stacks that dominated the city's skyline. The investors she needed were out there somewhere. If only she could find them, these men with the capital to pour into the factory's future.

But even then, how would she convince them that a widow was capable of securing that future? She felt like a rudderless ship in a storm, so far out of her depth.

A knock at the door drew her from her brooding.

Her assistant Robert entered. "Sorry to bother you, Mrs Fletcher. But your coachman has arrived at the gate."

Madeleine started. Midday already? Had she really been wrestling with those infernal ledgers for hours?

"Thank you, Robert. Please tell Bill I'll be right out."

Yes, a change of scenery would do her good. She was unlikely to find any answers by remaining here, surrounded by people who doubted her abilities.

Donning her hat and coat, Madeleine stepped outside into the bustling yard. The moment he spotted her, Bill climbed down from his box seat atop the carriage. Tipping his hat, he held open the door for her.

"Where to, ma'am? Home for lunch?"

"Not just yet, Bill. Let's stop at the cemetery first."

Visiting Benjamin's grave would settle her mind. Some peaceful tranquillity was just what she needed to face the challenges ahead.

Bill nodded understandingly as he helped her into the carriage. Soon they were rolling through the crowded streets of soot-stained Sheffield, leaving behind the weight of the responsibilities Madeleine wanted to escape from, if only temporarily.

After a while, they arrived at the iron gates of the cemetery, where Bill brought the carriage to a gentle halt. Madeleine gathered her skirts and stepped out.

"I shan't be long, Bill."

"Take as much time as you need, ma'am," the soft-spoken coachman replied with a short nod.

When Madeleine entered the cemetery, she was grateful to find it completely deserted. Only an elderly groundskeeper moved amongst the headstones, raking leaves and tending the simple landscaping.

She wound her way along the gravel path, dappled in sunlight and shadow, until she reached the slab of granite engraved with her husband's name.

Beneath it lay the body of her dear Benjamin, the faithful companion who had shared her hopes and dreams for nearly two decades.

"Hello, my love," she whispered into the air. "It's me again. I've come to ask for your guidance."

Kneeling at the base of his grave, she tenderly brushed away a few leaves from the cold, hard stone. There were days when Benjamin's loss felt as raw as the hour she had clutched his lifeless hand, begging him not to leave her.

Here at his final resting place however, she could almost imagine him sitting by her side, his eyes gentle and full of wisdom.

Madeleine poured out her doubts and worries, speaking of the dwindling profits and the multitude of accounting figures that made no sense to her.

"I won't lie to you, my love," she said. "It's hard for me to fill the void you created at the factory when you–"

Her voice faltered and a solitary tear ran down the side of her face.

"Meanwhile," she continued after a long sigh, "Ashton keeps badgering me about his turbine project and how I need to find new investors. But I don't know what the right choice is."

She caressed the engraved letters of her late husband's name. "You understood these things so much better, my sweet Benjamin. And the men respected you. But me? I can't lead them nearly half as well as you did."

Her voice dropped. "Some days I'm tempted to simply sell my share to Ashton. Let him take control and sort it all out. But I gave you my word I wouldn't do that."

Fresh tears slipped down her cheeks. "On your deathbed you made me promise not to relinquish my stake. You said you had confidence in me, that I was stronger than I knew."

She remembered how Benjamin had clasped her hand in his wasted one, his eyes burning with conviction despite his failing body.

"Ashton Redhurst is a brilliant engineer, but a poor administrator," he had rasped. "You have better sense, Maddie. A sharper instinct for people. Promise me you will not hand the reins to him."

And she had promised, half-convinced his words were the fevered ramblings of a dying man. But a promise made was a promise kept. And so she would not go back on her word – no matter how daunting the challenges might seem.

"And then there's our Ellie..." Madeleine's breath hitched. "Oh, Benjamin, I've lost her too. She and I have grown so far apart since you've been gone. She blames me, I know she does. Our home is fractured without you."

Lowering her head, she let her tears fall. She had been so strong these past months, carrying on through her grief and doubt.

But here, in this quiet sanctuary, she allowed herself to release the pent-up emotion that she usually kept locked away, hiding it from the world as if mourning the loss of a loved one was a thing to be ashamed of.

When the tears finally passed, she felt cleansed. Breathing in the cool, earth-scented air, she stood up and brushed the grass from her dress.

"I could probably do with a miracle, my darling," she spoke softly at Benjamin's grave. "So please put in a good word for me, up there in heaven."

Slowly, Madeleine turned and made her way back through the tranquil cemetery. At the gates, Bill was waiting patiently for her while his horse nibbled lazily at a few tufts of grass lining the street. The stolid coachman helped her into the carriage and then they drove back home.

When Madeleine arrived at her elegant townhouse, she found Charlotte in the parlour embroidering a handkerchief.

"There you are, dear," her cousin smiled, peering at Madeleine over her spectacles. "How was your day?"

"Rather trying, I'm afraid," Madeleine replied with a weary sigh as she settled onto the settee.

Charlotte set aside her embroidery. "Oh dear, what happened?"

As Madeleine recounted her argument with Ashton Redhurst and her meeting with Mr Underwood, Charlotte listened attentively, clucking her tongue in sympathy.

"It all sounds thoroughly unpleasant to me," her cousin said. "Shall we go and sit outside in the garden for a while? The fresh air might do you good. I'll ask Mrs Dobbs to bring out some tea and biscuits."

"No, I'm fine, thank you. I stopped by Ben's grave on my way home."

"Did it help to clear your mind?"

"Somewhat, yes," Madeleine nodded. She stared down at her folded hands. "I just wish I had Benjamin's wisdom to guide me. He always knew exactly what to do."

Charlotte leaned over and patted her arm. "There now, you mustn't be so hard on yourself. No one expects you to be like your husband, God rest his soul. But you're stronger than you realise, dear. Why, when we were girls, who was always the bold adventurer leading our youthful explorations?"

Despite herself, Madeleine chuckled at the memory.

"Ah, there's that pretty smile I love to see," her cousin said. "You'll figure this out, don't you worry. On that note, here's something else that ought to lift your mood."

She retrieved an elegant cream-coloured envelope from the side table and presented it to Madeleine with a playful flourish.

"This arrived for you while you were out. It's from Sir John."

Surprised, Madeleine opened the envelope and examined its contents. Sir John Bernard Wilton was a local squire, and long-time friend of the family. A kind-natured fatherly figure, he had always been very fond of Benjamin.

"It's an invitation," Madeleine said. "To a business salon, as Sir John calls it. He's gathering a group of business owners, manufacturers and investors for an informal get-together."

Charlotte's round face lit up with excitement. "How wonderful."

"I shouldn't accept," Madeleine sighed. "I'm still in mourning, and hardly fit for socialising."

"Stuff and nonsense," Charlotte huffed. "This salon is the perfect chance to demonstrate your competence amongst potential investors. You simply must go."

Madeleine hesitated. As a widow, attending a social function seemed inappropriate. Yet she knew that securing financial backing was critical for the company.

Sensing her reluctance, Charlotte grasped her hands. "You cannot hide yourself away forever, Maddie. Benjamin would want you to embrace life again."

"You may be right," Madeleine conceded slowly. "I cannot let fear stop me. This could prove to be important for the factory."

Charlotte smiled. "That's the spirit. I know you'll wear black, of course. But perhaps we could add that emerald necklace Benjamin gifted you. The one that brings out your eyes so beautifully."

Madeleine allowed her cousin's cheerful chatter to flow over her as she reread the invitation one more time. She hadn't socialised publicly since going into mourning many months ago. The prospect of mingling amongst strangers, all men at that, was deeply unsettling. Their scrutiny was sure to be critical, possibly even disapproving.

But hadn't she just prayed for a miracle at Benjamin's grave? Perhaps that's what this was: her best chance of saving the company her beloved husband had poured his heart and soul into.

She owed it to him to gather her courage and step back into society's spotlight, no matter how harsh its glare.

Chapter Four

With a fluttering heart, Madeleine stood on the stone steps before the Georgian façade of Sir John's impressive city residence. Nerves caused her stomach to twist into a knot as she reached for the polished brass door knocker. When she struck it against the plate, the sound echoed through the quiet street.

Moments later, the black lacquered door swung open and a liveried footman appeared. "Ma'am?"

"I'm Mrs Fletcher. Sir John invited me to his business salon."

With a polite nod, the footman stepped aside and bid her to enter the grand hallway. "Please wait here, Mrs Fletcher. I shall inform Sir John of your arrival."

Fighting the urge to fidget with her gloved hands while she waited, Madeleine let her eyes roam over the entrance hall. Sir John was one of those rare individuals who possessed great wealth as well as exquisite taste. And even in this hall, proof of both was on display.

A brief smile flickered across Madeleine's face as she remembered the numerous times she and Benjamin had been guests at Sir John's social events. Some were grand affairs, but there had also been many smaller, more personal gatherings – dinners, card games, and conversations between friends.

"Madeleine, my dear." Sir John's voice preceded the man himself into the hall.

Out of respect for his title, Madeleine bobbed a quick curtsy as he approached her with outstretched hands.

"Sir John, thank you for your invitation."

"The pleasure is all mine, child." He clasped her hands and smiled affectionately. "Come, let's have a quick private word. Before we throw you to the lions."

He led Madeleine to a small yet well-appointed parlour, where he gestured her towards a pair of armchairs. Once seated, he peered at her with concern in his ruddy features.

"Tell me – truthfully now – how are you these days?"

Madeleine stared down at her hands in her lap. "Some days are more difficult than others. I try to focus on caring for Ellie and managing the factory, but..."

"You miss him terribly," Sir John finished gently. At Madeleine's small nod, he sighed. "I understand all too well, my dear. When I lost my own beloved Catherine, I thought my world would end. We had shared so much together. Without her, I was utterly lost."

Madeleine looked up, eyes glistening. "Does it ever become any easier, Sir John?"

"Yes and no. You never stop loving them, or longing for them. But in time, the pain grows more bearable. You find yourself able to smile again and to take comfort in the happy memories."

Madeleine let out a shuddering breath. Perhaps one day her grief would stop weighing so heavy. For now, she could only cling to hope.

"Forgive me, Sir John," she said, dabbing at her eyes with a handkerchief. "You didn't invite me here to dwell on sad matters."

"There is nothing to forgive, my dear," he answered kindly. "I'm perfectly aware of the depth of your sorrow. But it does me good to see you out and about. So what do you say: are you feeling ready to join the other guests?"

"As ready as I'll ever be, I suppose." Madeleine twisted her handkerchief nervously. "Although I'm afraid I shall feel quite out of place."

"Whatever for?"

"Because I'm the odd one out amongst your guests."

Sir John waved a dismissive hand. "Nonsense, my dear. All those I've invited today are business owners, entrepreneurs, and people of means – just as you are."

"But I'll be the only woman present."

"That hardly makes you eccentric," he chuckled. "Rather, it makes you a pioneer. If you ask me, you're the normal one. I'm the oddity, truth be told."

Madeleine looked at him quizzically. "You, Sir John? What do you mean?"

"A member of the landed gentry taking an active interest in trade and business?" He let out a short laugh. "Why, some of my peers consider it most uncouth. But I say fiddlesticks to that. The old ways are dead and gone. A man like me ought to use his position and wealth to foster new industries and help others get ahead."

He reached over and patted her hand encouragingly. "So you see, my dear, you have nothing to feel self-conscious about. Together, we shall show them the way of the future."

Madeleine smiled, feeling bolstered by the older man's words. "You have a generous spirit, Sir John. I am honoured you would share your wisdom and connections so freely."

"Think nothing of it, my dear," he said, rising slowly to his feet. "Now, enough talk. We mustn't keep the wolves waiting too long, eh?"

He offered Madeleine his arm. With a deep, bracing breath, she stood and took it, allowing him to escort her from the cosy parlour.

"Take heart, Madeleine," he murmured as they approached the grand salon. "I have every faith that by the end of this afternoon, your company's prospects shall be much brighter indeed."

She nodded and gave his arm a grateful squeeze. Then, together, they made their entrance.

"Gentlemen," Sir John announced to the room. "This is Mrs Fletcher. Of the Fletcher & Redhurst Steam Engine Works."

Madeleine kept her chin high, though she felt exposed under the curious stares of those assembled. A few men nodded politely in her direction, while others seemed to ignore her presence altogether. But she also detected disapproval in one or two gentlemen's sideways glances.

Leaning in discreetly, Sir John muttered under his breath, "The wolves don't seem terribly keen today, do they?"

Madeleine had to suppress a nervous laugh. "Perhaps I shall refrain from petting any, lest they bite," she whispered back.

"Quite right, quite right," Sir John chuckled. "Well, no matter. I know just the fellow to introduce you to first. A bit less inclined to bare his teeth, I'd wager."

He steered her toward a gentleman who stood alone near the fireplace, gazing thoughtfully into his glass of brandy. When Madeleine and

Sir John drew nearer, the man looked up and smiled with a keen interest in his eyes.

"Sir John," he said. "Your selection of guests is even better than your choice of brandy." He spoke with an accent that Madeleine recognised as French.

"I am pleased that both are to your liking, my good fellow," Sir John replied. "Mrs Fletcher, allow me to present Mr Pierre Dubois, newly arrived in our fair city from Paris."

"*Enchanté*, Madame Fletcher," Mr Dubois spoke, bowing smoothly over her hand.

"How do you do?" Madeleine said. "Sheffield is a long way from Paris, Monsieur. What brings you here?"

"The prospect of doing business, Madame. Trade and commerce know no boundaries."

"Well, you've come to the right place, my good man," Sir John beamed. "Plenty of opportunity here. If you'll both excuse me – I need to mingle with my other guests for a bit, before they all grow envious of you."

The squire slipped away, leaving Madeleine and Mr Dubois to continue their conversation.

"Paris must be quite different from smoky Sheffield," Madeleine said. Studying his face, she thought his smile seemed genuine enough.

"Quite different, yes. Though both have their charms," he replied. "As a matter of fact, my business endeavours have brought me to your shores several times already."

"Have they? How interesting. What are your impressions of England, Monsieur?"

"The climate and the food always take some adjusting to," he chuckled. "But I find the English most hospitable. Some more than others, obviously."

She realised they were only making meaningless small talk, but it helped her to relax. And she had to admit Mr Dubois was easy to talk to. His calm and open manner made her feel at ease.

"Will you be staying long this time?" she asked.

"Longer than usual, I hope. I must confess I've grown a bit weary of Paris lately." A hint of sadness crossed his face as he gazed down at his brandy. But then he shook his head and smiled at her.

"Sir John mentioned that you own a steam engine factory?" he enquired.

"Half of it anyway. I inherited my late husband's share," Madeleine answered, her black dress rendering further explanation unnecessary.

"My condolences, Madame. Has your loss been a recent event?"

"Just over six months now."

Mr Dubois' expression turned thoughtful. "And how are you finding the transition to business ownership? I imagine it cannot be easy."

Madeleine hesitated, uncertain how much of her struggles she could share with him. "There are the usual challenges, to be sure. My business partner handles the technical operations, while I focus more on financial matters."

She allowed herself a small, wistful smile. "My late husband felt I had some skill with numbers and accounts."

"I detect a profound strength and grace in you, Madame. In that respect, you remind me of a famous pair of French widows: Madame Clicquot-Ponsardin and Madame Pommery."

"I'm afraid those names only sound vaguely familiar to me."

"You might have seen them on the label of a champagne bottle. Both ladies lost their husbands, and both took over the reins of the business. They became so successful that they revolutionised the entire champagne industry."

"Examples to live up to then," Madeleine quipped. "But you are too generous with your comparison, Monsieur. At the moment, the mere act of trying to balance the books is formidable enough for me."

Mr Dubois smiled sympathetically. "One day at a time, Madame Fletcher. Tell me, what do you hope to gain from this salon today?"

After a pause, Madeleine admitted, "I'm seeking investors. My partner in the business, Mr Redhurst, wishes to develop a new type of engine. But that requires a considerable amount of capital – which we currently don't have."

"What a wonderful coincidence," Mr Dubois replied with a twinkle in his eyes. "Attracting investors happens to be a specialty of mine. If you want, I could speak to a few potential backers on your behalf."

"That would be most kind of you, Monsieur," she said, wanting to trust yet fearing how much she needed his help.

"And in return?" she asked. "What would you want for your assistance?"

"I usually charge a small commission. But only when the financial support of your new investors materialises." As he set down his glass of brandy, a spark of excitement took root in him. "If I were to gather a group of interested parties, would you be willing to give them a tour of your factory?"

"Certainly. But–"

"Splendid. Madame Fletcher, I believe this could be the start of a most fortuitous partnership," Mr Dubois declared energetically.

Madeleine felt the tug of a hopeful smile on her lips. Perhaps Sir John had been right: her prospects were indeed beginning to look brighter.

She and Mr Dubois spent the remainder of the afternoon in deep discussion, hammering out the particulars. The Frenchman's enthusiasm was palpable as ideas and strategies tumbled rapidly from his lips.

And by the time the salon drew to a close, Madeleine felt considerably less burdened than when she had arrived.

"I noticed that the French gentleman seemed to be a good match," Sir John jested when Madeleine went to bid her farewell to their host.

"It would appear so, yes." She blushed slightly, but didn't quite understand why. "We're going to organise a tour of the factory for a group of investors."

"Marvellous," the squire beamed. "May your partnership be a resounding success."

"Thank you, Sir John. And thank you once more for your tremendous support."

"My dear child, if there's anything I can do to help – anything at all – promise me you will let me know."

"I promise," she nodded gratefully.

During her quiet ride home, a peaceful smile lingered on Madeleine's face. Because although she hadn't acquired any real funds yet, she had gained something far more important.

She had found hope.

Chapter Five

Madeleine woke up feeling refreshed after a full night's rest, a rare respite since losing Benjamin. She dressed with extra care, smoothing down her black dress and pinning up her hair. As she descended the stairs, the renewed optimism of the business salon still lingered.

In the sunlit breakfast room, Charlotte was already seated, chatting brightly while spreading jam on her toast. Across from her, Ellie sat scanning the newspaper, looking rather bored.

Normally, Madeleine would have disapproved of someone reading at the table. But she decided to hold her tongue about it just this once. Because if Ellie was reading, then perhaps there was less risk of any bickering for a change.

"Good morning, Maddie darling," Charlotte said cheerfully. "You look well-rested today. I take it Sir John's salon was a success then?"

"It certainly was. I am one step closer to finding new investors."

"Absolutely wonderful," Charlotte chirped happily.

"Investors, eh?" Ellie cut in sullenly without glancing up from her newspaper. "You'd better hope their purses are as deep as their words, Mother."

Before Madeleine could respond to her daughter, her cousin intervened. "Oh hush now, Ellie. Don't ruin your mother's moment."

Turning back to Madeleine, she said, "You'll have to tell us everything, dear. Ellie and I got back so late from the theatre last night, you'd already gone off to bed."

"I know. I waited up for a while, but I was very tired. Sorry. How was the play?"

"Dreadfully boring," Ellie replied from behind her newspaper. "Complete waste of time."

"It wasn't all *that* bad," Charlotte said. "But enough about the theatre. I want to hear all about this successful afternoon of yours. I'm sure everyone at the salon was scrambling to be the first to invest in Fletcher & Redhurst."

"Hardly," Madeleine said. "But I did meet a gentleman who offered to bring a group of potentially interested parties to the factory for a tour."

"Sounds like a smart man to me. Anyone local?"

"Not exactly. Mr Dubois is from Paris, actually."

Ellie looked up from her newspaper with a raised eyebrow. "A Frenchman? You'll want to be on your guard then, Mother. You know what the French are like."

"Eleanor," Charlotte tutted amiably. "That's not a very nice thing to say about someone you've never even met, is it?"

"Mr Dubois seemed a perfectly respectable gentleman, I assure you," Madeleine said, trying to keep her voice calm.

Ellie shrugged and disappeared behind her newspaper again. "Fine. But don't say I didn't warn you, Mother."

Madeleine gave her daughter a measured look before turning back to Charlotte. "Apparently, Mr Dubois is somewhat of an expert in securing investments. He was confident that if we organise a guided tour for the right people, some of them will be keen to invest."

"How exciting," Charlotte beamed. "With this new money coming in, you'll make the factory thrive like never before."

"We're not quite there yet," Madeleine cautioned. "And there are still plenty of things that could go wrong. But I'm hopeful."

Charlotte smiled and patted Madeleine's hand encouragingly. "I have great faith in you, Maddie."

"That's just because you're my cousin," Madeleine chuckled. "You'd have faith in me even if I told you I was going on an expedition to the North Pole."

"Of course I would," Charlotte replied earnestly. "And if you were the one leading the expedition, then I'd join you, too."

The two women giggled, until Ellie suddenly swore in a very unladylike fashion.

"Eleanor Fletcher," Madeleine huffed. "Mind your language, for heaven's sake."

"I'm sorry, Mother," Ellie said hotly. "But it's this article in the newspaper. It's about you."

"Me?"

"Yes, and I'm afraid to say it's absolutely vile."

Charlotte's hand flew up to her chest. "Oh, my. What does it say, dear?"

Ellie began to read out loud. "'The Folly of Female Emancipation: The Sad Case of Mrs Madeleine Fletcher' by Mr Charles Turner."

"*'It grieves me to witness the alarming moral decay which has infected our once upright British society of late. Under the dubious banner of emancipation, our women have become possessed of a dangerous spirit of overweening pride and disregard for the natural social order.'*"

"*'Where once the gentle female sex knew its proper place and duty, we now see misguided ambitions and a shameless aping of masculine virtues. This inversion of the naturally decreed roles of men and women can only lead to catastrophe if left unchecked.'*"

Madeleine let out a short groan. "Must we really listen to this nonsense, Ellie?"

"Wait, Mother. This is where he starts writing about you."

"*'As a perfect encapsulation of this folly, we may consider the case of Mrs Madeleine Fletcher, widow of the late Mr Benjamin Fletcher. In her quest for supposed liberation, Mrs Fletcher has taken it upon herself to assume control of her deceased husband's steam engine manufactory, plunging heedlessly into affairs far beyond her comprehension and natural abilities.'*"

Charlotte made a disapproving hissing noise. "I'd like to see this Mr Charles Turner try it for himself," she scoffed.

"It gets worse," Ellie said.

"*'This laughable display of arrogance threatens to undo all of Mr Fletcher's hard work, and it jeopardises the livelihoods of the hundreds of workers and families who rely upon the factory.'*"

Madeleine gasped. Ruining the lives of her workers and their families was indeed the very thing she was afraid of.

"*'Despite her delicate constitution, Mrs Fletcher deems herself capable of comprehending the complex mechanical workings and business operations of an industrial enterprise. Her delusions of competence risk driving the manufactory into the ground through mismanagement.'*"

"Rubbish," Charlotte bristled. "This horrible man doesn't know what he's talking about."

"He mentions Mr Redhurst as well," Ellie said as she continued reading.

"*'All the while, the true engineering genius behind the company's success, Mr Ashton Redhurst, is regrettably sidelined. His technical skills and brilliance stand to become collateral damage in this farcical charade of female empowerment.'*"

Madeleine frowned at the marked difference in tone. The attack was clearly aimed at her and her alone.

"*'It is our sincere wish that Mrs Fletcher shall come to her senses before lasting harm is done. But we must not get our hopes up too high. For wilful ignorance and hysterical fancy are the weaker sex's natural inclinations. Possessed of little wisdom or capacity for self-reflection, Mrs Fletcher will likely persist in her folly until utter disaster results.'*"

"I think we've heard enough," Charlotte said, reaching for the newspaper. But Ellie wanted to go on.

"This is the last bit," she said.

"*'Mark my words - no good can come of women abandoning their God-given roles as modest, dutiful wives and mothers. Mrs Fletcher's arrogance will only lead to ruin for all around her. Unless she renounces this dangerous spirit of emancipation, her husband's legacy shall surely fall victim to her conceit.'*"

"Poppycock," Charlotte declared fiercely. "What an outrageous pack of lies. This Mr Turner clearly loves dipping his pen in venom."

"He's a despicable worm," Ellie fumed, throwing down the newspaper on the table. "We ought to tell him exactly what we think of his revolting opinions."

Madeleine sat quietly as Charlotte and Ellie voiced their outrage. She was grateful for their support, but the journalist's cruel words stirred up her own doubts. Could she really carry on Benjamin's life's work?

"How dare they print such slander with no proof?" Charlotte tutted. "I've half a mind to write the editor a strongly-worded letter."

"Forget writing letters," Ellie said. "We should go straight to their offices and tell this Charles Turner he's nothing but a pompous windbag spreading codswallop." She slapped the table angrily.

"That's quite enough, both of you," Madeleine finally spoke up. "Getting ourselves worked up over some journalist's allegations will accomplish nothing."

Though she kept her tone calm, her stomach roiled. How had this man caught wind of her situation? Was her inadequacy as a factory manager that obvious? Were her doubts and struggles the talk of the town?

One thing she knew for sure: this cruel article had struck a nerve, stirring up all her fears. But involving Ellie and Charlotte would only make matters worse.

"Honestly," she continued lightly, "I cannot think why Mr Turner would take such an interest in my affairs. Perhaps he's simply trying to create drama and sell more newspaper copies."

"By ruining your reputation," her daughter grumbled. "We must speak up and defend your good name, Mother."

"I agree with Ellie," Charlotte said. "We can't let them print such nonsense unchallenged, Maddie."

"I appreciate you both wanting to defend me," Madeleine said with a grateful smile. "But getting dragged into a public spat won't help us. If we react, we'll only give Mr Turner more attention. Which is exactly what he wants."

She shook her head and added, "No, I believe it's best if we ignore this petty attack."

In truth though, the idea of responding made her weary. She didn't have the energy for a skirmish with some man from the newspaper. Not alongside everything else. With any luck, maintaining a dignified silence would allow the whole thing to blow over swiftly.

"Please promise me that we'll let the matter rest," she implored them. "Your love is all the support I need."

"You can count on us, dear," Charlotte said. "We believe in you. Don't we, Eleanor?"

Ellie nodded, vaguely staring at the newspaper on the table. "Of course," she mumbled.

"There you have it," Charlotte smiled broadly. "Now don't spare that vicious man another thought. A storm in a teacup, that's what this is. Why, tomorrow people will have already forgotten about it."

Charlotte's reassurances were comforting. Privately however, Madeleine was deeply worried. It was bad enough that she doubted herself. But now it seemed the word had got out. And she was afraid of just how far it might spread.

Chapter Six

Wringing her hands, Madeleine paced her office. Today the investors would come – strangers with the power to save or doom Benjamin's beloved factory. She glanced anxiously at the clock. So much hinged on the outcome of this visit.

Would these esteemed gentlemen see the potential that still remained in the soot-stained bricks and rumbling machinery? Or would they only see a struggling company headed by a woman out of her depth?

"We're wasting our time, you know," Ashton said. He sat lounging in Madeleine's chair behind her desk, reading the newspaper. "I don't for a minute believe that this Frenchman of yours will actually turn up."

"Mr Dubois will come. I know it," she replied. "He sent me a letter saying he had found several interested parties. We arranged for a visit today."

Ashton scoffed. "And when did you say you met him?"

"A fortnight ago. At Sir John's."

"Relying on some French charlatan to save us," he muttered. "The man will bleed us dry, as likely as not."

Madeleine stiffened. "Developing this new steam engine was your idea, Ashton. If it weren't for that, we wouldn't be straining our resources."

"Don't you dare put this on me," he bristled. "A more capable administrator would have secured those funds a long time ago."

Madeleine bit her tongue. An argument was the last thing she wanted just before the arrival of their guests.

But Ashton went on. "Have you seen today's 'Herald'?" he asked, tapping the newspaper. "More letters lambasting your leadership. 'A woman's duty is to her family, not to a company's finances.' Or this one: 'Women ought to run households, not steam engines.' And those are some of the politer ones."

His laugh grated.

Far from petering out, the personal attacks in the newspaper had continued unabated. Every day, 'The Herald of the North' printed letters from their readers about Madeleine. A few were supportive of her, but most agreed with the harsh opinion Charles Turner had expressed.

"This scandal taints us." Ashton leaned forward, fixing her with a dark gaze. "Perhaps it would be wiser if you resigned. Before you destroy our reputation and sink this company for good."

"Benjamin poured his life and soul into this company," she shot back angrily. "And I shall fight to protect what he built."

"What he and I built, you mean," Ashton snarled. "I'm the brains of this operation, my dear. All Benjamin ever did was push some papers around."

"He did much more than that, and you know it, Ashton! Benjamin is the one who kept the business going."

"Precisely. But now he isn't here any more, and look where it has got us. In serious trouble, that's where. I'll never understand what possessed him to pass his share on to you."

"Benjamin wanted *me* to look after his life's work," she replied sharply. "Me, Ashton. Not you. And so I promised him that I would."

"Some promise," Ashton sneered. "A woman handling complex mechanical and financial matters? Ludicrous."

"Ludicrous or not, I fully intend to respect Benjamin's dying wish. I'll weather the storm and see the factory through this difficult time."

Ashton opened his mouth to retort, but he was interrupted by a knock. Robert appeared at the door, blushing uneasily.

"I hate to interrupt, Mrs Fletcher, Mr Redhurst," Madeleine's assistant said apologetically. "But Mr Dubois and the guests have arrived."

"Thank you, Robert," Madeleine said. "Tell them Mr Redhurst and I shall be coming out to greet them in a moment."

The young clerk nodded, relieved to escape the icy tension that hung in the air between his two employers.

Ashton gave an arrogant little sniff and smoothed his hair. "No hysterics in front of the investors now. Calm and agreeable, like a proper lady."

His jab annoyed Madeleine.

"I'll be on my best behaviour, Ashton," she replied coolly. "And I'll expect you to do the same."

Wearing a mocking grin on his face, he walked off. Madeleine tried to shake off the irritation he had caused, and then strode out of her office.

With her head held high, she followed Ashton into the waiting area where her assistant Robert was talking to Mr Dubois and the visitors. Her gaze swept over the group: four gentlemen and – much to Madeleine's surprise – a lady.

She was a sturdy, broad-shouldered woman with piercing eyes and silver hair. Madeleine guessed her to be in her late fifties. Standing nearly as tall as the men, her presence dominated the room.

"Mrs Fletcher, *bonjour*," Mr Dubois smiled fondly when he saw Madeleine. "Mr Redhurst," he added, acknowledging the man with a mere nod. "Please allow me to introduce these kind people to you."

As he went around the group, Madeleine gave each of the men a polite smile and a few formal words of greeting. Then Mr Dubois came to the woman. "And this is Mrs Constance Pemberton-Thorpe," he said.

"A pleasure, Mrs Pemberton-Thorpe," Madeleine replied. When they shook hands, the woman's grip felt confident.

"So you're the brave woman who has taken on the daunting task of running a factory, eh?" Mrs Pemberton-Thorpe said, looking Madeleine up and down appraisingly. "I simply had to see this curiosity for myself."

Madeleine blushed under that intense gaze, but she kept her composure. "Then I hope this visit will prove enlightening for you, ma'am."

"I'm sure that it will, Mrs Fletcher – one way or the other," Mrs Pemberton-Thorpe replied somewhat enigmatically. "Incidentally, you and I have something in common."

"We do?"

"Yes, we're both widows. Although I understand your loss is more recent than mine?"

"Nearly seven months now," Madeleine said, desperately attempting to block out any sad memories.

"You get over it, eventually," Mrs Pemberton-Thorpe assured her matter-of-factly. "I lost my Hubert five years ago. Turned my life upside down, it did. But I made the most of it. You just have to take these things one day at a time."

"Thank you," Madeleine said, forcing a slight smile onto her face. "I'll bear that in mind."

Standing by their side, Mr Dubois politely cleared his throat. "Shall we begin the tour?"

"Yes, let's," Madeleine answered brightly, hoping her nervousness didn't show. This small group of people quite possibly held the future of Fletcher & Redhurst in their hands. Leading the way, she prayed she could win them over.

Once they were on the factory floor, the visitors gazed around at the enormous machinery, with the heat and the noise enveloping them.

Madeleine introduced Stuart Wainwright to the group. "One of our promising young engineering talents," she called him. "He shall explain to you how we succeed in producing some of the finest steam engines in the country."

Blushing crimson red from the neck up, Stuart stumbled over his words at first. But as he went on, his passion and expertise came shining through.

Madeleine smiled and nodded when she noticed how everyone appeared to be giving

Stuart their undivided attention. Ashton stayed in the background the whole time, remaining silent. But perhaps that was for the best, she thought.

When Madeleine shared just how many brand new steam engines the factory was producing every month, a smug gentleman named Mr Smythe harrumphed.

"If business is so robust, Mrs Fletcher, then why pursue investors at all?"

Mr Dubois laughed diplomatically. "An astute question, *Monsieur*. Bringing on investment partners is simply prudent business practice."

"Quite so," Mrs Pemberton-Thorpe cut in, giving Mr Smythe a razor-sharp look. "Success requires capital. Any savvy investor grasps that. Though you perhaps do not, Mr Smythe."

A few chuckles went round the group, while the man coloured at the mild insult.

"Have you considered taking up fishing or billiards, Mr Smythe?" Mrs Pemberton-Thorpe suggested airily. "Investing may not be the most suitable diversion for you."

"I know businesses need capital," the man grumbled. "But why not turn to the banks for a loan instead?"

Once again, Mr Dubois jumped to the rescue effortlessly. "In my experience, investors understand the needs and complexities of a business far better than the average banker."

"My sentiments exactly," Mrs Pemberton-Thorpe agreed. "My Hubert often lamented the bankers' lack of imagination when it came to financing. He used to say they all had the vision of moles, buried in their ledgers."

She gave a fond chuckle at the memory.

"When Hubert sought funding to install mechanised looms in all his textile mills, the banks hemmed and hawed endlessly. But a handful of investors understood the potential right away."

Turning to Madeleine, she said, "Trust me, my dear. You don't want to have anything to do with bankers."

Then she rounded on Mr Smythe. "You're not a banker, are you, sir?"

Indignantly, he shook his head in denial as another round of laughter silenced him. Madeleine hid her smile, but she was quietly grateful for this welcome support from the fierce widow and Mr Dubois.

Nearing the end of the tour however, another gentleman brought up the topic Madeleine dreaded the most.

"What about this piece by Mr Turner in The Herald of the North, Mrs Fletcher?" he asked. "Is there any truth to his allegations of incompetence in your handling of the company's finances?"

Mr Dubois intervened smoothly. "Never believe all you read, sir," he smiled. "Why, newspapers once claimed that passengers on steam trains would suffocate by travelling at speeds over 20 miles per hour."

"The article was right about one thing though," Ashton suddenly spoke up from the back of the group.

Every head turned.

"Which is?" the gentleman asked.

"My engineering genius," Ashton said with a patronising smirk. "Mr Turner was absolutely spot on about that, if I do say so myself."

The men among the visitors laughed at Ashton's joke. But Mrs Pemberton-Thorpe's feathers had been ruffled.

"I found it a disgusting, miserable piece," she declared. "Mr Charles Turner clearly has a passionate hatred for all women. It's distasteful."

With a mocking huff, she added, "Someone must have broken his heart very badly when he was younger. And who could blame a girl for scorning such a vile creature?"

Most of the men in the group looked away awkwardly.

But Madeleine silently cheered the fact that this formidable woman saw Charles Turner for the despicable serpent he was. She only hoped the rest of the investors would share a similar view.

Chapter Seven

Watching the investors depart in their carriages from her office window, Madeleine let out a deep sigh. The factory tour had gone wonderfully well, she thought: no major hiccups or embarrassments.

But now began the anxious waiting game: would any of the visitors commit their funds? And would the fresh capital be enough to turn the tide of the company's declining profits?

For a fleeting moment, Madeleine allowed herself to daydream. If the investments came through, she would be able to transform the factory. She tried to picture the new assembly hall they would probably need: an enormous space with a high vaulted ceiling of steel beams – almost like a cathedral of industry.

Closing her eyes, she imagined the new turbine engines leaving the factory with the 'Fletcher & Redhurst' name proudly embossed on their cast-iron exteriors.

The creak of the office door shook her from her reverie. She turned to see Ashton saunter in, with his usual arrogant stride and an irreverent grin on his face.

"Quite a show you managed to put on today, my dear," he said sarcastically. "I was particularly impressed that no one fell asleep. Especially since young Mr Wainwright was trying his hardest to sound utterly boring."

Madeleine bristled at his mocking tone, but she forced herself to remain calm. "The tour served its purpose," she said evenly. "It's a shame you didn't demonstrate more of that engineering brilliance Mr Charles Turner seems to admire you for."

A brief twitch at the corner of his mouth betrayed that her barb had stung him. "For those doddering old misers that this French frog of yours dredged up?" He let out a derisive snort. "That would have been like casting pearls before swine. I'd be surprised if any of them end up investing even a penny."

Before Madeleine could respond, a brisk knock sounded at the office door. Mr Dubois breezed in, smiling broadly.

"Speak of the devil," Ashton muttered under his breath.

"Congratulations, my friends," Mr Dubois beamed. "The tour has made an excellent impression on our visitors."

Infected by his cheerful enthusiasm, Madeleine returned a small smile. "Let's hope you're correct, sir. Although Mr Redhurst appears to remain sceptical."

"Come now, Monsieur Redhurst," the Frenchman said amiably. "No need to be gloomy. I detected sincere interest amongst several of our guests today."

"Your optimism is commendable," Ashton smirked.

"Thank you, Monsieur." Mr Dubois inclined his head, ignoring or not noticing Ashton's sarcasm. "Perhaps the three of us could discuss what to do next over a nice meal together? My treat, of course."

He smiled invitingly at Madeleine and Ashton in turn.

"Food and the French, inseparable as always," Ashton scoffed.

Mr Dubois simply shrugged. "In France, we believe in combining business with more pleasurable things. After all, one does not exclude the other."

Madeleine hesitated, wondering if it was proper for a recent widow to be seen having a meal in public with a gentleman.

Sensing her reluctance, Mr Dubois said, "We can talk business here if you prefer, of course. But the venison pie at The Red Lion is sure to make our conversation more enjoyable."

"I suppose discussing matters over a meal could be beneficial," Madeleine said slowly. "Very well, The Red Lion sounds lovely."

A small voice inside whispered a warning, but she chose to ignore it. This was just business, she reminded herself. And business was what she needed to focus on if she wanted to secure the factory's future. Benjamin would surely understand.

"As tempting as The Red Lion's pie may be," Ashton said smugly, "I'm afraid I have more pressing matters to attend to." Moving towards the door, he waved a dismissive hand. "But give my regards to the cook, won't you?"

With a final smirk, Ashton strode from the office, letting the door swing shut behind him.

"An intriguing character, this Mr Redhurst," Mr Dubois said with a wry smile.

"I do apologise on his behalf," Madeleine said. "Mr Redhurst has his quirks."

"It's of no consequence, Madame." With a short bow of the head, he gestured towards the door. "Shall we?"

After gathering her things, Madeleine let Mr Dubois escort her to the street, where they soon found a carriage to take them to the tavern.

She was worried what onlookers would think if they saw her sharing a cab with a man. But the busy street traffic paid them no mind. And Mr Dubois showed himself to be a perfect gentleman. He talked about the weather and his impressions of the city, which helped to settle her nerves.

His wit was catching, and Madeleine found herself smiling by the time they arrived at The Red Lion.

A few curious stares greeted them as they entered the tavern, but people quickly returned to their own conversations.

"A quiet table for two, please," Mr Dubois asked the waitress who came up to greet them.

When they were shown to their table, he held Madeleine's chair for her before seating himself.

"The venison pie here really is excellent," he said, glancing over the menu. "But please feel free to order anything that appeals."

Madeleine scanned the selections, simple tavern fare but with a few more elegant options added, to appeal to wealthier patrons.

"The roasted duck seems lovely," she decided.

When the waitress returned, Mr Dubois ordered the venison pie, Madeleine requested the duck, and he selected a decent red wine to accompany their meal.

"To new ventures," he said, raising his glass once the waitress had poured them each a drink.

"To hopeful futures," Madeleine replied, touching her glass to his.

The wine was full-bodied with hints of blackberry and spice. She took a small sip, feeling the warmth slide down her throat. It had been some time since she'd allowed herself to indulge in a glass with dinner. But the occasion as well as the cosy setting seemed to warrant it.

"Now, about today's visitors," Mr Dubois began, relaxing his hands on the table. "I'm confident that several of them can be persuaded to give us their support."

Madeleine raised an eyebrow in surprise. "Several, you say?" That was better than she had dared to hope.

"Oh, yes. Two or three of them seemed keen enough." He chuckled and added, "Mr Smythe, I'm afraid, will be a lost cause."

"No surprise there," she replied, remembering the testy gentleman and his cynical questions.

"I'll pay each of them a visit," Mr Dubois said. "Starting with the formidable Mrs Pemberton-Thorpe."

"I liked her. She had a sharp wit and a bright mind," Madeleine said, before taking another small sip of wine. "And as a widow, she may be more inclined to support our endeavour."

"Precisely." Mr Dubois gave an approving smile. "And that's why I shall call on Mrs Pemberton-Thorpe first. In fact, I already have an appointment with her. She invited me to have tea with her tomorrow afternoon."

"You don't waste any time, do you?" Madeleine said, barely able to suppress a small giggle.

"When something is worthwhile, I believe in pursuing it vigorously, Madame," he replied.

Madeleine blushed, but then their food arrived. A steaming hot venison pie and roasted duck with crispy skin. It looked and smelled delicious.

"I must say the cook here is surprisingly talented," Mr Dubois said, savouring his first bite.

"The duck is excellent as well," she replied. "I seem to have more of an appetite than I've had in some time."

"Good food and good company work wonders," he said, the corners of his mouth curling up in a charming smile.

"Is that a French saying?"

"Not really," he chuckled. "More my own experience."

He took a sip of wine. "I suppose I learned to appreciate life's finer things after a difficult start. Both my parents died when I was just a boy, you see."

"Oh my, I'm terribly sorry," Madeleine said.

"It was long ago," he said, casually waving away her concern. "I grew up in an orphanage, which wasn't always easy. But I tried to make the best of what came after."

Madeleine nodded slowly. She understood all too well. "I lost my mother and father as well when I was young. But I was lucky in one respect. My aunt Cordelia took me in and raised me as if I was her own daughter."

"How very kind of her."

"Yes, that was Aunt Cordelia's way," Madeleine replied fondly. "And my cousin Charlotte takes after her. Charlotte and I grew up together – more like sisters than cousins."

"You were fortunate indeed to have been brought up in such a loving home. It has clearly given you great inner strength."

She looked down, abashed. "Oh, I'm not so sure about that."

"But it's true," he insisted kindly. "Your strength and resilience are plain to see for anyone who cares to look closely."

Madeleine felt her cheeks grow warm at the unexpected praise. Searching for a way to redirect the conversation, she asked, "But what of you, Mr Dubois? How did you end up here in Sheffield? Wouldn't London have been a more likely destination for you?"

"Oh, I've done business in London in the past," he replied. "But this time round, I thought a change of scenery might do me good."

"I see. In that case, I hope the North won't disappoint you."

"So far, the North and its people have exceeded my expectations, Madame. There are treasures here waiting to be uncovered."

With a charming smile he refilled her wine glass.

"But speaking of expectations," he continued, "I have a feeling Mrs Pemberton-Thorpe will come through for us. If we can get her on board, the others will be easier to persuade as well, I believe."

His easy confidence drew Madeleine's attention back to more professional matters. But questions lingered. Questions he preferred to evade, she had the impression.

A man of many mysteries, she mused.

Mysteries could be dangerous in the business world. But with Mr Dubois they only served to make him more intriguing in her eyes.

Chapter Eight

The hansom cab rattled through the gaslit streets as Mr Dubois escorted Madeleine home after their dinner meeting. She sat awkwardly jammed next to him on the narrow seat, hands folded neatly in her lap.

Through the cab's small window, she watched the glowing street lights flit by in the night. It had been a long day, hosting the investors and then worrying about the outcome. But the pleasant conversation with Mr Dubois over a fine meal had left her feeling... happy.

Happiness, she thought with a tired smile. Now there was an emotion she hadn't counted on experiencing again any time soon.

"I must thank you for a perfectly lovely evening, Mrs Fletcher," Mr Dubois said, echoing her own sentiments. "It was the ideal conclusion to our successful factory tour this afternoon."

"Yes, it was an enjoyable dinner," she replied. "Though I hesitate to call the tour itself a success just yet. Our guests have not actually committed to anything."

"Have faith," he smiled. "I am certain they were thoroughly impressed with both your factory and your leadership. You may trust my instincts in these matters."

Madeleine looked down with a wry smile. "I wish I shared your confidence. I was a nervous wreck the entire time. I scarcely recall what I said to them."

"If you were nervous, then you managed to hide it well," Mr Dubois said reassuringly. "What came across was a savvy businesswoman in full command of herself. And a decidedly charming one at that."

Madeleine blushed at the compliment just as the cab rolled to a stop outside her home. Reluctantly, she had to admit that it was rather nice to receive a bit of flattery and encouragement from someone after so long.

Mr Dubois stepped down from the carriage and turned to help Madeleine. She accepted his hand and alighted gracefully.

"It was very kind of you to accompany me home, Monsieur," she said. "Now let us hope our efforts today will lead to success for the factory."

"Indeed," Mr Dubois replied warmly. "I, for one, look forward to our continued association, Madame." He took her gloved hand and placed a polite kiss upon it in farewell.

But as he did so, a movement at one of the windows of the house suddenly caught Madeleine's eye. With a twist in her gut, she saw the curtain twitching in Ellie's bedroom.

What had her daughter just witnessed? An innocent parting gesture, that's all it was. But she worried what Ellie would make of it.

Hastily, she bid goodnight to Mr Dubois and rushed inside. The house was quiet as she softly closed the door behind her. With any luck, she would be able to slip up to her bedroom without risking a confrontation with her daughter. She shrugged off her coat and placed it over a chair in the hallway, where Mary would take care of it in the morning.

"Mother, who was that man?" a voice at the top of the stairs demanded icily.

Madeleine's heart sank as she looked up to see Ellie glaring down at her, arms folded across her chest.

"Ellie, you're still awake," Madeleine said evasively, trying to keep her tone light.

"I was worried," her daughter bristled. "I don't like it when you stay out late without notice. Who was that man?"

"That was Mr Dubois."

"The Frenchman?" Ellie came thundering down the stairs.

"Yes, he kindly escorted me home after dinner. We were discussing business matters regarding the factory. You'll be pleased to know that the tour was a success."

"Don't play me for a fool, Mother. I saw him take your hand and kiss it right there outside our home. Haven't you got any shame?"

"Ellie, please. It was nothing. Merely a polite kiss on the hand. Sometimes a gentleman will do that when saying goodbye to a lady."

"Some gentleman he is," her daughter scoffed. "He has designs on you, Mother."

"That's very rude of you, Eleanor," Madeleine replied, taken aback by her daughter's accusations. "You know I am still in mourning for your father."

"Mourning didn't stop you from dining out with a rogue." Stepping in closer, Ellie sniffed at the air in front of her mother's face. "I can smell wine on your breath. Have you been drinking?"

"We shared a glass of wine over dinner. There's nothing unusual about that."

"Ah, so you admit it! Dinner, wine, kisses. What would Papa think?"

Stung, Madeleine drew herself up. "Mr Dubois is helping me secure investors for the factory. As a woman alone, I must be practical."

"Practical? Is that what you call making eyes at men and letting them paw at you?"

"Ellie," Madeleine gasped. "That's going too far, young lady. I shan't tolerate you speaking to me this way."

"And I will not tolerate my mother parading around with suitors less than a year after Papa's passing. Have you no decency?" Angry tears sprang up from the girl's eyes.

"Mr Dubois is not a suitor. I am simply conducting business – as your father would have wanted."

"Business is one thing. What I saw tonight was you preening for that scoundrel's attention."

Madeleine struggled to contain her outrage. "Clearly you misinterpreted a harmless exchange. I'll hear no more on this."

But her daughter wasn't done. "Misinterpreted? I know flirtation when I see it. It's a disgrace, Mother. Papa would turn over in his grave if he knew."

Something in Madeleine snapped. "Your father is gone," she shouted. "I need to make decisions for myself now. And I'll not have them questioned by an insolent child."

"Is that how little we mean to you?" Ellie spat, while tears rolled down her cheeks. "Yes, Papa is gone. But that doesn't give you the right to leap into the arms of the nearest man."

"Eleanor, stop this madness," Madeleine pleaded, blinking back her own tears. "I am still faithful to your father's memory. You know nothing of my burden."

"Perhaps not." Ellie glared at her mother with contempt. "But I do know that you don't care a whit for decency or good advice."

She whirled and ran up the stairs, slamming her door dramatically as she disappeared into her bedroom.

Defeated, Madeleine collapsed into a chair. With shaking shoulders, she buried her face in her hands and wept.

Had she really been that wrong? Had it been foolish of her to accept Mr Dubois' invitation to dinner?

And as for that kiss on the hand that Ellie had witnessed? Well, the man was French after all. It was simply how these Continentals did things.

Nevertheless, one thought echoed through Madeleine's mind: had she lost her precious daughter's love? Ellie had shown such anger and disgust.

"Oh, my dearest angel," Charlotte's voice sounded softly as her hand touched Madeleine's shoulder. "I hate seeing you so upset."

Madeleine looked up at her cousin through tear-filled eyes. "It was awful, Charlotte. The things she said..." Her voice broke off in a sob.

"I know. I heard most of it."

In a panic, Madeleine grabbed her cousin's hand. "Don't tell me you disapprove of me as well? Oh, Charlotte, please–"

"What's there to disapprove of, Maddie?"

"I mean, Mr Dubois–"

Charlotte smiled and knelt beside Madeleine. "You've done nothing improper. In my eyes, discussing business matters over a meal is perfectly respectable for a widow."

"That's not how Ellie sees it," Madeleine cried. "She seems to think I'm a fallen woman."

"No, she doesn't."

"But you heard what she said. She said I was a disgrace."

"That's just the foolishness of youth speaking. I'm sure she didn't mean those things. Not really."

Madeleine hesitated. She wanted to believe her cousin. But Ellie's words had hurt her so badly.

"She's worried about you," Charlotte continued. "And unfortunately, tonight her distress turned to anger. Young people can be silly like that."

"I worry about her, too," Madeleine said sadly. "What happened to that sweet little girl she used to be?"

"She grew up. And she lost her father. But she's strong. Just like her mother." Charlotte smiled at her.

Madeleine shook her head. "I'm not strong. I'm nothing without Benjamin."

"You mustn't say that, Maddie. You know it isn't true."

"Then why am I failing?" Fresh tears came rolling down her cheeks. "I'm failing Benjamin's factory and I'm failing Ellie."

"You're not failing anyone. Didn't I hear you say the factory tour was a success today?"

"It was – in a sense. Mr Dubois is confident he'll be able to persuade several of the guests to invest."

"See? That hardly sounds like failure to me."

"But what about Ellie? I just don't know how to make things right between us again."

"Be patient, dear. You and Ellie are both still grieving over Benjamin. Give it some time."

"Time," Madeleine echoed in despair. "Oh, Charlotte. To think that less than a year ago, we were all so perfectly happy. And look at us now. We're a broken family."

"It's only temporary, Maddie. You'll pull through. The pain will fade away and the wounds will heal."

Madeleine let out a long, sorrowful sigh. "That's what people always say, isn't it? But suppose it doesn't happen. What if Ellie keeps on hating me forever?"

"She doesn't hate you, Maddie. She never has and never will. Deep down in her heart she hasn't stopped loving you. No matter what she says or how she reacts."

Madeleine looked at Charlotte first and then she gazed up the stairs, thinking of Ellie. "We'll see," she said as she rose to her feet. "It's late and I'm tired. So I'd better be off to bed, I think."

"That's right," Charlotte smiled as she too stood up. "Get a good night's rest. You'll feel better in the morning. Do you want me to make you a hot cup of cocoa before you go up?"

"No, thank you," Madeleine replied wearily. With heavy feet she went up the stairs towards her bedroom. When she passed by Ellie's door, she paused.

Should she knock? Tell her daughter how much she loved her?

After some hesitation, Madeleine shook her head. No, she decided. She'd had her fill of emotions tonight.

In her room, she undressed, turned down the light and slipped into the empty bed. Feeling exhausted and lonely, Madeleine cried herself to sleep.

Chapter Nine

Piles of paperwork were spread out on Madeleine's large desk. Her shoulders sagged with exhaustion as she puzzled over the heavy ledger lying in front of her. When the numbers began to blur before her eyes, she sighed and pushed the book away.

"More tea, ma'am?" her assistant Robert asked gently. He was sitting across from her at the desk, taking notes.

Madeleine gave him a wan smile. "No, thank you, Robert. I fear no amount of tea will help make sense of these figures."

"Anything else I can do to help?"

She hesitated, not wanting to burden the young clerk with her troubles. But there was a weight that she needed to get off her shoulders.

"It's just that I'm anxious about Mr Dubois. It's been three days since the investors' tour and we haven't heard back yet."

"Don't lose heart, Mrs Fletcher," Robert said sympathetically. "I'm sure we'll have good news soon. Those investors seemed mightily impressed."

"You're right. My cousin Charlotte would tell me I need to be more patient. The trouble is...

Without fresh capital, I don't know how much longer we can continue."

She stared out the window at the factory yard, where men were busy unloading several flatbed wagons. Shaking her head, she turned back to the paperwork on her desk and frowned.

"I simply don't understand. Our sales keep falling while the costs seem to creep up and up. And yet the factory appears busier than ever."

Throwing down the pencil in her hand, she slumped back in her chair. "I suppose that only proves I have no head for numbers after all."

"Words of wisdom at last," Ashton laughed as he swept into the office without bothering to knock.

Instinctively polite, Robert stood up immediately. "Mr Redhurst, good morning, sir."

"Yes, yes," Ashton said dismissively. He looked at Madeleine. "Well, it seems your faith in that French frog was misplaced. No word from him yet, I gather?"

Robert glanced uncertainly at Madeleine. "Would you like me to leave, Mrs Fletcher?"

"No, please stay, Robert," Madeleine said. She turned to Ashton with forced politeness. "Mr Dubois has been exceedingly helpful. I'm sure we'll hear about his progress soon."

Ashton snorted. "Oh, please. I know his type: nothing but fancy talk and grand promises that lead to nothing." He sat on the edge of

Madeleine's desk. "I'll wager you ten guineas that he's too busy womanising. He probably got distracted by some tart with a pretty face, who's made him forget all about us."

Madeleine bristled at Ashton's rude manner, but held her tongue. Out of the corner of her eye, she saw her poor assistant shifting awkwardly on his feet.

"On second thought, Robert," she said, "Mr Redhurst and I have some matters to discuss privately."

"Of course, ma'am." Looking relieved, Robert quickly gathered his papers and left.

Alone with Ashton, Madeleine spoke up testily. "There's no call for such ungentlemanly speech. Mr Dubois has worked very hard on our behalf."

Ashton laughed derisively. "You're adorable in your innocence, Madeleine. Though I suppose you've always led a sheltered life. Ben would have shielded you from the darker side of the business world."

"I'm not a naive simpleton, if that's what you're implying, Ashton. Benjamin always shared both the good news and the bad news with me."

"Of course he would have. He was like that, our good old Ben – bless his soul." His voice took on a sympathetic tone. "It can't be easy on you, Madeleine. Suddenly having to run everything, while you're still grieving. Especially with a wayward girl like Ellie on your hands."

Madeleine stiffened. "My daughter is none of your concern. And I'm managing perfectly well, thank you."

Ashton held up his hands. "No need to put on a brave face with me, you know." Smiling, he got off the edge of the desk and sat down in one of the chairs instead.

"I've been thinking," he said. "Why don't you sell me your half of the company? Stop worrying about ledgers and contracts, and enjoy life. I'll make it worth your while."

"Absolutely not." Madeleine sat up and straightened her shoulders. "Benjamin explicitly left his shares to me in his will. I won't relinquish them."

"Be sensible," Ashton coaxed. "This world of commerce wasn't meant for gentle souls like you. Let me relieve you of that burden."

"I said no." Madeleine's voice was steel.

She noticed how the friendly smile vanished from Ashton's face. But before he could respond, there was a knock at the door.

"Mrs Fletcher," Robert breathed excitedly. "Mr Dubois is here. Shall I–"

"*Bonjour, mes amis,*" Mr Dubois said, jovially pushing past the young assistant. He had a large bouquet of flowers in one hand, and a bottle of champagne in the other.

Madeleine couldn't resist smiling at his lively entrance. "Mr Dubois," she said. "What a delightful surprise."

"I'll say," Ashton grumbled quietly.

"For you, Madame." With an elegant flourish, Mr Dubois presented the flowers to Madeleine.

"They're lovely, thank you." She blushed and accepted the bouquet, breathing in its rich fragrance with her eyes closed.

"I come bearing good news as well," Mr Dubois continued proudly. "Thanks to my efforts, we have secured the investment that you were seeking."

"How absolutely wonderful!"

"Three of the investors have agreed, including of course, the formidable Mrs Pemberton-Thorpe. Her commitment is by far the largest."

He looked round and then turned to Robert. "Young man, would you kindly fetch us three glasses, please?"

"Certainly, sir," the assistant replied before hurrying off.

"What a tremendous feat, Mr Dubois," Madeleine said, glowing with joy. "You said you'd be successful, and you were right. Bravo!"

She glanced over at Ashton with a little triumphant smirk, pleased that her business partner's crude comments had been proven wrong.

Aware of the man's sizeable ego, it didn't surprise her to see Ashton was looking daggers at Mr Dubois.

How awfully petty of him, she tutted to herself. *He wanted Mr Dubois to fail. So now he's sulking.*

"I couldn't find any glasses in a hurry," Robert said as he returned to the office holding a stack of three teacups and saucers. "So I had to get these instead. Terribly sorry."

Mr Dubois laughed. "French champagne in English teacups. Very fitting for our collaboration, I should think."

With a pop he uncorked the bottle and accidentally spilled some champagne over Madeleine's desk, as well as on Ashton's trousers.

"You blithering French buffoon," Ashton swore as he jumped to his feet. "Look what you've done to my suit."

"A thousand pardons, Mr Redhurst," Mr Dubois replied extremely politely. "How stupid of me. Please have your clothes cleaned and send me the bill."

"Never mind," Ashton grumbled while he tried to wipe down the wet stain in his trousers with his hand.

"Allow me to help," Mr Dubois said, setting down the bottle and taking a crisp handkerchief from his pocket.

"No, you've done quite enough already, thank you," Ashton said, raising a hand to stop the

Frenchman. He shot an angry scowl at Madeleine and then headed for the door.

"You are not staying, Monsieur?" Mr Dubois asked. "To celebrate our success?"

"I have work to do," Ashton snarled. "Good day, *Monsieur*." The sarcasm of his parting words was hard to miss.

But after Ashton had closed the door behind him with an angry thud, Mr Dubois merely shrugged. "His loss is our gain," he said with a slight chuckle. Then he proceeded to pour champagne in the teacups.

"Young Mr Adams, seeing as Mr Redhurst has left us and we have three cups, you will have to join us in our toast."

"Oh, I don't know if I should, sir." Robert blushed and cast a shy look at Madeleine.

"It's quite all right, Robert," she smiled.

"A toast," Mr Dubois proposed once everyone had their drink in hand. "To a bright future for 'Fletcher & Redhurst'."

They raised their cups and took a sip.

"Speaking of the Redhurst half of your company," Mr Dubois said, "I thought he would have been more pleased. This investment means there will be money to pay for his new turbine."

"You must excuse Mr Redhurst," Madeleine replied. "His behaviour can be somewhat...

erratic at times. But let me assure you that I, for one, am infinitely grateful to you."

In all honesty, she felt Ashton had been rude to Mr Dubois. And it irritated her that she had to apologise on his behalf – again.

Brushing aside any thoughts of Ashton, she turned her mind to more practical matters instead. "Please tell me, Monsieur. What happens next?"

"We should arrange another visit to the factory for our three investors. Something more in-depth and official this time. Shall we say one week from today?"

"Perfect. I will notify our solicitors to prepare the paperwork. Robert, will you see to that when we are done here?"

"Certainly, Mrs Fletcher," her assistant replied before jotting down a quick note.

"Excellent," Mr Dubois nodded approvingly. "I can see that 'Fletcher & Redhurst' is in good hands with a capable leader such as yourself, Madame."

Madeleine smiled. Mere weeks ago, she was increasingly afraid that the factory wouldn't be able to survive for much longer. But now, thanks to this kind and clever man before her, hope bloomed once more.

"A leader is only as good as the people she works with," she said, meeting his eyes. "I don't know what I would have done without you."

A touch of colour rose to his cheeks. Taking her hand, he placed a feather-light kiss on her knuckles. "It is my privilege, Madame."

His gesture sent a brief but pleasant shudder through Madeleine. *It must be the champagne,* she thought as he slowly released her hand.

"And now, *hélas*," Mr Dubois spoke with some regret, "I must be off. But please do let me know if I can be of any further assistance before our investors return next week."

He drained his cup and smiled. "And by all means, feel free to enjoy the rest of the champagne."

"You have been most kind and very generous, Mr Dubois," Madeleine replied. "I am in your debt."

With a gracious nod, the Frenchman took his leave.

"What an exciting day this has turned into," Madeleine said after Mr Dubois had left her office.

"It sure has, ma'am," Robert agreed. He drank up and looked appreciatively at his empty cup. "I've never had champagne before. Tastes delicious though. I'll have to tell Daisy about this."

"Daisy?"

Robert blushed. "Beg your pardon, Mrs Fletcher. Daisy is my fiancée. She's Mr

Wainwright's daughter. And Stuart Wainwright's younger sister."

"I didn't know you were engaged, Robert," Madeleine smiled. "How nice. If Daisy is anything like her father or her older brother, then she must be a lovely young lady."

"She is, ma'am. I count myself very lucky indeed."

"I'm sure you do. Now then, back to work. We have a lot to do before next week's visit." Staring at the paperwork scattered over her desk, she let out a long sigh. "The investors will probably want to have a look at the books as well."

"Leave it to me, Mrs Fletcher. I'll personally see to it that they are in perfect order."

"Excellent. I know you'll do a splendid job. Oh, and Robert? Please send word to my cook, Mrs Dobbs. I'd like her to prepare something festive this evening."

"Right away, ma'am," Robert said before leaving the office.

Madeleine sat down at her desk, smiling. It would be good to mark today's success with Ellie and Charlotte. The investors still needed to sign a formal agreement of course. But she felt she had earned this little celebration.

Most of all though, Madeleine hoped that a nice meal would help to thaw the chill between her and Ellie.

Chapter Ten

Madeleine let out a weary sigh as she entered the hall of her home, setting down her reticule on the small table by the door. After Mr Dubois' departure, the rest of her day at the factory had been spent poring over ledgers and figures that made her head spin.

"Welcome home, ma'am," Mary said, taking Madeleine's hat and coat. "Mrs Dobbs received your instructions for dinner. It's just about ready."

"Thank you, Mary." Madeleine made her way to the dining room, keen for a fortifying sherry before the meal. As she poured herself a glass, she heard Charlotte's cheerful voice approaching.

"The whole house smells of delicious food," Charlotte bustled in, rosy-cheeked. "Mrs Dobbs has been cooking and baking all afternoon."

Ellie was right behind her, avoiding her mother's gaze while looking as silent and brooding as ever.

"How was your day, my dears?" Madeleine asked, trying to put more cheer into her voice than she was feeling.

When Ellie didn't show any intention of answering, Charlotte quickly volunteered a bright reply. "Marvellous, as always. Ellie and I went for a walk earlier, didn't we, duck?"

Ellie merely nodded, staring with empty eyes at the dining table that had been beautifully laid out with their finest silver. The elegant setting couldn't disguise the obvious chill in the air though.

"Shall I serve the first course, Mrs Fletcher?" Mary asked when she briefly appeared in the room.

"If you would be so kind, yes," Madeleine replied. "We were about to sit down." She gestured for Charlotte and Ellie to take their seats.

Madeleine sipped her sherry nervously, wishing she could think of something to break the awkward tension. She and Ellie had barely spoken since their quarrel about Mr Dubois. The memory of her daughter's angry words that night stabbed at Madeleine's heart.

She wanted nothing more than to mend the rift. But where to begin? How could she say what was on her mind, without running the risk of Ellie taking it the wrong way?

Fortunately, in situations like these, her faithful cousin could be depended upon to engage in pleasantly meaningless small talk.

"I must say though," Charlotte prattled on. "The weather certainly was a bit on the chilly side today, wasn't it? Made Ellie and myself very grateful for a hot cup of tea afterwards. Didn't it, precious?"

Ellie offered only a short grunt in response, keeping her eyes down.

Madeleine suppressed a sigh, her heart sinking. Clearly this was not going to be the joyful, intimate family dinner she had envisioned. When she reached for her glass of sherry, she noticed her hand was trembling slightly.

"The first course is Windsor soup," Mary announced as she entered with a tureen. The young maid ladled the rich, creamy soup into their bowls before leaving the room again.

"Hmm, scrumptious," Charlotte said appreciatively after taking a spoonful. "Mrs Dobbs has outdone herself again." She savoured the aroma with a smile and then asked, "Tell us, Maddie. Why this fine meal? There must be a special occasion for it."

Madeleine brightened slightly. "I have some good news to share. We've secured the investment we needed to expand the factory – thanks to Mr Dubois."

"How absolutely wonderful," Charlotte beamed. "Well done, Maddie. I knew you were more than capable."

"It was Mr Dubois who did the hard work, really," Madeleine said. "But yes, it's an encouraging development. The future of the factory seems more certain now."

"And why wouldn't it be? With a strong woman like you at the helm," Charlotte said warmly. She turned to Ellie with an encouraging grin. "What do you say, Ellie? Isn't it brilliant the way your mother has pulled this off?"

"I suppose," the girl replied listlessly. Her eyes darted from Charlotte to Madeleine and then quickly went back down to her bowl of soup.

"Come now," Charlotte insisted. "Aren't you proud of your mother?"

"Of course." Ellie looked up and attempted a thin smile, but it didn't quite seem to reach her eyes. "It's great news, Mother."

Madeleine bit her lip. She wished she could read Ellie's true feelings. Was her daughter still upset over Mr Dubois' involvement? Or did she simply not care about factory affairs? Madeleine longed to know, but Ellie's flat tone gave little away.

An awkward silence threatened again until Charlotte intervened. "Well, I think this calls for a toast," she said, raising her glass. "To Madeleine, and a prosperous future for Fletcher & Redhurst."

"Yes, to your success, Mother," Ellie echoed feebly, touching her glass lightly to Madeleine's before taking a small sip.

"Thank you, my darling." Madeleine tried to look pleased, but inside, her stomach was in knots. Ellie's lukewarm reaction only made Madeleine's unease worse.

Charlotte set down her spoon. "I imagine Mr Redhurst was also quite pleased with this new investment?"

"On the contrary," Madeleine sighed. "He seemed rather put out. And he was terribly rude to Mr Dubois."

"That's odd," Charlotte said.

Madeleine snorted derisively. "That's Ashton Redhurst for you. Did you know, right before we got the good news, he even suggested that I sell my half of the company to him?"

Ellie's head jerked up, eyes flashing. "He did what? After Papa explicitly said–" She trailed off, then demanded sharply, "What did you tell him, Mother? You're not seriously considering selling out to that snake, are you?"

"I am not, rest assured," Madeleine said, surprised by her daughter's fierce reaction. "I told Ashton no. Quite firmly, too."

She reached out a tentative hand to her daughter, but Ellie immediately withdrew hers to the edge of the table.

"That's good," the girl muttered, reverting back to her meek demeanour.

"Ashton tried to make his offer seem very tempting though," Madeleine ventured cautiously. "He said it would mean I'd have more time to spend with you."

Holding her breath, she watched Ellie closely for a reaction. But a cold rock was easier to read, she thought.

"That sounds nice, I suppose," Ellie said while avoiding her mother's gaze. "But it's probably better if you devote yourself fully to the factory."

Madeleine opened and closed her mouth, unsure what to make of her daughter's reply. But as always, her cousin came to the rescue.

"Is that because you don't enjoy spending time with your mother, dear?" Charlotte asked kindly. "Or is it because you want her to succeed with the factory?"

"No," Ellie blurted out, caught off guard by Charlotte's frank question. "I mean, yes."

"Which one is it then?" Charlotte chuckled. "Yes or no?"

"What I mean is, yes, I'd like for us to spend more time together. But I also realise the company is more urgent and more important right now."

Madeleine felt a lump beginning to form in her throat. At last Ellie had created an opening.

"Ah," Charlotte said with a clever grin on her face. "So you still love your mother then?"

"Of course I do," Ellie murmured. Lowering her defences, she finally met her mother's gaze. "I want you to do well, Mama. And I want you to know... I'm proud of you."

Tears of happiness came rolling down Madeleine's cheeks. "Oh, Ellie."

This time it was Ellie who reached out across the table. Their hands found each other and their fingers twined together.

"I love you, Mama. And..." She lowered her eyes, looking ashamed. But she took a deep breath and looked at Madeleine again. "And I'm sorry for all those awful things I said to you."

"I forgive you, my precious angel," Madeleine said through her tears. "I love you, too. Very, very much. And I don't want you to think you're less important to me than the factory."

"I know," Ellie replied as tears stained her face as well.

"In fact," Madeleine said, "I'd love nothing more than to spend more time at home with you. But–"

"Please don't take Mr Redhurst's offer, Mama," Ellie said urgently. "You can't give up now. Things will get better soon with this new investment. And then you and I will have plenty of time together."

"I like the sound of that," Madeleine smiled.

"But you must promise me that you won't sell out to Mr Redhurst," Ellie insisted. "No matter what happens."

"I promise, darling. I would never do anything that might hurt or upset you."

They sat and gazed into each other's glowing eyes, hands clasped, revelling in their renewed connection.

Suddenly, a loud honking noise made them both jump. Charlotte was crying with joy and had needed to blow her nose into a handkerchief.

"Begging your pardon, my dears," she said, her voice thick with tears. "But all this bliss was just too much for my tender little heart. It's so lovely to see you two reconciled. Oh, happy day."

She sniffled and trumpeted into her handkerchief again. "Nothing worse for the constitution than family conflicts, if you ask me."

The rest of the dinner passed in high spirits. Laughter and lively chatter filled the room, while Mary served roast goose with all the trimmings, followed by a luscious trifle for dessert.

Later, after Ellie had hugged them both and retired upstairs for the night, Madeleine and Charlotte relaxed in the parlour with some tea.

"What a lovely evening this turned out to be," Charlotte smiled. "It was balm to my poor soul to see you and Ellie smiling again."

"All thanks to you, my dear cousin," Madeleine said. "Somehow you always seem to know the right thing to say."

Charlotte waved a hand. "Oh pish, it was nothing. Just a few gentle prods in the right direction."

"It was far more than that. You're the glue that holds this family together, Charlotte." Madeleine's voice grew thick with emotion. "After all that's happened this past year... Ellie and I would have been lost without you."

"You'd have managed just fine, I have no doubt," Charlotte tutted. But her eyes looked misty.

"Still, I don't think I can ever properly express how grateful I am for you." Madeleine leaned over to kiss Charlotte on the cheek.

"We're family, Maddie. United by fate. We may be cousins by birth, but in my heart, you're a sister to me."

"My heart feels the same about you... little Lottie." Madeleine grinned as she remembered what she used to call her cousin when they were girls.

Charlotte chuckled at the shared memory. "The adventures you and I had, eh?"

"I'll say," Madeleine giggled. "But no matter what scrapes we got ourselves into, you were always our saviour."

"Except that time when I accidentally glued Reverend Moore to his pulpit. Remember that one?"

The two women burst out laughing and then launched into reminiscing about their childhood. Several hours later, long after the clocks had chimed midnight, they went to bed.

And when Madeleine's head touched her pillow, she noticed she was still smiling.

Chapter Eleven

The next morning, as she stepped out of the carriage in front of the factory gate, Madeleine was unable to keep the smile from her face. The blissful memories of last night's dinner still warmed her heart. Ellie's loving words, her embrace, the two of them reconciled at last. It had been absolute heaven.

Humming softly, Madeleine made her way across the factory yard with a new spring in her step. But as she walked, the smiles and greetings she expected did not come.

Instead, the workers averted their eyes or offered only mutters and dark looks. Madeleine faltered, her cheer vanishing. What was this tension in the air? Had something happened? An incident at the factory perhaps? Troubling news from the city?

She glanced around, perplexed. *Bizarre,* she thought. *And frightfully chilling.* She would have to ask her assistant Robert about it as soon as she reached her office.

But as she pressed on, the hostile mood became clearer. Small groups of workers deliberately turned away as she approached, cutting short their conversations. One burly man even spat on the ground, missing her feet by mere inches.

Madeleine's breath caught. Shocked understanding dawned on her when she realised: all this resentment was aimed at her. But why? What had she done?

Her cheeks burned with shame while her heart thudded in fear. The cold disdain surrounding her was palpable now. Her happy glow had evaporated, leaving behind a sick feeling of dread.

She hurried inside, hoping to find answers for the workers' inexplicable hostility. But the mood indoors was scarcely better.

Angry shouts echoed through the vast production hall. Up ahead, she saw a small mob of people surrounding Ashton Redhurst and Jack Wainwright. Ashton's face looked dark and thunderous, but Jack was trying to calm everyone down.

So far however, the senior foreman didn't seem to be having much success.

"Blood, sweat and tears we've given this firm," one man cried. "And this is how you repay us?"

"It's a bloomin' disgrace, selling us out like this."

"Lying weasels, that's what you are. You and her both."

Madeleine trembled. She was certain those last words were referring to herself as well as Ashton.

"Gentlemen," she said, raising her voice to be heard above the noise. "What's the meaning of this? What's wrong?"

Heads swivelled in her direction, eyes flashing with bitter resentment.

"It's all your fault, Madeleine," Ashton barked hotly. "You should never have taken up with that frog of yours."

"Mr Dubois? What's he got to do with this? I don't understand."

Jack Wainwright stepped forward, cap in hand while giving her an apologetic look. "I'm afraid there's some unpleasantness about you in today's newspaper, Mrs Fletcher."

"Unpleasantness?" Madeleine's voice trembled.

"Here," Ashton grumbled before shoving a copy of The Herald of the North into her hands. "See for yourself."

Madeleine frowned and read the headline that Ashton was stabbing at with an irritated finger: *"Betrayal By Candlelight: Widow's Treachery Spells Doom for Family Firm"*.

An icy chill gripped her heart when she saw the name of the author: Charles Turner. The same man who had written that slanderous piece about her only weeks ago.

"Read it," Ashton urged her.

Startled by the commanding tone of his voice, Madeleine began reading the article out loud.

"*It pains me to report that the woeful lapse of judgement we cautioned against in regards to Mrs Madeleine Fletcher has now borne its bitter fruit.*"

"*In her misguided belief that she could competently run a complex engineering firm despite her feminine limitations, the widow Fletcher has taken negotiations with a dubious foreign gentleman to their disastrous conclusion.*"

Madeleine stopped and looked up. "A 'dubious foreign gentleman'? Does he mean Mr Dubois?"

"Who else?" Ashton scoffed. "But do read on. It gets better."

"*In a shocking development, credible sources have informed us that Mrs Fletcher intends to sell the Fletcher & Redhurst Steam Engine Works to parties unknown from across the Channel.*"

Madeleine let out a short noise in surprise and dismay. "Sell?! I have no intention whatsoever of selling the company. Where does Mr Turner get such fancies?"

Ashton grinned. "It would appear that your little dinner with Mr Dubois did not pass unnoticed." He nodded at the article, prodding her to keep reading.

"Mrs Fletcher has been observed dining with a mysterious French businessman of questionable character. Flashing his slick continental charm and plying the bereaved widow with honeyed words, he has seemingly bewitched her into relinquishing her late husband's legacy."

Madeleine gasped. "Scandalous."

"Quite," Ashton agreed. "But scandalous of whom, I wonder?"

"What?! Do you honestly think that Mr Dubois and I–"

"I wouldn't dream of thinking such things," Ashton interrupted her smugly. "But if you feel that's outrageous, wait until you see the end of Mr Turner's article."

Reluctantly, Madeleine continued.

"It is a travesty that one of the brightest jewels in the crown of British industry may soon belong to foreign hands. The blood and sweat of generations invested in building the famous Fletcher Works shall be tossed away on the misguided whims of a woman."

Shaking her head, Madeleine gave an annoyed sigh. "What a dreadful bore this man is." Against her better judgement, she went on.

"Craving male companionship, the lonely widow opens her heart and the factory ledgers to the first dubious gentleman who smiles at her. Such is the irrationality bred by misplaced female ambition."

She stopped reading, feeling deeply hurt and offended. "I've had enough of this filth," she said as she lowered the newspaper in disgust.

"Then allow me to finish it for you." Ashton snatched the paper from her hands and read the final part out loud.

"If only Mrs Fletcher had heeded our earlier warnings instead of stubbornly pursuing this disastrous course. Alas, there seems little hope of reversing this folly now that negotiations are in their advanced stages. The sun may soon set on a once proud pillar of British engineering."

"So ends the sorry tale of Madeleine Fletcher's conceit. Let it stand as a cautionary reminder that society courts calamity when our women stray beyond the limits of their gender."

"I don't understand half them fancy words," someone in the mob grumbled. "But I gets the gist right enough: some foreign devil's getting 'is thievin' hands on our factory."

"That's not true," Madeleine cried. "Not a single word of it is true."

"What about your French fella' then?" someone else shouted. "We've seen 'im sniffin' around. Don't tell me 'e were just a figment o' me imagination."

The man folded his beefy arms across his broad chest, while several other workers murmured their angry agreement.

"Mr Dubois has only been helping us to find new investors," Madeleine said with an increasingly desperate edge to her voice. "But no one is buying the factory."

"What're we needin' investors for then?" someone demanded to know. "You told us everythin' was apples 'n pears, money-wise."

"Aye," another voice chimed in. "Where there's smoke, there's fire, I says."

"A load o' rubbish, that's what this is," one bald labourer bellowed. "Pretty talk don't mean nowt to us. We got families to feed."

Madeleine shrank back, feeling cornered. She racked her mind for the right words to say, but she was still too shocked by the viciousness of Charles Turner's lies.

A sudden commotion by the entrance drew everyone's attention. Mr Dubois appeared in the crowd, and several people didn't fail to voice their anger at him. Quickly, he pushed his way through the disgruntled workers to Madeleine's side.

"I came as swiftly as I could after reading that dreadful article," he told her. "Are you all right, Madame?"

She gave him a weak, yet grateful smile. "I'm managing, thank you. Though matters are rather tense, as you can see."

"Let me help," he said before turning to address the men. He held up his hands, waiting for quiet.

"Good people of Sheffield," he began, his voice steady and strong. "Don't let the cheap words of some newspaper man turn you against each other. You know Mrs Fletcher: she always thinks of you and your welfare first. Has she ever given you any cause to doubt that?"

The workers shuffled uncertainly. "It's true she's always treated us fairly," someone piped up.

"Exactly," Mr Dubois said. "And do you know why? Because Mrs Fletcher is proud of you. She's proud of the strong men who have helped to build this factory into the success it is today."

"Hear hear," a lone voice shouted. Madeleine thought it had sounded like Stuart Wainwright, the young engineer.

"You are Northerners," Mr Dubois declared. "Throughout the world, you are known as honest and hardworking. Men of grit who stand tall together, come what may."

Heads started nodding and an approving murmur rippled through the crowd. Mr Dubois smiled encouragingly.

"Have faith, I tell you. Money is needed for progress. But the real power that drives this factory–"

He paused and looked round at the listening faces. "Why, that's you! Your skills and your labour. It's your hands that shape the future. Never doubt your worth. And never let yourself be deceived by the lies printed in some newspaper."

Jack Wainwright stepped forward. "You heard the gentleman, lads. Standing around raising our voices and shaking our fists isn't going to help anyone. So how about we get back to work, eh?"

Despite some muttered grumbling here and there, the crowd slowly dispersed as everyone returned to their stations.

"Thank you, Monsieur," Madeleine whispered after letting out a long sigh of relief. Her head felt dizzy, but she couldn't show any sign of weakness now.

"My pleasure, Madame," Mr Dubois replied.

"Well spoken, Dubois," Ashton grinned. "But then again, you Frenchmen always have a way with words, don't you?"

"Ashton, please," Madeleine begged. "I've had my fill of venom and hostility today. So I'll kindly ask you to bite your tongue."

"In that case, I'll take my tongue elsewhere," he scoffed. "I could probably do with a drink after all this excitement."

He turned to leave, but then stopped. "You may have convinced these simple workers, but the investors will be another matter. They're sure to abandon us over this."

"And that is why," Mr Dubois said, "I will be paying each of them a personal visit – today, in fact. To put everyone's mind at rest and dispel any doubts."

"Good luck," Ashton replied with a smirk before sauntering off.

Madeleine was glad to see the back of him. That man could be so impossibly rude, she thought.

"Mr Dubois, won't you join me in my office?" she asked. "We have much to discuss."

As she led him up to her office, each step felt like a monumental effort. The clamour and chaos had drained all her energy.

Walking past Robert, who sat in the outer office with a concerned look on his face, Madeleine entered her own office and closed the door behind them. She staggered to her desk and leaned heavily on its edge.

"Madame, you appear unwell," Mr Dubois said softly. "You are pale as a ghost."

"I'm fine," she said automatically, though the room seemed to sway and blur around her.

Mr Dubois stepped closer. "You have been under tremendous strain. Please, allow me to fetch you some water at least."

As he turned toward the pitcher, Madeleine tried to straighten her back. But then her legs gave out. With a startled gasp she collapsed, only to find herself being caught in Mr Dubois' gentle embrace.

For a suspended moment they remained frozen, their faces inches apart. Madeleine gazed up into his dark eyes, struck by their unexpected warmth.

"F–forgive me," she stammered as the two of them sprang apart awkwardly. "I don't know what came over me."

"The fault is entirely mine," he replied quickly. "That is to say... I–" He cleared his throat. "Let me get you that glass of water."

Suddenly, the door flew open and Charlotte burst in, her eyes wide with panic. "Maddie," she cried, gasping for breath. "It's Ellie: she's been arrested!"

Chapter Twelve

"Arrested? My Ellie?" Madeleine stumbled back. Once more, the room began to spin around her. But Mr Dubois took hold of her arm and deftly guided her to the nearest chair.

"What happened?" Madeleine asked Charlotte weakly.

"She just up and disappeared from the breakfast table, in a frightfully agitated state. But I couldn't send Bill to go after her, because he was driving you to the factory."

"My girl ran away? Where to?"

"The offices of The Herald, apparently."

Madeleine gave a short and painful groan. "Where Charles Turner works..."

Charlotte nodded. "An hour after Ellie had vanished, a constable came to our door. He said Ellie was down at the police station: she'd been arrested for having caused a disturbance at The Herald."

Madeleine's hand flew up to her chest. "It's that dreadful article. Ellie probably read it, too. I remember how angry she was about the first one. So I can only imagine how furious she must be over this one."

"Oh, Maddie," Charlotte lamented. "What shall we do?"

"I have to go to the police station at once. See if I can get the police to release her." She jumped up, but she swayed on her feet.

"Madame Fletcher, forgive me," Mr Dubois said, rushing to her side. "You are still faint. Please allow me to escort you to the police station."

"That's kind of you, sir. But I wouldn't wish to impose," she said, even though the room tilted dangerously.

"I insist, Madame," he replied politely. "Besides, the police might be more inclined to listen to you when there's a calm gentleman with you." He gave her an apologetic smile. "You know what they are like."

"You're right," Madeleine said. "I would be grateful for your company, Mr Dubois."

He nodded and helped her to gather her things.

Charlotte wrung her hands anxiously. "I'll hurry back to the house and wait for word." She embraced Madeleine. "Bring her home – please?"

It was Mr Dubois who replied, calmly and confidently. "We'll do whatever it takes to secure Mademoiselle Ellie's release."

Madeleine leaned heavily on his arm as he escorted her outside. In her disoriented state, the sun seemed overly bright and the street noises painfully loud. But Mr Dubois' steady presence guided her along until they reached the waiting carriage.

"To the police station, Bill," Madeleine told her coachman. "Quick as you can, please."

Mr Dubois handed her up and climbed in after her.

"I pray Ellie is unharmed," she said as the carriage rolled into motion. "What on earth might have possessed her?"

"Don't fret, Madame. I'm sure we'll be able to resolve this misunderstanding."

"I hope you're right." Madeleine twisted her gloved hands together. "Ellie hasn't been the same ever since her father died. But I fear she may have done something truly rash this time."

"It's in the nature of youth to be impulsive. I'm sure your daughter meant no real harm."

Madeleine sighed. "She has such a fiery spirit. I suppose this latest piece of slander pushed her over the edge."

Mr Dubois nodded. "No doubt she wished to defend your honour. An admirable impulse, if somewhat misguided in its execution."

"I suppose. But goodness me, getting arrested..." Madeleine pressed a hand to her forehead. "And of course this whole episode will only provide more fodder for that awful journalist."

"Let's try not to worry about that for the moment. First, we need to focus our efforts on your daughter's release."

"Yes," Madeleine sighed. "I'm worried the police won't let her go very easily."

"Have faith, Madame. We'll make an earnest and heartfelt case for freeing Ellie. Her young age and family name should help us."

"Do you think so?"

"Mademoiselle Ellie is hardly a penniless street urchin," he chuckled. "In my experience, the police are often rather biassed. Ruthless and mean with the poor, but fairly accommodating towards members of the better classes."

"Let's pray you're right," Madeleine said. She stared hard into the distance, wishing she could see the way out of this horrible mess. "Ellie is a good girl at heart. Just a bit quick-tempered at times."

"I have yet to make her acquaintance," he said. "But if she takes after her mother, then I'm sure she is a delightful young lady." He smiled at her, trying to put her at ease.

Madeleine made a miserable attempt to return his smile. But her mind was weighed down by the memory of the bitter row she'd had with her daughter. A row that had started because Ellie had seen Mr Dubois bringing Madeleine home after dinner.

How would she react now, when Madeleine showed up at the police with Mr Dubois by her side? If Ellie was still angry or upset over the newspaper article and her subsequent arrest... Wouldn't Mr Dubois' presence irritate her even further?

Madeleine shivered at the prospect.

"Have no fear, Madame," Mr Dubois said, misreading her gesture. "I will use every skill of persuasion at my disposal to secure Ellie's freedom."

"You are too kind, sir. I don't deserve such loyalty from a near stranger."

"Nonsense. Helping those in need is the duty of any gentleman. And I would hope that you see me more as a friend than a stranger."

Just then the carriage rolled to a stop. Madeleine took a deep breath and accepted Mr Dubois' hand to descend.

Side by side they climbed the worn steps of the police station and then entered through the heavy oak doors. In an instant, Madeleine's senses were assaulted by a wave of noise and the smell of tobacco.

Two policemen jostled past from behind, almost knocking her over as they wrestled with their struggling suspect. Instinctively, Madeleine moved closer to Mr Dubois.

"I'll do the introductions," he said as he offered her his arm. She nodded, grateful for his reliable cool-headedness.

Navigating through the press of bodies, Mr Dubois led her to the front desk where a gruff police sergeant sat scribbling in a ledger. The man glanced up as they approached.

"Good day, officer," Mr Dubois said smoothly. "I've accompanied Mrs Fletcher here regarding her daughter, who I understand is currently in your custody."

The sergeant set down his pen and cleared his throat, while trying to look very official. "Ah yes, the Fletcher girl. Caused quite a ruckus down at The Herald earlier."

"Oh please, sir," Madeleine blurted out frantically. "Ellie's just a child. She's prone to foolish outbursts. Surely, we can resolve this without punishment."

The sergeant's stern face remained impassive. "You do realise, don't you, ma'am, that a serious offence has been committed? If every member of the public were to assault the press simply because they didn't like something the newspapers printed..."

"I understand that, sir," she replied, close to tears. "And you must believe me: my Ellie isn't that type of girl. Not normally. But ever since she lost her father–" Madeleine's voice faltered.

"Miss Fletcher comes from a good family, sergeant," Mr Dubois said calmly. "She doesn't pose any threat or nuisance to society." He threw a critical glance at a trio of unsavoury suspects who sat waiting on a hard bench nearby. "Unlike some of your other guests here."

The policeman scoffed. "From what I've heard, she acted like a hellcat over at The Herald."

"Please, sir," Madeleine pleaded through her tears. "Ellie would never–"

"But if you'll let me finish," he interrupted. "Mr Turner has very graciously declined to press charges. And therefore, Miss Fletcher is free to go."

Madeleine nearly collapsed in relief. "Thank heavens."

"There is however one condition," the sergeant cautioned. "Mr Turner has requested that you call on him in person, Mrs Fletcher."

Madeleine paled, but she nodded. "I shall do so, I promise." She would happily face that horrid man if it meant Ellie could escape any prosecution.

"Very well then." The sergeant turned to a nearby constable. "Andrews, bring over the Fletcher girl. She's going home."

Giving Madeleine a dark look, he added, "None too soon, in my opinion. Quite a demanding young lady, this precious daughter of yours. My constables have been running to and fro for her the entire time: tea, biscuits, a pitcher of clean water so she could refresh her face and hands."

"I do apologise," Madeleine blushed. "Must be the effects of her distress, I'm sure."

"Oh, take her home already," the sergeant sighed wearily. "And please don't tell me you have any more children like her?"

"Mama!"

Madeleine whirled to see Ellie rushing towards her, looking somewhat dishevelled but none the worse. She drew her daughter into a fierce embrace.

"Oh, my dear girl," she murmured, stroking Ellie's hair. "Thank the Lord, you're safe."

Ellie clung to her tightly for a long moment before pulling back. "I'm sorry, Mama. I don't know what came over me."

"Hush now, my darling. We'll discuss this later." Madeleine cupped her daughter's face tenderly. "First, let's leave this place."

"Our sincerest thanks for your willing cooperation, sergeant," Mr Dubois said to the police officer. "Time we were on our way, I believe," he told Madeleine and Ellie as he motioned them towards the door.

When they stepped outside, the sunlight momentarily blinded Madeleine. Closing her eyes, she breathed deeply, relieved to have her daughter by her side.

Ellie shuffled her feet and cleared her throat. "Thank you, Mama, for coming to get me."

"You might say it was a team effort," Madeleine replied, inclining her head towards Mr Dubois. "Eleanor, I don't think I've introduced you to Mr Pierre Dubois yet? He has been a tremendous help today."

The Frenchman executed a short, courteous bow. "Miss Fletcher, the pleasure is mine."

Ellie blushed and hardly dared to look him in the eye. "How do you do, sir? It would seem I'm in your debt."

"Not at all, Mademoiselle," he responded kindly. "I'm pleased that I was able to be of some assistance to you and your mother in this difficult situation."

An awkward silence ensued while Ellie studied her shoes intently. Madeleine had to hide an amused grin at her daughter's discomfort.

"Well then," Mr Dubois said lightly. "I suppose you both will be wanting to head home after this ordeal?"

"Actually, there is one more difficult matter to resolve first," Madeleine sighed. "Mr Turner expects me to call on him, Eleanor."

"You cannot be serious, Mother," Ellie bristled. "After all the horrible things he wrote about you."

"It was his condition for not pressing any charges against you," Madeleine replied evenly. "A small price to pay, I felt."

"Can't it wait until tomorrow?"

"Why delay the inevitable? The sooner we get this over with, the better."

"I'm assuming you want me to come with you?" Ellie asked, lowering her eyes.

"Correct. So you can apologise to Mr Turner."

Ellie merely nodded. Even though she had stopped protesting, Madeleine could tell her daughter was dreading the idea.

"Shall I accompany you as well?" Mr Dubois suggested.

"That's very kind of you to offer," Madeleine said. "But I'm afraid your presence might only spark more gossip, given the nature of Mr Turner's articles."

"You have a point there," he agreed.

"And besides, you've done more than enough," she continued warmly. "Thank you once again for rushing to my aid today."

"Think nothing of it, Madame. I'm happy I could be of service."

After exchanging a few gracious parting words, Mr Dubois helped them into their carriage. Madeleine gave him a short wave of the hand and then called out to her coachman.

"To the Herald of The North, Bill."

Where the infamous Mr Charles Turner awaits us.

Chapter Thirteen

"I really don't want to go, Mama," Ellie grumbled, sitting by Madeleine's side as their carriage made its way to the newspaper's offices. "Charles Turner is a dreadful man. He's bound to gloat over our humiliation when we come to grovel before him."

"Who said anything about grovelling?" Madeleine asked with a determined grin on her face.

"That's how he'll see it anyway."

"Then let him, if it makes him happy. We are merely going to offer Mr Turner our apologies. But I have no intention whatsoever to throw myself at his feet or anything dramatic like that."

"Good."

"You'll see there's great personal strength in dignity."

"If you say so, Mama. But I'm still not looking forward to this visit."

"Perhaps you should have thought of that before you rushed off and caused a scene," Madeleine said, unable to resist the small barb.

"I only did it because I wanted to stand up for you," Ellie replied defensively. "When I read that horrible article about you... Well, it made my blood boil. And I felt I had to do something."

"I appreciate the sentiment, my darling. I truly do. But please, next time, try to think before you act."

"I know," Ellie said with a guilty pout on her lips. "I'm sorry."

"It's all right, my angel. You're still so young. But tell me, what exactly happened at The Herald?"

"I might have shouted and screamed at Mr Turner," Ellie admitted. "But I certainly didn't do anything that would have warranted involving the police. I just wanted to make my point clear."

"With words? And nothing more?"

"Precisely. Words, that's all it was. I swear."

Madeleine gave her daughter a long look. "I believe you," she said. "I know you're honest and that you care for things like fairness and justice."

She smiled. "And if Charlotte were here, she'd probably tell you that I was like that as well when she and I were young: bold, fiery and a bit too impulsive at times."

Ellie chuckled. "Really, Mama?"

Madeleine nodded. "If you ply Charlotte with cake and ask her about our childhood, I'm sure she could tell you a mad story or two."

"I might just try that," Ellie laughed.

"Then hopefully, hearing about some of the silly mistakes from my youth will help you not to make them yourself."

The carriage wheels clattered on the cobblestones as they turned the corner to The Herald's offices. Ellie gazed out the window. "We're here," she said nervously.

Madeleine gave her daughter a warm smile. "Chin up, my darling. We'll get through this, you and I together. We can handle whatever awaits us."

Side by side, they marched into the building.

"Mrs Fletcher to see Mr Charles Turner, please," Madeleine announced to the nearest clerk.

"First floor, third door to your right, ma'am," the young man answered politely. If her name sounded familiar to him, his face didn't show it.

Madeleine and Ellie climbed the stairs and knocked on Charles Turner's door.

"Come," a grumbling voice answered.

Taking a deep breath, Madeleine opened the door and stepped inside.

Sitting behind his cluttered desk, Charles Turner looked every bit the bitter old man Madeleine had expected him to be. His hair was slicked back with pomade in a vain attempt to hide his thinning pate. Flinty eyes peered up at them from behind spectacles sitting atop a ruddy, vein-crossed nose.

"Ah, the little hellion and her mother," the journalist sneered. "Have you come to plead for mercy? Or to threaten me again? Either way, I'm thrilled for the entertainment."

"We've come to offer you an apology, Mr Turner," Madeleine replied, refusing to be baited by him.

"An apology, eh?" He leaned back, sporting a snarky grin. "I must admit I'm surprised, Mrs Fletcher."

"About what, sir?"

"Why, about you coming here at all, of course. I rather thought you wouldn't have the courage for it. Or is it arrogance that drove you here today?"

Madeleine smiled politely. "I'd say I was motivated by decency, Mr Turner. I take it you're familiar with that virtue?"

"I am indeed." He scoffed. "In fact, every day our newspaper's columns are full of reports about people who all claim to be decent and virtuous members of society."

"Reports?" Ellie grumbled. "Gossip and scandal-mongering more like."

"Still intent on stirring up trouble, are you, Miss Fletcher?" Turner smirked. "So much for that apology of yours then."

"The apology is sincere, I assure you," Madeleine intervened quickly. "But Eleanor became very distraught when she read that article of yours. Understandably so, I might add."

"You approve of your daughter's actions?"

"Not her actions, no. But I can see what motivated them."

Turner laughed. "And what would that be? A hot-headed temperament? A natural inclination towards hysterical outbursts?"

"No, Mr Turner," Madeleine replied calmly. "A daughter's love and devotion to her mother."

"Love and devotion," he said, rolling his eyes. "That's another fine pair of virtues."

"They most certainly are, wouldn't you agree?"

"So love and devotion is what propelled your daughter to come barging in here and threaten me?"

"Eleanor's emotions got the better of her, I'm afraid."

"A typical female affliction," Turner mocked.

"Men can be equally guilty of acting without thinking," Madeleine replied pointedly. "And surely, Mr Turner, you weren't frightened by a delicate young lady like my daughter, were you?"

"Of course not."

"And yet," Madeleine grinned, "you felt it necessary to call on the help of the police."

A thunderous expression briefly crossed his face. *Touché,* Madeleine thought with some glee. *I had you there, didn't I?*

"Only to protect the girl from her own neurotic self," he snarled.

"Most thoughtful of you."

"I can see where your daughter got her flair for theatrics from," Turner said. "You sure have a way with words, haven't you, Mrs Fletcher?"

"At least I have the courage to speak my words directly to someone's face, Mr Turner. Instead of hiding behind the printed sheets of a newspaper."

"Everyone has their special skills, I suppose. Some of us excel at running a business into the ground while gallivanting about with French investors. Whereas others see it as their duty to inform the public."

"Is that what you call it: informing the public? Spreading lies is what I think you mean."

"I merely report the facts as they come to me. If you've taken offence, perhaps the truth touched a nerve?"

"The truth? Your articles were full of wild distortions."

He shrugged. "Every good story requires a bit of colourful embroidery, my dear Mrs Fletcher. There's an art to maintaining readership that you clearly fail to appreciate."

"It may well be artful to weave half-truths into your writing, Mr Turner. But it hardly embodies integrity."

"Integrity? Bah, humbug. The public craves scandal and sensation. I simply provide what the masses demand."

"And that's your excuse for slandering a lady's good name, is it?"

With a grin, he held up his hands. "Why don't we cease these hostilities between us? I'm not an unreasonable man. If you feel my articles distorted the truth, then perhaps we ought to let you tell your side of the story."

Madeleine narrowed her eyes, cautious of a potential trap. "Explain yourself."

"A personal account – exclusive to The Herald of course – giving you the opportunity to share your views with the public."

"You wish to interview me for your newspaper?"

He nodded. "Our readers would love it, I'm sure. After all, they've heard so much about you already."

Studying his face, Madeleine considered his offer. Given the viciousness of his previous articles, she was distrustful of his motives in this matter. Did he really want to give her a fair chance?

"And as a further enticement," he added with a smile, "I will gladly gloss over your daughter's regrettable actions... if you agree to this interview. Let bygones be bygones, I say."

"Very well," Madeleine said. "I agree to those terms."

She still didn't trust the man. But if sitting down with him to answer his questions meant that Ellie would be spared any more unpleasantness, then Madeleine was determined to play along.

"Excellent," Turner said. "You've made a wise decision."

Let's just hope I don't end up regretting it, she thought. "Where and when would you like for us to have this exchange, sir?"

"I don't wish to inconvenience you any more than needed. So if you prefer, we can have our conversation in the comfort of your own home?"

Madeleine didn't know how she felt about letting Charles Turner into her house. On the other hand, it was a better option than to invite him to the factory, where he would likely want to snoop around and start asking questions to the workers.

So she accepted his proposal and they arranged to have the interview three days later.

"You were wonderfully brave in there, Mama," Ellie said once the two of them were safely back in the carriage and on their way home. "How you stood up to that mean old bully. I wish I could be as clever with my words as you were."

"Maybe Mr Turner had hoped that I'd be a frightened, jittery mouse," Madeleine smiled. "He would have loved to write about that in his next piece, no doubt. But I suppose we showed him wrong."

"Not only that, now you'll also have a chance to tell everyone the truth. Just think, Mama: you'll be able to set the record straight after all those lies he wrote."

"Perhaps," Madeleine murmured.

Privately however, she had her doubts that speaking with the sneering journalist would do much good. Turner probably had his own underhanded reasons for suggesting this interview. The man lived to dig up secrets and spin tawdry tales. She didn't trust his motives one tiny bit.

Chances were slim that a dishonest scoundrel like him planned to trade in fair reporting anytime soon. Not when there was more profit to be made in dragging names through the mud instead.

Chapter Fourteen

Three days later, Madeleine was pacing the floor of her living room. Moving in agitated circles, she wrung her hands as she cast yet another worried glance at the clock on the mantelpiece.

"He's late," she said. "He should have been here half an hour ago."

"Were you expecting punctuality from a man like him?" Charlotte asked in a soothing tone. "Charles Turner has no manners, dear. He's probably doing this on purpose. To make you even more nervous."

"If that's his intention, then I must say he's doing an excellent job."

"Do sit down and have some tea." Charlotte gently patted the spot next to her on the sofa. "You'll wear a hole in that fine Persian rug at this rate."

With a sigh, Madeleine sank onto the settee beside her cousin. "Drat that man and his confounded newspaper. My stomach has been doing somersaults all morning."

She accepted the tea that Charlotte gave her, but the cup rattled against the saucer, so she quickly put it down again.

"Look how my hands are shaking. I'm in no state to face anyone, let alone a cruel and cunning journalist."

"Just breathe easy," Charlotte said, placing a reassuring hand on Madeleine's arm. "I know you'll handle yourself beautifully in front of that dreadful scribbler."

"Do you really think so? What if I end up stumbling over my words like a simpleton when he starts asking his questions? Already his contempt for me is clear as day in those nasty newspaper columns of his."

"Rise above him, Maddie. You'll be marvellous, believe me." Charlotte gave her cousin a warm, reassuring smile. Madeleine tried to return the gesture, but all she seemed capable of was a brief and painful grimace.

"Everything is ready, isn't it?" she asked anxiously.

Charlotte nodded. "Down to the smallest detail. There's tea and biscuits aplenty. And if you need anything, the bell is here beside you."

"And Mary? She knows what to do as well?" Madeleine had personally informed the maid on the importance of today's visitor. But she desperately needed the confirmation from Charlotte.

"Of course," her cousin answered patiently. "The girl is staying close to the front door, so she can let Mr Turner in the minute he arrives."

"Good, good," Madeleine murmured while her eyes darted around the immaculately tidy sitting room.

"Stop worrying, Maddie," Charlotte said. "All will go well. I'll be close by, in the small parlour. If that rogue gives you any trouble, just shout for me and I'll come rushing over."

Madeleine couldn't keep herself from chuckling affectionately when she pictured the vision of her dear cousin storming into the room and threatening Turner with an umbrella.

"Bless you, my sweet Charlotte. Your support means ever so much to me, it really does."

Suddenly, the doorbell sounded, making Madeleine start. "He's here," she gasped.

"Chin up, girl," Charlotte said. She gave Madeleine's hand a final encouraging squeeze and then withdrew to the adjoining parlour.

Trying her hardest to appear calm, Madeleine arranged herself elegantly on the sofa.

Mary entered, bobbing a curtsy. "Mr Charles Turner to see you, ma'am."

"Do show him in."

A moment later the journalist bustled inside. Rising, Madeleine extended a polite hand. "Mr Turner, thank you for coming. Please have a seat."

Turner's eyes glinted as he appraised the room before settling himself in the wingback chair. "Good afternoon, Mrs Fletcher. So very kind of you to make time to speak with me."

His oily tone made her skin crawl, but Madeleine maintained a cordial front. "May I offer you some tea?" She lifted the pot with a smile that felt more like a wince.

"Not much of a tea drinker, I'm afraid. You wouldn't happen to have anything a bit stronger, would you?"

Suppressing the urge to frown at his brazen request, she offered him a glass of brandy instead. He accepted it eagerly and took a sizeable gulp.

I'm surprised he doesn't smack his lips as well, Madeleine thought with some contempt for his poor social manners.

"Shall we get straight to business then?" he asked as he put aside his glass and produced a notebook from his old, worn briefcase.

"By all means," she replied, mentally bracing herself for his questions.

Turner flipped open his notebook, pencil at the ready. "You'll have gathered from my articles that I'm not exactly a great supporter of yours. But please, tell our readers – in your own words – what motivated you to take on this momentous task of running your late husband's factory?"

"Plain and simple: it was Benjamin's dying wish."

"But why? There's no male heir to take over the reins. You only have a daughter. Why would your dearly departed husband place such a huge burden on you?"

Madeleine bristled at his dismissive tone regarding Ellie. As if a daughter was merely second-rate offspring. But she kept her voice steady when she replied.

"I never questioned my husband's wishes. I can only assume he wanted me to look after his life's work and legacy."

"A widow's duty, eh? And would you say you're acquitting yourself well? It must be a formidable challenge for someone lacking in knowledge and experience."

Madeleine faltered briefly. She thought of her own doubts that nagged at her constantly. But of course she couldn't tell him about those.

"Although I admit it's difficult," she said after clearing her throat, "I strive to honour Benjamin's faith in me. I work hard every day. And I shall persist, no matter what."

Turner's mouth curled up in a grin as he scribbled down her words rapidly. Madeleine rather suspected that her momentary hesitation would come back to haunt her.

"Forgive me for saying so, Mrs Fletcher, but that doesn't sound overly confident, does it?"

"I'm sorry if that was your impression, Mr Turner," she replied with a thin smile. "I confess

I have little experience in speaking with the press. I suppose I just don't have a silver tongue like some other people do."

The journalist barked a laugh. "A woman who doesn't have a way with words? Ha, now there's a first."

While she tried to smile politely at his crude joke, Madeleine began to regret that she had agreed to this interview so easily. The man was impossible.

"Seeing as we're on the topic of women," he went on, "I was wondering if you'd care to share your perspective on the women's rights movement?"

"Women's rights, Mr Turner? I'm afraid I don't understand."

"Oh, you know: all this nonsense about making men and women equal by law. What are your views on those radicals stirring up trouble lately? Do you consider yourself to be a suffragette for instance?"

"Good grief, no. I'm far too busy with the factory to be involved in any of that sort of thing."

"The hard-working, groundbreaking widow," he grinned. "Paving the way for future generations of girls and women intent on conquering the world."

"I don't see myself as a role model, if that's what you're implying, Mr Turner."

"Then how *do* you see yourself, Mrs Fletcher?"

"As I've already told you, I'm simply a widow trying to fulfil my late husband's wishes. It was fate rather than any personal ambitions that made me the co-owner of a large factory."

"And was it fate as well that sent this French chap your way? Meeting him has proven quite fruitful to you, hasn't it?"

"Mr Dubois has been most helpful in securing the investment we were looking for, yes."

"Awfully kind of him. But tell me, Mrs Fletcher, how well do you know this gentleman?"

Madeleine frowned, suspicious of any hidden motives behind the question. "Well enough to conduct business together. We've talked on several occasions to discuss–"

"Yes, yes, I'm sure you have," Turner interrupted. "But I'm referring to the man himself. What do you know about his past?"

"I do not like to pry unduly into the personal affairs of business associates, Mr Turner."

"And yet you've welcomed him into the heart of your affairs," the journalist said. "Rather unwise, I should think, considering the whispers one hears."

"Whispers? What sort of whispers, sir?"

His eyes glinted eagerly. "Why, the rumours that your charming French associate has something of a shadowed past. That his business dealings haven't always been... legitimate."

"I don't concern myself with rumours, Mr Turner." Madeleine tried to keep her tone of voice even. But her mind was swarming with doubts. It was true that Mr Dubois had always remained rather vague about the finer details of his past.

"I've been asking around about this Mr Dubois of yours," the journalist explained. "And while I haven't found any hard evidence against him yet, I've managed to trace several former clients of his."

He paused, deliberately dragging out the suspense of the moment.

"And?" Madeleine asked. "Did they speak highly of him?"

"Hardly," Turner grinned. "They all lost large amounts of money because of your Mr Dubois."

"Bad investments happen, unfortunately. Success is never guaranteed in these matters."

"True. These people however, or victims as we might call them, they felt they were duped."

"I suppose no one likes to admit they made a poor decision. It's easier to blame others when something goes wrong in our life, isn't it?"

"That's one explanation, I guess. But I have a special sense for these things." He tapped the side of his nose. "And I suspect your Frenchman is a swindler, Mrs Fletcher. Someone who tricks wealthy people out of their money and then disappears."

Madeleine gasped. "That's a serious accusation, Mr Turner. Even for someone like you. Do you have any proof?"

"I do not," he conceded with a grin. "And that's why I haven't reported the story in our newspaper yet. We wouldn't want to be sued for libel. But I know a fraud when I see one."

Madeleine shook her head. "And I'll take Mr Dubois' word over a piece of unfounded gossip any day. I'm sorry, Mr Turner, but I don't believe what you just told me."

"As is your right, Mrs Fletcher. But if you're so sure about your chap's trustworthiness, then why don't you ask him about these so-called rumours?"

He drained his glass and rose to his feet. "Well, it's been lovely talking to you. Our chat will make for an interesting piece in The Herald soon."

Madeleine stood up as well and called for Mary with a short tinkle of the hand bell. "Thank you, Mr Turner. The maid will see you out."

Sporting his usual smug grin, the journalist followed Mary out of the room, leaving Madeleine alone with her frantic thoughts. Could Turner's claims about Mr Dubois possibly hold any truth?

With a racing pulse, she went to the sideboard where the bottle of brandy stood and poured herself a double measure. The dark amber-coloured liquid burned as it slid down her throat.

Was that despicable journalist merely trying to stoke up trouble? Or had Mr Dubois bewitched her with his charm?

Chapter Fifteen

Madeleine drained the last of her brandy just as the sitting room door creaked open behind her.

"Goodness me," Charlotte gasped as she hurried inside. "Drinking spirits at this hour?"

Madeleine set down the empty glass and turned to see her cousin's round face pinched with concern, one hand fluttering at her chest.

"Oh, Charlotte," she sighed. "It was awful."

Her cousin bustled forward, skirts swishing. "That ghastly journalist rattled your nerves, didn't he?" Charlotte clucked her tongue. "I should have stayed in the room with you."

Madeleine's hand reached for the bottle of brandy, desperate to ease her distress. But Charlotte gently caught her arm.

"No more of that now, Maddie," her cousin chided softly. "Let's get you comfortable, so you can tell me everything."

With a gentle nudge Charlotte guided Madeleine towards the sofa and helped her to sit down. She fluffed up an embroidered pillow and tucked it behind Madeleine's back, before settling down next to her cousin.

"There. That's better, isn't it?"

Madeleine nodded, still feeling numb from Charles Turner's shocking revelation.

"Now then," Charlotte said, her kind brown eyes glowing with sympathy. "Tell me what happened. It must have been quite bad for you to be this upset."

"That dreadful Mr Turner," Madeleine began. "He said the most troubling thing about Mr Dubois."

"What did he tell you? Did he invent some vile nonsense about anything improper going on between you and Mr Dubois?"

"No, nothing like that," Madeleine replied as a blush of shame coloured her cheeks. "He claims Mr Dubois may not be as trustworthy as he seems. And that in the past, Mr Dubois has swindled people out of their money."

"Preposterous. Don't believe a single word of it. Why, Mr Dubois has been nothing but a gentleman. Securing that investment for you, coming to your aid in front of the workers."

"Yes, I know." Madeleine bit her lower lip. "And yet..."

She rose and started pacing before the fireplace. "What do I truly know about the man? He's certainly charming, exceedingly friendly, and helpful too. But he did remain rather vague about his past."

She halted and turned to her cousin. "The investors are due to sign the paperwork in a few days, Charlotte. What if Mr Turner spoke the truth?" Distress cracked her voice. "Have I allowed myself to be fooled by a scoundrel?"

"Now, now, Maddie. You've had a nasty jolt. Your mind is too clouded for rational thought. Some refreshments are in order, I believe." Charlotte took the hand bell and rang it to summon the maid.

"Mary, dear," she said when the girl appeared. "Bring us a fresh pot of tea, please. And two generous helpings of that delicious sponge cake Mrs Dobbs made earlier."

She turned to Madeleine and smiled. "Nothing like a good piece of cake to clear the mind and help you think straight again."

Madeleine rather suspected cake wouldn't ease her worries, but she indulged her cousin's sweet tooth. Patiently she waited until Mary returned with the tea tray.

"I can't stop thinking about Mr Turner's allegations," she said as Charlotte passed her a piece of cake. "If Mr Dubois turns out to be a fraud... Why, my reputation would be ruined. And even worse, it would put the future of the factory at stake."

As nice as Mrs Dobbs' cake seemed, Madeleine was too nervous to eat any of it. So she set her plate down again.

"Firstly," Charlotte said between bites of cake, "don't work yourself into a state. Not before you've determined the truth."

"But that's the crux of the matter, isn't it? How do I tell the truth from a lie?"

"Why don't you invite Mr Dubois to come and see you? Speak with him directly about these allegations."

Madeleine paled. "Confront him? I cannot simply ask the man if he is a swindler."

"No, of course not. But you could tell him Mr Turner has made certain claims. Claims that have upset you and that you would like to clarify with him."

Pondering her cousin's idea, Madeleine took a sip of tea. "What if he grows angry at the accusation?"

"Any true gentleman would understand your concerns," Charlotte said. "If Mr Dubois cares for your good opinion, then he will accept the chance to put your mind at rest."

Madeleine considered this as she continued to drink her tea. Charlotte did make an excellent point. And Madeleine would not feel easy until she heard Mr Dubois' response from his own lips.

"Very well," she decided. "I shall write him an urgent note requesting to see him. And I'll send Bill to deliver it straight away." She rose to her feet. "If you'll excuse me, I'll go and write my note in the study."

Charlotte longingly eyed the piece of cake Madeleine hadn't touched. "You're not finishing that then, are you?"

"You can have it," Madeleine smiled. "Thank you for the good advice. You're an absolute angel."

Her cousin shrugged and picked up Madeleine's plate. "I told you cake would help."

In the study, Madeleine quickly penned her note and then she handed it to her coachman. Bill soon returned with an elegantly handwritten reply from Mr Dubois, stating that he would be delighted to call on her at eleven o'clock the very next day.

True to his word, the Frenchman arrived promptly at the agreed time the following morning. Madeleine sat waiting for him in the living room, still unsure about how to broach the subject.

"Mrs Fletcher, what a pleasure to see you again," he beamed when Mary showed him into the room.

"The pleasure is mine, Monsieur." Madeleine gestured to the tea service as he took a seat. "Would you care for some tea? Or do you prefer coffee?"

"Tea will be splendid, thank you."

Madeleine tried to keep her nervous hands from trembling as she poured two cups of tea. How on earth was she supposed to bring up the questions she was burning to ask?

Cream and sugar for your tea, Mr Dubois? Oh, and by the by, is it true that you're a swindling crook?

No, that would never do.

"I hope you are finding Sheffield agreeable, Mr Dubois?" she enquired politely. "Are your lodgings to your satisfaction?"

"Yes, they're quite pleasant, thank you," he replied smoothly. "And my landlady is a very kind woman. When she heard I was from France, she went and purchased a French recipe book. Just so she could prepare the sort of dishes that make me feel at home, she said."

"How awfully sweet of her."

"I thought the same," he smiled before raising his cup to his lips to take a careful sip.

A short and awkward silence followed. Madeleine stared into her own cup of tea, grasping for the right words. But her mind drew a blank.

Looking at her with those clever yet tender eyes of his, Mr Dubois set down his cup. "Forgive my boldness, Mrs Fletcher, but I sense something is troubling you. And I'm fairly sure you didn't invite me here simply for tea and idle chatter."

Madeleine flushed. "I– That is–" She faltered, then met his gaze. "I had a visit from Mr Turner yesterday."

"The journalist? He came to see you?"

"It was part of the agreement he and I made: he wouldn't press charges against Eleanor in exchange for me granting him an exclusive interview."

"That strikes me as a fair enough bargain. And this was yesterday, you said? How did it go?"

"Charles Turner isn't a very agreeable person, I'm afraid," she sighed. "And I shan't be surprised if he ends up twisting and turning every single word I spoke."

"I do hope the scoundrel doesn't misconstrue your words too badly. You deserve better than to be mistreated by the likes of him, Madame."

Madeleine cleared her throat. It was now or never, she decided. "But he also told me something that I found most upsetting," she said. "Something about you, Mr Dubois."

He raised an eyebrow in surprise. "About me?"

"Yes. He claims you are a fraud who misleads wealthy people and tricks them out of their money."

To Madeleine's surprise, Mr Dubois was dumbstruck. The man who was always so eloquent and well-spoken now seemed to struggle with words. She swallowed, fearful of what his tense silence meant.

"Is this true, Monsieur?"

With a heavy sigh, Mr Dubois nodded. "I am afraid there is truth to the accusations, Madame."

Madeleine gasped, one hand flying to her mouth in shock.

"In the past," he admitted, "I did make a living through... dishonest means. I charmed my way into the lives of wealthy individuals, gaining their confidence and trust. And when the moment was right–" He paused and cleared his throat. "Then I relieved them of substantial sums."

Though his words remained steady, regret flickered in his dark eyes. "I was a different man then, caught up in a vicious cycle of greed and pride. I convinced myself the deception was necessary and justified."

He smoothed a hand over his lapel, gaze turned inward. "But that changed some months ago. An incident in Paris convinced me that I had to change my ways. Two small children nearly died and an innocent young woman would have been sentenced to death for it."

Madeleine sucked in a sharp breath. Could it really be that the truth was even worse than she had imagined?

"All because one of my schemes went wrong," he continued. "The young lady was completely innocent. And she was one of the brightest, happiest souls I'd ever met. But she almost paid the ultimate price."

Silence hung between them. The ticking mantle clock suddenly seemed overly loud.

"After that I wished to become an honourable man," Mr Dubois said. "But old habits do persist. I struggled to earn an honest living. So when I came here, I reverted back to my old swindling tricks."

"Is that why you attended Sir John's salon?"

His voice dropped. "Yes, it was an excellent hunting ground. And you were the perfect mark. A wealthy widow alone – vulnerable, trusting. An ideal target."

His callous words pierced her like an arrow. Being seen as easy prey was bad enough. But there was another element to her pain as well. She had begun to like this man. She had given him her trust. This betrayal felt like he was trampling on her heart.

"You saw me as just another fool," she murmured, blinking back tears. "Someone to be duped and discarded once you'd had your way."

Shame flooded his features. "My plan was to take your investors' money for myself. But then..."

"Then what?" Madeleine demanded in a strained whisper. "What stopped you from deceiving me as you have so many others?"

"My heart," he said simply. "Being with you these past weeks has changed me."

Suddenly, he rose from his seat and dropped down on one knee in front of her. "Your warmth, your compassion and your goodness: they all appealed to the man I wish to become."

He tried to take her hand, but she shrank back.

"Alas," he said with a melancholy shake of the head. "Against my better judgement, I violated every rule of my old swindling ways: I fell in love with you."

"Love?" she said, gasping for breath. "You cannot expect me to believe—"

"I know it sounds improbable. I can scarcely believe it myself. But this is the truth I'm speaking now, from the depths of my penitent heart. I love you, Madeleine."

Confused, she got up and went over to the fireplace.

"I love you like I have never loved another," he insisted as he too rose to his feet.

She couldn't bring herself to meet his fervent gaze. And so she kept her back to him while she spoke.

"What a shameless scoundrel you are, Monsieur. After all the lies you just confessed, you dare speak of love?"

Hesitantly, he approached her. "Madeleine, I swear to you–"

She whirled to face him, eyes flashing with rage. "This is just another scheme of yours. Another dirty trick to sway me. I was a fool ever to trust you. To think that I..."

She turned her face away while a tear escaped down her cheek.

"Madeleine," he said as he closed the distance between them. "My feelings for you are true." He placed a hand on her shoulder. "Please, you must–"

"I have heard enough," she hissed, shaking free of his grasp. "From this moment, sir, our association is ended."

"I understand your anger," he said softly. "And I realise I don't deserve your forgiveness. But I am truly and deeply sorry for misleading you."

"Just leave, Monsieur." She refused to look at him, and instead kept her eyes fixed on the mantelpiece. "And don't ever come back."

After a brief moment of silence, she heard the quiet rustle of his clothes as he turned round and went to the door.

"Adieu, Madame Fletcher," he murmured sadly before leaving.

As soon as he left and closed the door behind him, the dam containing Madeleine's emotions burst. She collapsed onto the sofa and wept for her shattered hopes.

Chapter Sixteen

Madeleine stared out the factory office window, watching smoke curl from the tall chimneys. The familiar sight usually comforted her. Today however, it only deepened her sadness. She took a sip of tea, but its warmth barely registered. All she felt was the bitter ache of betrayal.

She should have known better than to trust Mr Dubois' honeyed words and ready charm. How she had hoped that he might be different. And that she had found not just a friend, but a new ally – something she was far more desperate for than she cared to admit.

What a fool I've been, she muttered silently to herself.

The man was nothing but a conniving crook. She thought back to their last meeting, and to the earnest light in his eyes when he had declared his love.

Ha! As if a liar like him could truly love anyone except himself. She had simply been another pigeon for him to pluck.

And yet...

She couldn't deny that a small part of her heart had begun to warm to the clever Frenchman. When they first met, his attentiveness and interest in her work had felt genuine. Their shared orphan pasts had only brought them closer over long talks and confidences.

But it had all been artifice and trickery, she realised now. Mr Dubois excelled at gaining trust, so he could more easily worm his way into unsuspecting souls. Likely she had never been more to him than a profitable scheme.

Curse that snake and his pretty lies.

She dashed away the tears that welled up, angry at herself for crying over a cad unworthy of her grief. Had she learned nothing from dear Benjamin's passing? Life was too short. She shouldn't waste hers on those who would use her heart for their own ends.

Suddenly, the door crashed open and Ashton Redhurst strode in, his face flushed from the heat on the factory floor.

"I must congratulate you, Madeleine," he said sarcastically, throwing down a newspaper on her desk. It was today's edition of The Herald. And Madeleine already knew what was in it.

"Ashton, I'm not in the mood for any games today," she warned him tiredly.

"I hope you're in the mood for a bit of local fame though," he smirked. "Because your interview with Turner is sure to be the talk of the town."

His smug expression made her insides clench. "I've read it, thank you very much," she said. "It's a piece of garbled nonsense from beginning to end."

"Oh, I wouldn't dismiss it so quickly," Ashton admonished with a wag of his finger. "I felt it was a most entertaining read."

Madeleine huffed. "That dreadful man twisted everything I said."

"Did he, now? Well, that would explain some of your more outlandish statements." He snatched up the newspaper and scanned the pages. "Ah yes, here's a fine sampling."

"I told you I've already seen it, Ashton."

Ignoring her, he cleared his throat theatrically and quoted, "'I openly admit that trying to run this factory has proven far too difficult for someone like me. I'm truly struggling under the burden my late husband placed on my shoulders.'"

"I never said any such thing," Madeleine bristled. "All I did was admit that it was difficult. Nothing more."

"What about this one?" he continued with barely hidden glee. "Apparently, you said: 'Speaking to the press is all rather new to me. I'm afraid I don't have a way with words like some, or any real understanding of how the world works. I've lived a very sheltered life up until now.'"

"Distortions and lies. Charles Turner has no shame or scruples whatsoever."

"Undoubtedly," Ashton said with a short snigger. "But my favourite part has to be this one: 'I am merely a bereaved woman attempting to carry out my husband's final request. Running this factory was never my own choice or ambition. It was simply the hand fate dealt me.'"

"That's probably the closest he comes to using my real words in the entire interview. But even then he makes me sound like some helpless old biddy, doddering about without a clue."

Ashton laughed unpleasantly. "Except when he mentions your views on women's rights of course. You come across as a deranged firebrand in that part."

"Enough," she snapped angrily. "What's your point, Ashton? You clearly seem to think this is all very amusing."

Ashton's arrogant smile faded. "Not at all, Maddie. And neither will our investors. This interview of yours could jeopardise the factory's prospects. What in heaven's name possessed you to agree to it?"

"I only did it for Eleanor's sake," she replied with a frown. "Turner said he wouldn't press charges against her if I gave him an exclusive interview."

"Perfectly decent of him. I only hope that saving your wild and ill-mannered daughter was worth the damage these twisted words of yours will do to the company's reputation."

Madeleine shot him an angry glare. How on earth had Benjamin ever put up with this irritating man, she wondered?

"Ashton–"

A polite knock at the door put an end to the scathing reply she wanted to give to her business partner.

"Excuse me for interrupting, Mrs Fletcher," her assistant Robert said as he popped his head round the door. "But I have the paperwork you urgently requested. Would you prefer me to come back later?"

"No, it's fine, Robert. Please come in. Mr Redhurst and I were just about done anyway."

Ashton glanced over at the young man with thinly veiled disdain. "Ah, Maddie's intrepid assistant arrives. Come in, come in, there's a good boy."

Robert flushed under the mocking attention, but he maintained a polite tone. "Good day, Mr Redhurst." Turning back to Madeleine, he gestured at the leather folder he was carrying. "These are the draft contracts for your final approval, Mrs Fletcher."

"Never any shortage of paperwork, eh?" Ashton said, his grin oozing false charm. "I trust everything has been sorted out for the investors' visit tomorrow? You've refilled the ink bottle, sharpened the quills, and stocked up the refreshments trolley?"

He laughed at his own joke, too loudly. Madeleine pressed the palms of her hands down onto the surface of her desk, to contain her anger.

"Of course," she replied coolly. "All preparations have been seen to."

"Marvellous," Ashton smiled. "Wouldn't want any embarrassing hiccups when the moneymen arrive."

He checked his pocket watch. "Well, I shall leave you to it. Many details to attend to before our grand day. Your Monsieur Dubois will be present as well tomorrow, I presume?"

"No, he will not," she said, keeping her voice steady.

Ashton's eyebrows shot up in exaggerated surprise. "He won't? My, oh my. Other fish to fry, has he?" His mocking laughter bounced off the walls as he strode out of the office.

Madeleine sighed irritably and shook her head.

"Those papers you requested, ma'am," Robert said softly while he carefully laid down the folder in front of her.

"Thank you, Robert." She opened it and began to leaf slowly through the sheets of paper.

"Is it true then, ma'am?" her assistant asked awkwardly. "Mr Dubois won't be joining us tomorrow?"

"Correct." She pretended to be studying a particular paragraph, so she could avoid meeting his eyes. "Mr Dubois and I felt that his role in this matter had come to an end."

"That's a bit of a shame," Robert said innocently, oblivious to the true meaning behind her words. "I was rather looking forward to seeing him again. He always seemed like such a friendly gentleman."

"Hmm, yes, quite." Madeleine kept her eyes fixed on her paperwork, swallowing the lump in her throat. "Speaking of tomorrow, did you manage to get everything in order for the visit?"

"Most certainly, Mrs Fletcher." Robert brightened, pleased to be the bringer of good news. "I've personally checked off every item on your list of preparations, ma'am. Everything's ready. Down to the last detail."

"Excellent work. I knew I could rely on you, Robert." She bestowed him a grateful smile.

"My pleasure, ma'am." He turned to leave, but then stopped. "Oh, there was something peculiar I meant to mention to you though. I was checking our financial records, in case the investors wanted to see them. And I noticed a few discrepancies."

"Tell me." Mentally, she braced herself for a boring explanation on some minute accounting detail that went over her head.

"Nothing major, mind you," he blushed. "At least not from what I could tell. A few sales entries here and there that don't seem to align between the factory logs and our ledgers in the office. Small inconsistencies, really."

"I see. Anything I ought to be concerned about?"

"No, I shouldn't think so, ma'am." With an apologetic grin, he rubbed the back of his neck and turned a deeper shade of red. "To be honest with you, it's likely just me misreading the numbers. Mr Underwood does have rather atrocious penmanship."

"Yes, I've noticed his scribbles can be hard to decipher sometimes," she said with a thin smile.

"Brilliant accountant though," Robert babbled. "Why, Mr Underwood could do those figures in his sleep. Yes, I'm sure the books are shipshape."

Madeleine couldn't help giving a little chuckle at his apparent awkwardness. "You're nervous for tomorrow, aren't you?"

"I am," he admitted sheepishly. "It's such an important day for you and the company, ma'am. And I–"

"It's fine, Robert. I appreciate your care and your attention to detail."

"Thank you, Mrs Fletcher," he replied with obvious relief. After a parting smile, he saw himself out and softly closed the door behind him.

Alone in her office again, Madeleine stood and went back to the window. Gazing out over the factory yard, a renewed sense of hope took hold of her.

She refused to dwell on the betrayals and setbacks of late. The future awaited, shining bright with promise. Because tomorrow, the company would turn the page on a difficult chapter.

And she would lead it. Not for her own personal glory, but for the humble people whose livelihoods depended on the factory's success. All she needed now was a few signatures to make it happen.

Chapter Seventeen

The clip-clop of hooves and the rumble of ironclad wheels on cobblestones echoed through the carriage as Madeleine gazed pensively out the window. Beside her, Ellie fidgeted with her gloves, glancing at her mother.

"You look amazing, Mama," Ellie said. "And I love the brooch you're wearing. Isn't it the one that used to belong to Grandmama?"

Madeleine smiled and touched the jewel tenderly. It was one of the very few items she had been able to keep out of the debt collectors' hands when both her parents had died so unexpectedly.

"Yes, it is. I wanted to wear it today for good luck."

"It's so beautiful with that delicate silver filigree," Ellie said admiringly.

"I'm glad you like it, dear. It'll be yours one day."

"A true family heirloom," Ellie breathed excitedly. Then she checked herself when the unintended implication dawned on her. "Of course, I hope I'll be an old woman by the time I inherit it from you."

Madeleine laughed. "Perhaps you won't have to wait *that* long. I might give it to you sooner."

"I'll wear it with pride, when the time comes," Ellie beamed. "The main thing is that it looks wonderful on you now. Those investors are going to be so impressed with you."

"Because of my brooch?" Madeleine giggled.

"No, because you're a strong and capable woman."

"That's very kind of you, my darling. But I must admit: I'm awfully nervous about today."

"Well, you shouldn't be. And I want you to know I'm tremendously proud of you, Mama."

"Thank you, Ellie." Affectionately, she touched her daughter's hand. "I'm very grateful you wanted to come with me. Although I'm afraid it'll probably be an exceedingly dull affair. There's nothing exciting about watching people sign a few documents."

"But it's such a big moment for you. I wouldn't miss it for the world."

Madeleine smiled at her and let out a happy sigh, feeling ever so thankful that she and Ellie seemed to have put the worst of their turbulent phase behind them. Soon after, their carriage rolled to a gentle stop when it reached its destination.

"Shall we?" Madeleine asked after taking a deep breath.

"Always," Ellie smiled.

They stepped out into the mid-morning sun, the sooty brick façade of the Fletcher & Redhurst Steam Engine Works rising before them.

As soon as they entered the main factory building, Madeleine's assistant Robert detached himself from a small group of people he was talking to. Sporting a bright smile on his happy face, he came hurrying over.

"Good morning, Mrs Fletcher." He turned to Ellie and nodded politely. "Miss Fletcher, so very nice to see you."

"Good morning, Robert," Madeleine replied warmly. "You look particularly dapper today."

His hair was neat and shiny with pomade and he had put on his best Sunday suit.

"I thought this special day was worth the extra effort," he blushed.

"Everything's ready then, I take it?"

"Absolutely, ma'am. I was just speaking to Stuart Wainwright back there, and he said he'll be available should the investors have any questions of a more technical nature."

"Wonderful. And what about Mr Redhurst? Is he around as well?"

"Of course I'm around," Ashton's voice grumbled from behind her. "I do own half of this company, you know."

Madeleine turned around with a cordial smile. "Good morning, Ashton."

"Yes, yes, it's morning alright," he muttered.

She noticed his normally pristine suit had several smears of grime on it. "I see you've already been hard at work," she said, maintaining her pleasant tone.

Distractedly, he brushed at the stains. "Been inspecting things left and right. After all, we're running a factory here. Not a ladies' tea party."

Madeleine bit back her reply, knowing that silence was the best response to his sarcasm.

"And besides," he added, "I'm sure you won't have any need for me when those fancy peacocks come to scribble their names on a scrap of paper."

"Ashton," she chided. "That's no way to talk about our investors. It's thanks to their generosity that *you* will be able to work on that precious turbine project of yours."

"They'll get their fair share of the profits," he sneered. With a final humph, he stomped off and nearly knocked over a passing worker. "Mind where you're going, you stupid oaf," Ashton snapped at the poor man.

"Why is Mr Redhurst in such a foul mood?" Ellie asked. "He should be excited."

"I'm afraid that man will always be a mystery to me," Madeleine sighed. "His temperament is more changeable than the wind."

"Perhaps he's merely nervous," Robert suggested. "Mr Redhurst was already busy on the factory floor when I arrived early this morning. So I'm sure he's just as excited as we all are. In his own unique way, I mean."

Madeleine wasn't quite as convinced as her assistant, but she liked the young man's unwavering positive spirit. "Mr Redhurst can go and hide in the boiler room for all I care," she said. "Then at least he won't get in our way or ruffle any feathers."

Ellie chuckled and Robert hid an amused grin behind the palm of his hand. When the three of them arrived in Madeleine's office, she was happy to see the preparations her assistant had made.

A vase with freshly cut flowers adorned the large desk, adding a cheery splash of colour. Next to it was a tray with a variety of small sandwiches and canapés, as well as a neat row of tea cups and glasses.

And even more importantly, several copies of the investment contracts were laid out with pens at the ready to make things official.

"Excellent work, Robert," Madeleine said, picking up one of the contracts and glancing casually at the pages. "Everything looks perfect."

"Thank you, ma'am," her assistant replied, visibly pleased with her praise.

"Now all that's left is to wait for our guests to arrive," Madeleine said as she carefully placed the contract back on the table.

"Speaking of whom," Ellie said. She was standing by the big window that overlooked the factory yard. "I think the first of the investors might have arrived. A sleek black carriage has just pulled up outside the gate."

Robert let out a nervous little yelp and rushed towards the door. "I must go and welcome them," he said. "I shall be right back, Mrs Fletcher."

"Is Mr Adams always this excited?" Ellie giggled.

"He's a fine young man and a very capable assistant," Madeleine smiled. "But you must understand, Ellie. To him and everyone else in this factory, the signing of those contracts means that their livelihood and their future will be a bit more secure."

"Good thing they've got you at the helm then. Today's events will prove once again what a champion you are, Mama."

"I pray you're right, dear. I won't truly relax until I see the ink of those signatures drying on paper."

Before they could continue their conversation, the door to Madeleine's office swung open and Mrs Pemberton-Thorpe came striding in.

"Tremendous day for us to be formalising our agreement, wouldn't you all say?" the energetic widow beamed.

"Mrs Pemberton-Thorpe," Madeleine said cordially. "How very nice to see you. Welcome."

After she had introduced Ellie, tea was offered. And then the other two investors, Mr Bancroft and Mr Collins, arrived a short while later. Soon, a happy mood filled the room and the group was engaged in cheerful small talk.

With a smile, Madeleine thought about how lucky she was to have found these three financial saviours.

Thanks to Mr Dubois, a voice in the back of her mind reminded her painfully.

But that's in the past, she told herself. *I should only look to the future now.*

A quick glance at the waiting contracts sent a flutter of nerves through her stomach. She desperately wanted this to be over. But she didn't want to appear rude either by speeding things along.

"Shall we relieve you of this terrible suspense?" Mrs Pemberton-Thorpe asked when she caught the direction of Madeleine's gaze.

"Oh, I wouldn't want to press–"

"Nonsense. It's what we're here for after all, isn't it?" The widow turned to the other two investors and said, "Gentlemen, shall we?"

"Ladies first," Mr Bancroft replied politely.

"With pleasure," Mrs Pemberton-Thorpe said as she swept over to the desk.

Heart thumping in her throat, Madeleine handed the formidable lady a pen.

"One swift stroke and we're partners, eh?" the widow said with a good-humoured twinkle in her eye. "Suppose I'd better use my best handwriting then."

Madeleine held her breath as she watched the pen inching closer to the paper.

But then, a tremendous boom suddenly shook the room. The floor trembled beneath their feet, while the teacups and cutlery made ominous clattering noises.

"Was that an explosion?" Ellie gasped when the rattling had stopped.

"It sounded like it came from the factory floor," Robert said, his face draining of colour.

"I must go and see what's happened," Madeleine said as she made for the door.

Ellie grasped her mother's arm. "I'll come with you, Mama."

"No, stay here where it's safe, darling. All of you wait here, please." Madeleine gently peeled her daughter's fingers away.

"But what if you need help?" the girl protested.

"Robert, please entertain our guests while I'm gone. I'm relying on you."

"Of course, Mrs Fletcher." Putting on a weak and unconvincing smile, he ushered the investors away from the door.

With a final nod, Madeleine hurried from her office toward the factory. As she raced down the long hallway, panicked shouts echoed from up ahead. Acrid smoke stung her nose – a smell that turned her blood to ice.

Bursting through the large doors that led to the production hall, she reeled back instantly when a thick cloud of black smoke threatened to swallow her.

Squinting through the suffocating haze, she searched desperately for the source. Fiery cinders rained down over shadowy figures racing to and fro.

"Mr Wainwright," she cried out hoarsely for the senior foreman. "Mr Wainwright, where are you?"

Only garbled shouts answered. Men clutching fire buckets rushed by, their faces black with soot. Madeleine pressed a hand over her mouth, eyes watering.

Panic welled up inside her chest, until a figure emerged from the smoke. "Mrs Fletcher," the voice of young Stuart Wainwright called. "Over here, ma'am!"

She rushed toward the engineer, heart pounding. "Stuart! What on earth has happened?"

"One of the new engines exploded during a test firing," he cried, wiping grease and sweat from his brow. "At least three men are badly injured."

"Dear Lord..."

Around them, several more workers came stumbling through the haze. Their eyes were wide with shock, their clothes torn and stained with smears of something dark. Oil or blood, Madeleine wondered?

"What should we do, ma'am?" Stuart asked. "We don't have a nurse or a doctor on staff. And the fire is spreading."

Men began to crowd around Madeleine, their frightened faces pleading for instructions. Her pulse thundered as she scanned the chaotic scene. The sheer horror of the sights and sounds around her made it impossible to think.

But she could sense everyone's eyes were fixed on her. She had to act now – or lose everything.

Chapter Eighteen

"What in heaven's name?" a voice cried out from behind. Madeleine spun round in surprise to see Mrs Pemberton-Thorpe emerging from the smoke. The other two investors were on her heels, followed by Robert and Ellie. All of them were staring, wide-eyed and horrified, at the nightmare that surrounded them.

"Eleanor," Madeleine gasped. "You shouldn't be here. It's dangerous."

Robert shot her an apologetic look. "I'm so sorry, Mrs Fletcher. I tried to keep them in your office, but Mrs Pemberton-Thorpe insisted on coming down."

"I wanted to see if there was anything we could do to help," the widow said.

"Sweet Lord," Mr Collins exclaimed when an injured worker stumbled past with a limp arm hanging uselessly at his side.

"That man needs medical attention," Mr Bancroft said. "Surely, there must be a physician who–"

"You're quite right, sir," Madeleine replied, snapping back to her senses. She gestured to one of the onlooking workers. "Run and fetch Doctor Brown in Bridge Street. He's the closest by, I think. And you–" she pointed at another man, "Go get the fire brigade at once. Hurry!"

As the men raced to obey, Madeleine surveyed the turmoil and panic around her. Smoke and embers swirled through the air, while cries for help came from different directions. *What an absolute mess.*

"We ought to start dousing the fire ourselves," she decided. "Stuart, where's your father?"

They could really do with the senior foreman's help to organise the men, she thought.

"I haven't seen him since the explosion, ma'am," the young engineer replied. "But he was working close to that engine before– before it blew up."

An icy shiver ran down Madeleine's spine. "Let's not jump to any hasty conclusions," she said, trying to put on a brave face. "In the meantime, round up as many men as you can, Stuart. Form a line and make them pass down buckets of water to wherever the fire is."

She realised it probably wouldn't be enough to put out the fire. But it was better than watching her factory burn down to the ground until the fire brigade arrived.

Stuart nodded and ran off, taking the handful of gathered workers with him.

"Robert?"

"Yes, ma'am?"

"Once help arrives, we'll need to find all the wounded and take them someplace safe where they can be treated."

Robert considered this. "The workers' dining hall is mostly empty right now. We could set it up as an infirmary."

"Good thinking," Madeleine approved. Though lacking in supplies, at least it offered adequate space. "When Doctor Brown gets here, take him there straight away and prepare the area for the injured."

"Shall I go and wait for the doctor by the gates then, ma'am?"

"Yes, please do," she replied before sending him off on his task.

"I want to help too, Mother," Ellie spoke up eagerly.

Madeleine shook her head. "It's too dangerous, darling. You should return to the office where it's safe." She turned to her guests. "In fact, I must urge you all to withdraw back to safety until this dreadful business is resolved."

Mr Bancroft and Mr Collins exchanged uneasy glances.

"It seems this will take quite some time to sort out," Mr Bancroft said dubiously, eyeing the chaos.

Mr Collins nodded. "And there may not be much of a factory left standing when all is said and done."

Madeleine lifted her chin. "I assure you that I have matters well in hand, gentlemen. I will do my utmost to bring everything under control as swiftly as possible."

But the investors shook their heads gravely. "Under the circumstances, Mrs Fletcher, I'm afraid we must withdraw from the agreement," Mr Collins declared. "We will not be investing in your company at this time."

Mr Bancroft murmured his assent. "Our sincere regrets, Mrs Fletcher. But I trust you can see how this disaster would give us cause for concern."

Madeleine bit her lip. Another setback. She loathed the unfairness of it all. She was trapped in a weak position, and there wasn't anything she could do about it.

"Cowards," Mrs Pemberton-Thorpe grumbled after the pair of men had departed. "Fleeing at the first sign of trouble. Why, if my dear Hubert had still been around today, he would have had a few choice words to say to those two gentlemen."

"Regrettable as it may be, I understand their decision," Madeleine replied sadly. "And really, Mrs Pemberton-Thorpe, you don't have to stay onboard either. Mr Collins had a point when he said–"

"Tut, tut, my dear. Let's not dwell on that for now. You have more pressing worries at present.

Your injured workers for instance. What do you intend to do with them?"

"Doctor Brown can treat the most urgent cases in our temporary infirmary. And then I suppose we'll have to move them to the hospital."

"May I suggest a better solution?"

"Of course."

"I know what those hospital wards are like: they're overcrowded and understaffed. Your men would be much better off if you kept them here, in this improvised infirmary of yours."

"But we have no medical supplies. And who would care for the men? We don't have a nurse or–"

"I'll do it," Mrs Pemberton-Thorpe replied, straightening her back.

"You?! But–"

"I did a fair bit of nursing back in India when my Hubert was stationed there, you know. Stood my ground through several outbreaks and all sorts of injuries."

"I had no idea." Madeleine was pleasantly surprised, but she didn't dare to get her hopes up yet. "Are you sure you want to do this though?"

"Absolutely positive."

"You'll need help, ma'am," Ellie blurted out. "So I'd like to volunteer."

Madeleine began to protest, but Mrs Pemberton-Thorpe spoke up first. "Wonderful! That's the sort of plucky spirit I like to see, young lady. And we'll ask the men to spread the word at home. There'll be plenty of wives and daughters to lend us a hand as well."

Madeleine sighed, but then she nodded her assent. In truth, they were going to need all the help they could get. And at least this meant Ellie would be kept out of harm's way.

"Very well," she relented.

"Splendid!" Ellie smiled and clapped her hands, delighted that she'd be able to be of use.

"Now then," Mrs Pemberton-Thorpe said crisply. "We'll need bandages, carbolic soap, blankets. Perhaps you could dispatch a few men to the nearest chemist? We ought–"

She was interrupted by the sudden appearance of a distressed worker who came hurrying over.

"Begging your pardon, Mrs Fletcher," the man said, trying to catch his breath. "But we've found old Jack Wainwright."

"Good," Madeleine said, her excitement growing. Could it be that the tide was slowly turning in her favour? "Where is he? Is he all right?"

But the man looked down at the ground and shook his head. "I'm afraid he's done for, ma'am. The blast got him."

"No," she groaned in horror. "Does his son know?"

The man grimaced and nodded. "Stuart's the one who found him, ma'am."

"Oh, poor soul," Mrs Pemberton-Thorpe commiserated. "That must have been awful for him."

"Took it pretty badly, he did," the man replied.

"Take me to him," Madeleine said resolutely.

Following the man's lead, Madeleine, Ellie and Mrs Pemberton-Thorpe rushed through the billowing smoke toward the tragic scene. As they drew nearer, she could make out a small cluster of workers standing solemnly over a prone figure on the floor. Her pulse quickened with dread.

Lying motionless amidst twisted steel wreckage was the body of loyal Jack Wainwright. Battered and burnt, his face retained a look of surprise, as though death had claimed him swiftly. His men now stood around him with their heads bowed respectfully.

Kneeling by his dead father's side, Stuart clutched the older man's hand. His face was ashen and when he lifted his head to look up at Madeleine, she was struck by the raw anguish in the engineer's crying eyes.

"I'm so sorry," she murmured.

"He always joked he wanted to die on the job," Stuart said with a broken voice. "But I don't think he meant for it to happen like this."

He hung his head and sobbed.

Madeleine reached out to lay a comforting hand on his shoulder. But as she did, she noticed a patch of dark blood crusted near his hairline.

"Stuart, you're injured!"

He put a hand to his head absently. "It's just a scratch..."

"Even so, you need to get that seen to straight away," Madeleine said firmly. Seeing him hesitate, she added gently, "Please."

"I can't," he said, rising to his feet. "I have to stay here. Without my father, the men need–"

Mrs Pemberton-Thorpe slid up to his side. "We're setting up a field hospital in the factory dining hall. Perhaps you could first show Miss Fletcher and myself how to get there?"

Taking her cue, Eleanor went over to Stuart's other side and linked her arm through his. "Let's have a quick look at that head injury of yours and then you can rejoin the men later."

The young engineer lingered a moment, unable to tear his eyes away from his dead father. But then he allowed himself to be led from the tragic scene by the two women.

Madeleine watched them go with a measure of relief. Seeing Mrs Pemberton-Thorpe and

Ellie take charge of the situation made her realise that she wasn't alone. There were friends and allies she could rely on, even in the middle of this catastrophe.

Sadly though, that very same disaster had also robbed her of at least one ally. Turning back to the sight of Jack Wainwright's dead body, she let out a sigh.

"Old Jack was a good man," one of the men said.

"He most certainly was," Madeleine agreed. "I'll make sure his family is taken care of."

"A fat lot of good that'll do the poor bugger," a grumbling voice sounded out of nowhere. Like a phantom, the figure of Ashton Redhurst emerged from a plume of smoke and vapour.

"Ashton," Madeleine breathed, laying a hand on her chest to steady her racing heart. "You're safe. Thank heavens."

"Yes, I'm still alive. What a pity the same can't be said about old Jack here." He gave a curt nod at the body lying on the floor. "The man should never have died. This is your fault, Maddie."

She jerked back, shocked by his callous accusation.

"Oh, don't act so surprised." Ashton waved a hand at the surrounding destruction. "This whole bloody mess is your doing, Maddie. You knew we desperately needed that investment. But you were too timid and too slow. And now look." He pointed angrily at Jack Wainwright's dead body by their feet. "Good men have lost their lives because of your dithering."

Several of the workers around them quietly muttered their agreement.

Seething, Madeleine clenched her fists. "How dare you, Ashton? For months I've been working hard to–"

But just then she was interrupted by shouting voices at the entrance. The fire brigade had arrived and they were hauling in long hoses and heavy equipment.

"We'll continue this discussion some other time, Ashton," she hissed. "Right now, I have a factory to save."

Raising her chin, she turned away from her business partner. "And you," she said, addressing the small group of workers around her, "take poor Jack's body to an empty storeroom. We'll mourn for the dead properly later."

With grim determination, she strode off towards the firefighters. This catastrophe had already taken so much. She wasn't going to let it take the livelihoods of those who remained.

Chapter Nineteen

The grandfather clock in the foyer chimed one o'clock just as Madeleine and Ellie stumbled through the front door, exhausted after the endless day. Despite the late hour, Charlotte came rushing from the drawing room.

"Oh, thank heavens," she cried, throwing her arms around Madeleine. "I've been worried sick ever since Bill came back with the awful news. Are you both all right?"

"Just tired, that's all," Madeleine sighed, returning her cousin's embrace.

Charlotte let go and studied them both with concern in her eyes. "You must be famished after everything you've been through. When was the last time you ate?"

"Breakfast, I think," Madeleine said.

Her cousin gasped and a look of genuine horror appeared on her round face. "Breakfast?! But that's ages ago. Lucky for you, I had Mrs Dobbs leave out some supper in the dining room before she went to bed."

"Charlotte, you're a saint," Madeleine said gratefully.

"Breakfast," Charlotte tutted to herself, shaking her head disapprovingly as she herded the two of them into the dining room.

Madeleine's empty stomach growled when she saw the spread of cold meats, cheese, boiled vegetables and bread on the sideboard.

"Sit, sit," Charlotte said before she began loading two plates with food.

"There now, eat up," she instructed with a kind smile, placing the heaped plates in front of them and pouring them each a glass of sherry. "You need your strength after the day you've had."

Then she nabbed a piece of cheese from the sideboard and sat down across from them. "Bill has told me some of what happened when he came back from the factory," she said, nibbling at her cheese. "But he's not much of a talker, I'm afraid. So please do fill me in. It must have been horrendous from what little I've heard."

Between mouthfuls, Madeleine recounted the chaos of the explosion and its aftermath – the billowing smoke, the cries of the wounded, the tragic loss of life.

"We've set up an infirmary in the workers' hall for now. Three dead so far and over a dozen injured, though thankfully no more casualties since this evening."

"May the Lord have mercy on their souls. What about the factory itself? How bad was the explosion?"

"Once the fire brigade arrived, we managed to put out the fire fairly quickly. So the factory is still standing. But I dread to see what it'll look like in the light of day tomorrow morning."

"And you, Ellie?" Charlotte asked. "I was surprised, and more than a little worried, when Bill told me you chose to stay behind as well. Weren't you frightened, dear?"

"Not really," the girl replied proudly. "I felt my place was by my mother's side. And I volunteered to help Mrs Pemberton-Thorpe."

"She's one of the investors," Madeleine explained to Charlotte. "My only investor, I should say. Because the other two walked away after the explosion."

"Oh, Maddie," Charlotte said. "I'm so sorry to hear that."

"It doesn't matter now, I guess. At any rate, it was Mrs Pemberton-Thorpe's idea to set up an infirmary at the factory. She said it was better than sending our wounded to the hospital."

"Clever woman." Charlotte turned to Ellie and asked, "And you stayed to help her, you said, dear?"

"Yes, I did. She showed me how to clean and dress a wound."

"How very brave of you," Charlotte smiled. "You'll be the new Florence Nightingale next."

"I just wanted to do my part," Ellie replied, covering her mouth while she chewed on a bite of bread and cheese. "Poor Mr Wainwright though."

"Who's he?"

"The senior foreman," Madeleine answered heavily. "He was killed in the blast."

"Tragic," Charlotte shook her head sympathetically. "Did he have any family?"

"He did, yes. In fact, his eldest son Stuart works at the factory as well."

"Stuart was actually the first person I helped," Ellie spoke up. "He was awfully brave about the whole business."

"Was he badly hurt?" Charlotte asked.

"Oh no, just a cut on his forehead from some falling debris." Ellie traced a line above her own brow. "But there was so much blood. I had to clean the wound thoroughly before I could bandage it."

"How dreadful for the poor young man to lose his father that way," Charlotte replied.

"Yes, it's all very sad." Ellie twisted a lock of hair around her finger. "And yet Stuart was determined to get back to the men as soon as possible. He kept thanking me for my help, even as he hurried out of the infirmary."

She sighed and stared down at her plate, with a dreamy expression on her face. "I do hope he didn't overexert himself afterwards. Perhaps I ought to go back first thing in the morning to check on him."

Looking up at Madeleine and Charlotte, she blushed and quickly added, "Him and the other patients at the infirmary, of course."

"You want to return to the factory tomorrow?" Charlotte asked in surprise.

"Oh, yes," Ellie nodded eagerly. "There's still so much work to be done. I couldn't possibly rest easy knowing that Mrs Pemberton-Thorpe worked through the night without relief."

Madeleine gave her daughter a weary smile. "You should get enough rest first, darling. We don't want *you* to overexert yourself either."

"But Mrs Pemberton-Thorpe is staying up all night to look after the wounded. I feel I should be there to assist her."

"She's got a handful of women who volunteered to help. But if you want to go back, you may do so. *After* a good night's sleep."

"And a decent breakfast," Charlotte added.

"Thank you," Ellie said, rising from the table. "If you'll please excuse me, I'll wish you both good night." With a smile still lingering on her lips, she hurried off to her room.

Madeleine watched her daughter depart with a shake of her head. "That girl. She's grown so much recently."

Feeling the weight of the day pressing down on her, she rubbed her right temple with her hand. "As for me though, I doubt sleep will find me anytime soon. My mind is still spinning."

"Why don't we head to the drawing room for a cup of tea then?" Charlotte suggested. "I happen to know Mrs Dobbs left us some cake, too."

Madeleine managed a weak smile. "Cake does sound rather lovely right now."

Soon the two women were settled into a pair of comfortable armchairs in the drawing room. On the low table between them stood two steaming cups of tea and several pieces of Victoria sponge.

Charlotte tucked into her first piece with fervour. After she had savoured a bite with closed eyes, she turned to her cousin. "Maddie, how I admire you. Lesser women would have fallen to pieces dealing with such a tragedy. But you handled it with remarkable strength and grace."

Madeleine stared down into her tea, shoulders slumping. "I felt anything but strong today," she admitted. "When I consider everything that needs managing in the coming days and weeks, I feel overwhelmed."

Without having drunk any of her tea, she put the cup and saucer back on the low table. "There are wounded to care for, families to support. Not to mention figuring out how this will impact the factory."

She threw up her hands in dismay. "The repairs are bound to be costly. And with at least two of my investors gone... Oh, Charlotte, how will I cope?"

"There, there, now. Don't work yourself into a state," Charlotte said while she calmly continued to work her way through her piece of cake. "One thing at a time, as they say."

Daintily, she wiped a stray crumb from her mouth. "You have some good and capable people to help you at the factory, don't you? Like this assistant of yours, Mr Adams?"

"I suppose so, yes. But–"

Charlotte held up a hand. "Let's cut up this great big problem of yours into smaller pieces." Spearing her fork into the Victoria sponge, she neatly sliced off a bite-sized portion. "What will you do first when you go to the factory tomorrow?"

"I should check on the wounded in the infirmary. Check if everyone made it through the night."

"Sounds like the decent thing to do," Charlotte nodded. "What's next?"

"Then we have to ascertain the damage. See how much of a factory I've still got left."

"And who would be the right person for that task?"

"That'd be Ashton, I guess. He's the head engineer after all."

"Good," Charlotte said before forking another bit of cake into her mouth.

Madeleine picked up her cup of tea again and took a thoughtful sip. "The investors will have to wait until the dust has settled. We have to know the extent of the damage first."

"There, you see? One thing at a time." Charlotte gave her an appreciative grin. "No need to fret about everything all at once, is there?"

"You're right, of course," Madeleine murmured. But then she trailed off and stared into her tea once more.

"You don't sound very convinced to me," Charlotte smiled. Leaning in closer, she lowered her voice and asked, "What are you *really* afraid of, Maddie?"

"Money," she replied in a hoarse voice. "The factory was struggling already. And now this happens."

Charlotte nodded and then patiently waited for Madeleine to continue.

"Benjamin left us well provided for. But if I pour that money into the factory–" She felt tears beginning to prick behind her eyes. "I'm afraid I'll jeopardise Ellie's future."

"Ah," Charlotte merely replied, understanding her cousin's pain.

"If I lose the business, it would ruin everything for her, Charlotte. Her prospects, her security in life. She'd have nothing because of me." Her voice broke. "What a miserable failure of a mother I'll be then."

Charlotte carefully placed her empty plate on the low table and dabbed at her mouth with her napkin.

"Money isn't the measure of your worth, Maddie," she said gently as she picked up her cup of tea. "You've shown tremendous leadership managing the company so far."

Madeline shook her head doubtfully. "The facts seem to tell a different story."

"Nonsense. Even the most prosperous businesses hit difficult patches on occasion. Ups and downs are only natural. Rather like the tides."

She sipped her tea and then continued, "The trick is to hold steady through the lows. Take things slowly and stay true to your own wisdom."

Part of Madeleine wanted to believe in the truth of her cousin's words. But the doubts still lingered.

"So you feel I should keep going?" she asked quietly. "You don't think I'm just being stubborn and making a fool of myself?"

"If you're caught in a storm, the only way to reach safety is by pushing forward one step at a time." Charlotte gave her an encouraging smile. "You've come this far already, Madeleine. Why stop now?"

"But Ellie–"

"What about Ellie? Have you seen how strong and invigorated she was this evening? The girl's got your spirit, Maddie. She's a fighter. She too will find the path that's right for her. Come what may."

"That must be a trait she inherited from her father then," Madeleine said. "I'm more the timid type."

"Timid? You?" Charlotte let out a little snort. "Not a chance. Do you remember that time when you pushed Reggie Miller into the duck pond for making fun of me?"

They shared a laugh at the memory, which helped to ease some of the tension in Madeleine's shoulders.

"How do you always manage to be so wise, my darling Charlotte?" she asked.

"I have plenty of time on my hands. So I eat cake and read lots of books. Occasionally, you pick up useful tidbits left and right."

"Then by all means, continue eating and reading for many more years, please," Madeleine smiled. She rose to her feet. "Thank you for listening and for your kind words tonight, Charlotte. They mean the world to me."

Giving her cousin a kiss on the cheek, she added, "*You* mean the world to me."

Once she was up in her bedroom, she quickly changed into her nightgown and slipped underneath the warm blankets. Before turning down the light by her bed, she cast a last glance at her late husband's portrait.

"Oh, Benjamin," she whispered into the gloom. "If you can, please send me a sign. Show me what to do."

When the portrait didn't reply, she let out a long sigh and lowered her head onto the soft pillow. Moments later, she fell into a deep sleep – hoping that the new dawn would bring forward a clearer path.

Chapter Twenty

The morning sun was already climbing through the bright skies when Madeleine and Ellie climbed into their waiting carriage. Ellie stifled a yawn as she settled onto the tufted leather seat next to her mother.

"Are you sure you wouldn't rather stay at home and rest today?" Madeleine asked. "You seem awfully tired, darling."

"And leave Mrs Pemberton-Thorpe shorthanded? I couldn't possibly. A strong cup of tea will see me through."

After coachman Bill had softy urged his mare into motion and they began to drive past all the tidy houses, Ellie gazed dreamily out the window.

"Poor Stuart," she sighed. "Can you imagine what a horrible night he must have had? Losing his dear old father so suddenly."

"Yes, Jack Wainwright's death was a dreadful thing," Madeleine replied. "We'll have to offer the family what help we can in their grief."

"Stuart was ever so brave yesterday, didn't you think? The way he kept his composure in front of the men," Ellie prattled on. "But I daresay today the shock will set in. And when that happens, he may need a bit more looking after. A listening ear. Perhaps even a shoulder to cry on."

She turned her large, sympathetic eyes on her mother. "I'll go and see him as soon as we arrive. Having some company might lift his spirits. Don't you think, Mama? Or would that be... improper?"

"There's nothing improper about wanting to help, I suppose," Madeleine said slowly. "But do take care not to become overly familiar, dear. You scarcely know the young man."

"Oh, I wouldn't dream of it, Mama," Ellie replied hastily. "I only wish to offer him a bit of friendly support. It must be such a difficult time for him and his family."

Madeleine nodded and pursed her lips, eyeing her daughter shrewdly. Perhaps there was more to Ellie's eagerness than a mere desire to be helpful. Something of a more romantic nature?

We'll cross that bridge when we come to it, she sighed to herself. And besides, Stuart Wainwright was an honest and upright young man. A safer choice than many others if her daughter was indeed developing an adolescent fancy.

Ellie turned her gaze back to the window, her cheeks slightly flushed. Madeleine studied her daughter a moment longer before letting her own thoughts wander.

One matter at a time, she thought, recalling her conversation with Charlotte the previous night. Today, she would have her fair share of challenges, no doubt. But she refused to be daunted by the prospect, no matter how unpleasant.

They spent the rest of their journey in a peaceful, companionable silence while the carriage continued to wind its way through the familiar streets.

But when they rolled to a stop near the factory's tall iron gates, Madeleine frowned at the sight that greeted them. A large group of workers had gathered at the entrance. And as soon as the men spotted the carriage, they raised their voices in anger.

"There's trouble brewing, ma'am," Bill said. "Shall I come with you? To keep you and Miss Eleanor safe?"

Madeleine considered the situation only for a moment before shaking her head. "That won't be necessary, Bill. These are my employees after all. I'm sure I have nothing to fear from them." She straightened her hat and made to get out of the carriage. "Please return for us this evening as usual."

"Very good, ma'am." Bill tipped his cap, though he looked uncertain.

Madeleine stepped down from the carriage without hesitation, Ellie following close behind. She recognised many familiar faces from the factory floor as she drew near. There was Simmons, the toolmaker. Wilkes and his apprentice. Mason from the machine shop. They all looked distraught, bitterness simmering in their eyes.

As Madeleine and Ellie walked up to the gates, shouts went up from the crowd. In an instant, the seething mob had surrounded them. Madeleine's breath caught, a jittery nervousness flashing through her.

Mustering all her bravery, she raised her voice above the clamour. "Good people! What seems to be the matter here?"

The men responded with another angry surge. "The matter?" Henry Mason roared, his barrel chest puffed up. "The matter is we ain't workin' in a ruddy death trap no more."

Simmons shook his fist, face mottled with rage. "That's right. And we ain't takin' orders from the likes of petticoated business folk either."

There were loud shouts of agreement. Madeleine felt her stomach drop. A strike? And such bitter hostility toward her? She raised her hand entreatingly.

"Good sirs, please," she implored, pitching her voice to carry. "I understand emotions are running high after yesterday's tragic events. But surely we can discuss this in a more civil manner? There must be—"

The men cut her off with another swell of outrage, pressing closer. Behind her, she felt Ellie grasping at her arm.

"Mama," her daughter whimpered, "I'm frightened."

"The newspaper's got the right of it," someone shouted. "Women aren't fit to run a factory."

Rough hands shoved a copy of The Herald of the North in Madeleine's face. The tabloid headline screamed at her in lurid type:

"WOMAN'S FOLLY AND PRIDE LEAVES MEN DEAD"

And below it, the subtitle accused her in stark terms:

"Fletcher Widow's Incompetence To Blame For Factory Disaster"

Turner, Madeleine seethed inwardly. That scandalous journalist had wasted no time apparently. How dare he use this awful tragedy as yet another excuse to print lies and slander about her?

"Gentlemen," she shouted, trying to keep her voice steady, despite the shock and distress inside her. "You don't honestly believe that I caused this accident, do you?"

"Three men are dead," Simmons grumbled loudly. "That sort of thing never happened when Mr Fletcher were still alive."

"But that's ludicrous," Madeleine replied. "Charles Turner is lying. Can't you see?"

"Mama, please," Ellie hissed from behind her. "It's no use. They won't listen to you. Can we please leave?" The girl's terrified eyes darted over the unruly mob.

"They must understand–" Madeleine insisted.

But before she could think what to do, a sharp voice cut through the noise. "That's enough from all of you!"

The crowd parted to reveal Ashton Redhurst, his face set like a thundercloud. None too gently, he pushed past the men to reach Madeleine and Ellie.

"Get back to work, you louts," he barked at the mob. "Or I'll personally sack every single one of you."

When no one reacted, Ashton grabbed Madeleine by the elbow and propelled her toward the factory entrance.

"You men ought to be ashamed of yourselves," he snarled at the workers. "Accosting two innocent women like this."

Ellie hurried after them through the reluctant crowd as Ashton pulled Madeleine through the tall double doors of the main building.

In the sudden quiet of the large hallway, Madeleine slumped against the wall, her heart still pounding.

"Are you all right, Maddie?" Ashton asked. His face was still flushed with anger, but his tone grew gentler. He released her arm and raked a hand through his hair.

Madeleine nodded, trying to calm her breath. "What got into those men?"

"Mindless rabble," he grumbled. "I'm surprised they were able to even read that newspaper."

Madeleine turned to her daughter. "And you, Ellie? Are you all right, dearest?"

"I'm fine now, Mama," the girl replied, though she still looked rattled. "I was just frightened they might do something dreadful to us out there. But I'm grateful to be inside." She straightened her dress with as much dignity as she could muster. "I'll go and see if Mrs Pemberton-Thorpe needs any help in the infirmary."

"Yes, you do that," Madeleine said. "I'll be along shortly." She watched her daughter hurry off and then looked at Ashton again.

"Thank you, Ashton. For saving us."

"You're welcome. Let's go to your office, shall we?"

Madeleine nodded and let him escort her down the hall. As they entered the outer office, the handful of clerks who had braved the angry crowd outside were standing around in a small group, whispering. Now they sprang apart, faces guiltily turning toward their desks.

Ashton glowered at them. "What's all this loitering about then? The ledgers won't balance themselves, you know?"

The young clerks shuffled their feet.

"Begging your pardon, Mr Redhurst," Robert said hesitantly. "It's just, with so many of the workers on strike, and operations halted– Well, there isn't much work for us to be getting on with, sir."

Ashton grumbled under his breath. Shooting the clerks one last stern look, he ushered Madeleine into her office and closed the door firmly behind them.

"Madeleine, I owe you an apology," he said while she peeled off her gloves and coat. "I shouldn't have spoken so harshly to you yesterday. It must have been the shock of the explosion, you see. Caused me to speak out of turn."

She frowned and sat down at her large desk. "I understand, Ashton. It was a terrible shock for all of us." The memory of his accusations still stung. But she had more important things to do than holding useless grudges.

He cleared his throat and glanced around the familiar office as if he was seeing the ledger books and wood panels only for the first time.

"Such devastation," he sighed miserably. "Years of hard work, destroyed in a flash. Dreadful. Makes you stop and think, doesn't it?"

"About what, Ashton?" she asked while leafing through a pile of paperwork.

"How tenuous this business can be, I mean. Especially with the difficult financial straits we were already facing."

He came striding over to her desk with a grave look on his face. "And now this confounded strike will put the company in an even more precarious state."

Placing both hands on her desk, he leaned in closer towards her. "Maddie, what a tremendous burden all this must be for you. Please, for everyone's sake, reconsider selling your shares to me. Before things get out of hand and the pressure breaks you."

She straightened her shoulders and met his gaze. "Benjamin had his reasons for leaving his half of the company to me. Walking away now would feel like betraying the trust he placed in me."

"His dying wish," Ashton said, rolling his eyes. "Yes, you've told me all about it. But he wouldn't have wanted any of this for you." He pointed in the general direction of the mob outside. "Ben never could have foreseen this sort of nightmare happening. Or he wouldn't have asked you to take the reins."

"Nevertheless," Madeleine insisted, "I must see this through. The business will recover in time."

He let out an exasperated groan. "You're just as stubborn as old Ben."

"I'll take that as a compliment then," she replied evenly, returning her attention to her paperwork. "In the meantime, Ashton, why don't you make yourself useful by assessing the extent of the damage?"

A muscle twitched in his cheek, though he quickly buried his irritation. "Very well," he said. "I'll go and survey the state of things. And I'll speak to Mr Underwood about estimating the repair costs."

"Excellent idea. Thank you, Ashton," she replied without looking up from her work.

Turning on his heel, he brusquely strode out of the door. When it closed behind him with a slight thud, Madeleine stopped shuffling papers and sighed.

At least she'd won the argument, she thought.

"I'll visit the infirmary first," she murmured out loud as she rose from her desk. Hopefully, she wouldn't find any new tragedies or emergencies there.

When she walked into the outer office, the clerks looked up at her. They were sitting at their desks this time, but Madeleine could tell they were still feeling as lost as before.

"Ma'am?" her assistant Robert ventured as he jumped to his feet. "Seeing as business is virtually at a standstill this morning, is there anything you'd like us to do?"

She considered the anxious faces staring at her. "Perhaps you could all lend a hand in cleaning up the factory floor? The sooner we can get operations started again–"

"Wonderful suggestion, ma'am," Robert smiled. "We're eager to help."

"Splendid," she replied.

"And Mrs Fletcher? I was wondering if perhaps I would be allowed to dash out for an hour or so around lunchtime?"

"Of course, Robert. Get some fresh air."

"Oh, it's not that. It's Daisy, you see."

"Your fiancée?"

"Yes. The poor girl is taking her father's death quite badly. And I thought–"

"Go and visit her, Robert. It's fine." She gave him a warm smile to show that she really did understand.

"Thank you, ma'am," he breathed excitedly. "I won't be too long, I promise. And afterwards, I'll also tidy the books a bit more. To follow up on those odd discrepancies I noticed before?"

"Ah yes, I must admit I'd forgotten about those."

"I'd say that's only normal, ma'am. With everything that's going on at the moment. But since I have some extra time on my hands, I thought I might as well."

"By all means, feel free to look into the matter, Robert. But don't push yourself too hard, please."

"Certainly, ma'am," he replied with a happy smile.

"And now I really must be off to the infirmary," she said. "Let's hope and pray Mrs Pemberton-Thorpe has some good news for me."

Chapter Twenty-One

"All our patients are alive and well, my dear."

Madeleine let out such an audible sigh of relief it made Mrs Pemberton-Thorpe chuckle.

"Were you that worried about my nursing skills?" the widow quipped.

"Of course not," Madeleine replied, not wanting to offend her sole remaining investor. "But with so many other things going wrong–"

"I was merely teasing you," Mrs Pemberton-Thorpe smiled. "You'll be happy to hear that Dr Brown expects everyone to make a swift recovery. In fact, I reckon half of these men will be able to go home by the end of the day."

"Thank heavens for that."

"Some will probably bear scars for the rest of their lives. But that's only a small price to pay compared to what could have happened."

"It is indeed," Madeleine nodded. "I am in your debt, Mrs Pemberton-Thorpe. The way you have stepped forward in this time of crisis–"

"Call me Constance, dear. And I merely did what I felt was right and proper. When there is suffering, one must always lend a hand." With a rueful grin, she added, "But then again, I'm old-fashioned in that respect, I suppose."

"Not at all. I think your views are very refreshing. But you must be exhausted, Mrs Pemb– Constance, I mean. Did you get any sleep at all? Or did you stay up the whole night?"

"I managed a few brief naps. But I spent most of the night on my feet. A few of the men had a fever, so I wanted to keep an eye on them."

"You're a true guardian angel. But please, you shouldn't risk your own health. We need you to remain hale and hearty."

"Your concern is appreciated, my dear. But at my age one tends to require less sleep, you know. Why, at home I often rise before the staff are up and about." She chuckled and added, "Much to Cook's dismay."

"Even so, you really ought to get some rest."

"I will, not to worry. There won't be that much for me to do here the remainder of the morning anyway. Especially since my best and brightest volunteer-nurse has now arrived."

With a slight nod of the chin, she gestured towards the far end of the infirmary. When Madeleine looked over, she saw Ellie standing by Stuart Wainwright's side. The young engineer was talking to one of the injured men.

"She's a very devoted and talented girl, your daughter," Mrs Pemberton-Thorpe smiled.

"You're too kind," Madeleine said, beaming at the praise for Ellie. "Now please, get some well-deserved rest. Before you succumb to fatigue."

"I'm not about to collapse just yet," the widow laughed. "This old battleaxe still has some fight left in her."

Shaking her head in amusement, Madeleine took her leave and made her way across the large hall towards Ellie and Stuart.

"Mama," her daughter said with a bright smile and sparkling eyes. "Stuart– that is, Mr Wainwright, is going round speaking to all these men. Isn't that simply wonderful of him? Trying to cheer up others despite his own misery and grief?"

Stuart blushed at Ellie's gushing words. "It's what my father would have done," he said with an apologetic shrug.

"I'm pleased to see you're recovering well," Madeleine said. "That head wound of yours seemed quite nasty yesterday."

"Oh, I'm fine, Mrs Fletcher," Stuart replied earnestly. "It looked worse than it actually was. And your daughter's care was beyond reproach."

Ellie's cheeks flushed pink with delight at his words.

"Well, I'm very glad to hear you're feeling better," Madeleine said.

"Yes, ma'am. I'm ready to get back to work straight away." He shook his head sadly. "A shame about this strike business though. It's halted everything. My father would have disapproved most sternly of that sort of thing, I can tell you."

Madeleine sighed. "Yes, and the trouble is I don't quite know yet what to do about it. The men are saying the factory is dangerous. A death trap, they called it."

Ellie gave Stuart a little nudge. "Tell my mother what you told me earlier."

"Oh, I don't know, Miss Eleanor," he hesitated. "It's probably not worth bothering your mother with."

"What is it, Stuart?" Madeleine asked now that her curiosity was roused.

"Just a notion of mine, Mrs Fletcher. Nothing serious. I wouldn't want–"

"Stuart thinks the engine was tampered with," Ellie blurted out.

"Sabotage?" Madeleine gasped.

But the young engineer held up his hands. "I didn't say that. All I said was that the engine shouldn't have exploded the way it did. We've built so many of them over the years and nothing has ever gone wrong."

"You suspect foul play?" Madeleine could scarcely believe she was asking the question.

"Too early to tell, ma'am. Someone would need to take a closer look at the wreckage first."

"Stuart could do that, couldn't he, Mama?" Ellie suggested eagerly. "He's very clever."

"I'm not sure if I'm the right person, Miss Eleanor," he said. "The blast killed my father. That might cloud my judgement."

"I suppose I could ask Ashton instead," Madeleine said.

"Mr Redhurst has ordered the debris to be cleared up as soon as possible, ma'am." Stuart sighed and dropped his shoulders. "I shouldn't have brought up this senseless idea of mine in the first place. It's probably merely a trick of my conscience. To make me feel even more guilty."

"Guilty?" Madeleine asked. "You? But why?"

"I'm one of the engineers, ma'am. It's my responsibility to ensure the safety of our operations. But I failed and now my father is dead."

Madeleine could see his jaw clenching as he tried to hold back his tears. "You shouldn't blame yourself, Stuart. None of this is your fault."

"But–"

"Tell you what," she said. "You have my permission to move the wreckage somewhere out of the way. Investigate them at your leisure. Would that help to ease your mind?"

"It would, Mrs Fletcher. Thank you."

"Just make sure you do it discreetly," she cautioned. "Out of Mr Redhurst's sight." The man's temperament was volatile enough, she thought. No sense in antagonising him needlessly.

"I could use one of the big storehouses," Stuart said. "There should be plenty of space in number three. That one's enormous."

"Very good. And please, don't–"

But just then Robert came rushing into the infirmary, slightly out of breath. "Pardon the interruption, Mrs Fletcher. But you have a visitor. It's Sir John."

Madeleine raised an eyebrow in surprise. Sir John was here?

"I know he's an old friend of yours," Robert continued. "So I took the liberty of showing him into your office to wait."

"Thank you, Robert. I'll go and see him at once." She turned back to Stuart. "My apologies, I must cut our conversation short. Do let me know if you find anything that seems amiss."

"Of course, ma'am," the engineer nodded.

Madeleine bid them all a good day and swiftly made her way to her office, wondering about the purpose of the elderly squire's unexpected visit.

When she entered, Sir John rose from his chair with a benevolent smile.

"My dear Madeleine," he said, clasping her hands fondly in greeting. "When I read about the dreadful accident in the papers this morning, I simply had to come and offer my sympathies."

"You are too kind, Sir John," Madeleine replied as they both took a seat. "It was a terrible tragedy. To lose so much in so little time." She shook her head sorrowfully.

"Terrible indeed. You must be carrying a heavy burden in the aftermath of this catastrophe. How are you holding up?"

Madeleine sighed. "We're managing for now. Though operations have entirely halted because of the strike."

Sir John frowned. "Yes, I saw the ridiculous accusations by that vile journalist of The Herald. The nerve of the man, disparaging your good character and leadership so callously."

"His words upset me, I'll admit," Madeleine said quietly. "But I cannot dwell on petty grievances now. I must find a way to convince my workers that the factory is safe and get them back to their posts. And we also have to make repairs as swiftly as our funds will allow."

"A daunting task, I have no doubt. But if anyone has the capability and strength of will to set things right, then I believe it is you."

"Your faith in me is much appreciated, Sir John," she said, giving him a faint but grateful smile.

"And remember, my dear," he went on. "If you should ever require assistance – monetary or otherwise – you need only ask. My door shall always remain open to you."

"Thank you," Madeleine replied warmly, feeling touched by his offer. "You are an exceedingly generous and kind-hearted soul. It's no wonder tales of your wisdom and compassion are so widely known."

"You're not wrong about my reputation being well-known, it seems. You'll never guess who came to see me recently." He paused, eyeing her intently. "Mr Dubois."

Madeleine stared at Sir John, shock and disbelief written plainly across her face.

"The name causes you some distress," he remarked, not unkindly.

"Mr Dubois and I have parted ways. Not on the best of terms, I might add."

"I know."

"You know? But how? What did he want of you?"

"He came seeking my counsel," Sir John explained calmly. "During our conversation, he readily confessed the nature of his prior questionable dealings to me. And he expressed his deepest remorse."

A scornful sound escaped from Madeleine's lips.

"He claims to be a reformed man now," Sir John said. "Eager to make righteous amends, as he called them."

"And how exactly does he intend to make these 'righteous amends'?" Madeleine's shock was slowly turning to anger.

Once a villain...

"That's why he wanted my advice," the squire replied. "To find a suitable way to atone for his past sins."

"The audacity. I hope you showed him the door?"

"On the contrary," Sir John smiled. "I hired him."

Madeleine sat bolt upright in her chair. "Surely not?"

"I have tasked him with raising funds for my charitable works," Sir John said.

"But the man is a criminal."

"Not anymore. The charm and cunning that once served him so well in his swindling days are now being used for good. Doesn't that sound like true redemption?"

She shook her head, deeply worried. "I implore you to be cautious, Sir John. That man is not to be trusted. This display of guilt and regret might very well be another one of his schemes."

But Sir John merely laughed, his eyes crinkling at the corners. "My dear Madeleine, I may seem like a trusting old fool to you, but I've been around long enough to know a thing or two about people."

He winked and tapped the side of his nose. "You don't get to my age without learning to be an excellent judge of character. I'm convinced Mr Dubois is sincere in his desire to reform."

Seeing her about to protest, he held up a hand. "And rest assured, I've taken precautions. The funds he raises will be supervised closely. He won't have direct access to a single penny."

Madeleine sucked in her breath, still sceptical despite her dear friend's confidence. "I do hope you know what you're doing, Sir John."

"I appreciate your concern, my dear. But trust me, I have this well in hand."

He rose from his seat, Madeleine following suit. "Now, I must be off. But remember what I said. If you ever need anything, anything at all, you need only ask."

She tried to chase the worried frown from her face with a small smile that felt contrived. "Thank you, Sir John. Your support means the world to me."

He bowed slightly. "Think nothing of it, my dear. I have the utmost faith in you." With a final reassuring nod, he took his leave.

When the door had closed behind him, Madeleine went back to her desk, her mind whirling. Sir John's unwavering belief in her was heartening. But his trust in Mr Dubois? That left a sickening knot of unease in her stomach.

She could only hope that the squire's judgement was as keen as he claimed. Because if he was wrong about the Frenchman... She shuddered to think of the consequences.

With a sigh, she turned back to the mountain of paperwork on her desk. There was still so much to be done. But for now, all she could do was press on.

Press on and pray.

Chapter Twenty-Two

The carriage creaked and swayed as it trundled through the city streets, but Madeleine scarcely noticed the familiar rhythm. Her eyes felt gritty and her head throbbed dully: the price of a restless night spent tossing and turning, chasing elusive sleep that never came.

Beside her, Ellie chattered away with the bright energy of youth, her words tumbling out in an eager rush. "Mrs Pemberton-Thorpe said I have a real knack for nursing, Mama. She even let me change some of the bandages yesterday, including Mr Wainwright's. His wound is healing nicely. Disinfecting it must have hurt a bit, but he didn't complain."

Madeleine made a soft sound of acknowledgement, her lips curving into a distracted smile. She knew she ought to be paying more attention, to share in her daughter's enthusiasm. But her mind felt as heavy as her limbs, weighed down by a jumble of worries that refused to be ignored.

Sir John's revelation about Mr Dubois churned uneasily in her stomach. The charming Frenchman's betrayal still stung like salt in a wound. So the notion that he was now supposedly a changed man? It simply defied belief.

And yet, the kind-hearted squire seemed convinced of Mr Dubois' sincerity. The whole situation left Madeleine reeling, unsure what to think.

"Mama? Are you even listening?" Ellie's voice pierced through the haze of her thoughts.

Madeleine blinked and turned to her daughter with an apologetic smile. "Of course, my dear. Forgive me, I was daydreaming. You were saying something about Mr Wainwright?"

"Only that he's been ever so brave in the face of his loss," Ellie said, her eyes shining with admiration. "He works so diligently, never stopping even though he must be hurting dreadfully inside."

"Mmm." Madeleine made another vague noise of agreement, her mind already starting to drift once more. Ellie's innocent chatter faded into the background as the carriage rolled on, bearing them toward the factory and the challenges that awaited her there.

The moment the carriage lurched to a halt near the gates, the distant rumble of angry voices reached Madeleine's ears. Her heart sank as she peered out the window, taking in the sight of the gathered workers, their faces set in stubborn lines.

"Looks like the strike is still on, ma'am," Bill said from the driver's seat, his brow creased with concern. "Shall I stay with you and Miss Eleanor until you're inside? Just to be safe?"

Madeleine hesitated for a moment, weighing her options. The memory of yesterday's unruly mob still sent a shiver down her spine. But she couldn't hide away forever. She needed to face her workers, to try and make them see reason.

"Thank you, Bill," she said at last. "We would appreciate the escort."

Squaring her shoulders, Madeleine stepped down from the carriage, Ellie close behind. As they approached the gates, the murmurs of the crowd grew louder, more agitated.

"Please, everyone," Madeleine called out, raising her voice to be heard above the din. "I understand your fears, truly I do. But this strike will only harm us all in the long run. I implore you, return to your posts. Let us work together to rebuild and move forward."

But her words were met with a fresh wave of grumbling, the men's faces hardening with distrust. A tight knot of anxiety settled in Madeleine's chest, constricting her breathing. How could she hope to lead them if they wouldn't even listen?

With a heavy sigh, she allowed Bill to usher her and Ellie through the gates, the weight of her workers' discontent bearing down on her shoulders.

But as they began to head for the main building, a familiar figure emerged from the crowd, a smug smile playing on his lips.

Charles Turner, the journalist who had been hounding Madeleine relentlessly, stepped forward, his eyes gleaming with malice.

"Mrs Fletcher," he called out, his voice dripping with mock concern. "How does it feel to know that your own workers have turned against you? Do you still maintain that a woman is fit to run a business? Or have you finally realised your folly?"

Madeleine gritted her teeth. She knew engaging with Turner would only encourage him, but his barbed words needled at her frayed nerves nonetheless.

"Tell me, Mrs Fletcher," he continued, playing to the crowd. "How do you plan to convince these men to return to work – when they clearly have no faith in your leadership? Or are you content to watch your late husband's legacy crumble to dust?"

The gathered workers jeered and shouted their agreement, their anger finding a new target in Turner's goading questions. Madeleine felt Ellie's hand slip into hers and she gave it a little squeeze in response.

"Perhaps it's time to admit defeat, Mrs Fletcher," Turner pressed on. "Surely even you must see that your inexperience and womanly sensibilities have no place in the world of industry. Why not hand the reins over to someone more capable? Like your partner Mr Redhurst?"

Madeleine's cheeks burned with indignation, but she refused to be baited. With a curt shake of her head, she turned away from Turner and the jeering crowd, her grip on Ellie's hand tightening.

"Come along, Bill," she said quietly, her voice strained but determined. "Let's go inside."

With the coachman's solid presence at their side, Madeleine and Ellie made their way through the hostile throng, ignoring the taunts and insults that followed in their wake.

"Running away, Mrs Fletcher?" Turner called after her. "Perhaps you should consider running all the way home, and leave the real work to the men."

The crowd erupted in laughter, their jeers growing louder and more vicious. Feeling exposed and vulnerable, Madeleine's steps faltered. But she was intent on denying him the satisfaction of a response. With a resolute set to her jaw, she pulled Ellie closer and crossed the threshold into the factory. Bill quickly closed the heavy doors behind them, muffling the cruel cacophony outside.

"Thank you, Bill," Madeleine said sincerely. "Ellie and I felt safer having you near."

Bill touched the brim of his cap. "Think nothing of it, ma'am. I'm just glad I could be of help." He glanced back at the closed doors, his brow furrowing. "If that's all, ma'am, I'd best be getting back to old Bess. I don't like the thought of leaving her alone while that unruly lot is out there."

Madeleine nodded, understanding his concern for his trusted mare. "Of course, Bill. Please, go back to the house. We'll be fine from here."

With a final tip of his cap, Bill slipped out through a side door, leaving Madeleine and Ellie alone in the echoing entrance.

"I should go to the infirmary," Ellie said, her voice sounding small in the vast space. "Mrs Pemberton-Thorpe will be waiting for me."

Madeleine mustered a smile for her daughter, despite the heaviness in her heart. "I'm sure your presence will be a great comfort to the patients again."

Ellie gave her mother's hand a quick squeeze before hurrying off down the corridor, her footsteps fading into the distance. Madeleine watched her go, drawing strength from her daughter's resilience.

My brave, sweet girl, Madeleine thought, a surge of love and pride swelling in her chest.

Then she turned and made her way towards her office. With any luck, Ashton would have finished his survey of the damage to the factory. But Madeleine very much doubted that his findings would cheer her up.

Chapter Twenty-Three

As she neared the door to her office, voices drifted out from within – Ashton's deep baritone, overlaid by the reedy tones of Mr Underwood. Madeleine's steps slowed, a prickle of apprehension raising the hairs on the back of her neck.

Bracing herself for whatever news awaited her, she drew a deep breath and reached for the door handle. As she stepped into her office, both men turned to face her, their expressions grim.

In that moment, she knew with a gloomy certainty that her day was about to take a turn for the worse.

"Morning, Madeleine," Ashton greeted her, his usually arrogant voice tinged with solemnity. "You'd better sit down. I'm afraid we have some rather troubling news to discuss."

Madeleine's gaze flicked between the two men, noting the tension in their postures. Mr Underwood fidgeted beside Ashton, his fingers plucking at the cuffs of his sleeves.

Moving round her large desk, she could feel her insides twisting. She sank into her chair, the leather creaking softly beneath her, and then folded her hands on the polished surface. When she tried to swallow, her mouth felt as dry as old parchment.

"I've had a good look at the damage from the explosion," Ashton said. "And I asked Mr Underwood to run the numbers. To give us a clearer picture of what we're facing."

He nodded to the accountant, who cleared his throat nervously. "Yes, well, you see, Mrs Fletcher," Mr Underwood began, his voice quavering slightly. "I've done my level best to estimate the costs of the necessary repairs. Of course, it's always a bit of a challenge to arrive at precise figures in these situations. What with the variable costs of materials and labour to consider, not to mention the potential impact on production schedules and–"

"Skip all that, Underwood," Ashton interrupted, barely concealing his impatience. "Just show Mrs Fletcher the numbers, will you?"

The accountant blinked, seeming to deflate a little. "Ah, yes, of course." He fumbled with the sheaf of papers in his hands, nearly dropping them in his haste. "I have the final estimates right here, ma'am."

With a trembling hand, he held out a single sheet filled with neat columns of figures. "It's the number at the bottom right corner you'll want," he said helpfully as Madeleine took the page from him.

When the figure registered, a sharp gasp escaped her lips. It was a staggering amount, far exceeding even her most pessimistic predictions. Her mind reeled as she tried to process the implications.

"As you can see," Ashton said, his voice low and grave, "the financial impact of this disaster is quite severe."

Madeleine gave a nod, staring blankly at those awful numbers on the sheet in front of her.

"Can we manage it?" She looked up from the page, her heart sinking at the grim set of Ashton's jaw. Mr Underwood shifted uncomfortably beside him, his gaze darting away when she tried to catch his eye.

"Ashton? Mr Underwood? Can we afford this?"

"At this point," the accountant croaked, "I am not convinced we have the necessary funds."

A sharp, icy pain lanced through Madeleine's heart, and a bitter taste rose up to the back of her mouth.

"But surely there must be a way," she said, hating the note of desperation that crept into her voice. "Perhaps we could secure a loan. Or raise new capital–"

Ashton shook his head, his expression almost pitying. "It may not be that simple, Madeleine. With the factory's operations halted and our workforce in revolt, we hardly present an attractive prospect for potential lenders of any sort."

Madeleine's fingers tightened on the paper, the figures blurring before her eyes. It felt as if a crushing weight pressed down on her, constricting her chest and throat. How could she possibly lead the company through this crisis when the odds seemed so thoroughly stacked against her?

"And to make matters even worse," Ashton said, "this arrived today." Reaching into his coat pocket, he withdrew a letter. "It's from the solicitors of Wilson & Harris."

Madeleine frowned. "The textile mill?"

"The very same," Ashton confirmed grimly. "Who also happen to be our biggest customer." He held out the letter to her.

Madeleine took the proffered letter and unfolded it. Her eyes quickly scanned the neatly handwritten lines, each word hitting her like a physical blow.

"They're... cancelling their order?"

Ashton nodded, his mouth set in a thin line. "Citing safety concerns and doubts about our ability to deliver."

Madeleine looked up at him, a cold dread seeping into her bones. "But we've always fulfilled our contracts with them. We've never let them down."

"That was before the explosion," Ashton pointed out. "Now, they've lost confidence in us. And I can't say I blame them."

Mr Underwood cleared his throat, drawing their attention. "If I may, ma'am," he said hesitantly. "Losing the Wilson & Harris contract will have severe repercussions for our cash flow. If our income stream dries up..." He trailed off, swallowing hard.

"What are you saying, Mr Underwood?" Madeleine asked, though she feared she already knew the answer.

The accountant's shoulders slumped, as if the weight of his words was too much to bear. "The company will run out of money within a month or two. We won't be able to pay our workers, our suppliers... or anyone else."

Madeleine felt as if the floor had dropped out from beneath her, a yawning chasm of despair opening up at her feet. Her heart pounded in her ears, a deafening drumbeat that drowned out everything else.

"Is there nothing we can do?" she asked, her voice sounding small and far away to her own ears. "We can't just give up."

Ashton paused, his expression softening. "Well, there is one alternative, Madeleine. Remember my offer to take over your half of the company?"

She nodded, a flicker of unease passing through her.

"I know it's not what you wanted to hear," he continued, his voice taking on a sympathetic tone. "But perhaps it's time to consider it more seriously. For your own wellbeing and happiness."

He took a step closer, his eyes searching hers. "Think about it, Maddie. How much longer will you be able to put up with this burden? And do you really want to watch the business descend into ruin? Is that what Benjamin would have wanted for you?"

At the mention of her late husband's name, Madeleine felt a sharp pang in her chest. "I don't know," she admitted, her voice barely above a whisper.

Ashton's face turned thoughtful. "You know, I seem to remember Ben telling me once how much you loved to play the piano. When was the last time you sat down to play?"

"Not since he passed away," she sighed. The idea of losing herself in the joy of music had felt wrong to her.

"Imagine how much easier and happier your life could be without the weight of this factory on your shoulders. You could devote your days to your music. You could spend more time with Ellie and pursue any passion that catches your fancy."

Stepping in closer, he placed a hand on her shoulder, the warmth of his touch seeping through the fabric of her dress. "I would treat you fairly, Maddie. You know I would. We could have Mr Underwood estimate the current value of the company, and I would offer you a generous price for your share."

He turned to the accountant. "You could do that, couldn't you, Underwood?"

Mr Underwood straightened, pressing his sheaf of papers against his chest. "Certainly, Mr Redhurst. The valuation process would involve a thorough analysis of the company's assets, liabilities, and projected future earnings. We would need to consider various factors—"

As Mr Underwood droned on, Madeleine felt a heavy weariness settle over her. The relentless barrage of setbacks, the crushing burden of keeping the factory afloat, and now, the devastating blow of their financial ruin. It all crashed over her like a tidal wave threatening to drag her under.

She raised a hand, cutting off Mr Underwood's rambling explanation. "Thank you, gentlemen," she said, her voice strained. "I need some time to think about all of this. Could you please leave me?"

Ashton exchanged a glance with Mr Underwood before nodding. "Of course, Madeleine. Take all the time you need. But remember," he added, "the longer you wait, the more dire our situation becomes. Don't let this opportunity slip away."

With that, the two men took their leave, softly closing the door behind them. Alone, Madeleine slumped back in her chair and let out a deep, shuddering sigh. She closed her eyes, fighting against the headache that was setting in.

Perhaps Ashton was right.

Perhaps selling her share was the only way to save herself from this impending disaster.

Chapter Twenty-Four

You've come this far already, Madeleine. Why stop now?

As the memory of Charlotte's loving words rose up in Madeleine's mind, her eyes fluttered open again. Her darling cousin had been right. She had fought too hard, come too far, to give up at the first sign of trouble.

The trick is to hold steady through the lows, Charlotte had told her.

Yes, this was undoubtedly a low point. But if she could just hold on, if she could weather this storm.

Madeleine rose up from behind her desk. She couldn't give in to despair, not yet. There had to be a way to salvage the situation, to reassure their customers and bring the workers back.

"We have to know what caused the explosion," she decided. That was the key that could unlock this dreadful nightmare.

With renewed determination, she left her office and made her way to the storehouses. She needed to find Stuart, to see if he had made any progress in his investigation of the wreckage.

As she went into storehouse number three, she spotted Stuart standing amidst the twisted metal and debris, his brow furrowed in concentration. And there, right by his side, was Ellie, a tray of tea and biscuits in her hands.

Madeleine paused, quietly observing the pair from a distance. Ellie leaned in closer to Stuart, holding out the tray with an earnest expression. "Have another biscuit, Mr Wainwright. It'll help you think better."

Stuart, his gaze never leaving the wrecked engine, reached out absentmindedly and took a biscuit from the tray. He bit into it, chewing slowly as he continued to study the mangled remains of the machine.

"It's impossible," he muttered, shaking his head. "This shouldn't have happened. Not like this."

Madeleine stepped forward, her curiosity piqued. "Stuart? Have you discovered something?"

Both the young engineer and Ellie started at the sound of her voice, turning to face her. Stuart quickly swallowed his mouthful of biscuit, a faint blush colouring his cheeks.

"Mrs Fletcher," he said, inclining his head respectfully. "I was just examining the wreckage. Trying to make sense of it all."

Madeleine nodded, moving closer to inspect the twisted metal herself. "And have you? Made sense of it, I mean?"

Stuart hesitated, his eyes clouding with worry and guilt. "I'm afraid I have, ma'am. And it's not good."

He led Madeleine closer to the wrecked engine, pointing out where a series of valves and pipes had been. "See here? The only way this engine could have exploded is if someone had failed to secure those valves properly. It's a critical step in the assembly process, one that should never be overlooked."

Madeleine frowned, trying to understand the implications of his words. "Are you saying it was an accident, then? A mistake made by one of the workers?"

Stuart shook his head, his expression pained. "That's the odd thing, ma'am. This engine? It was part of a batch of three. All of them were set aside and inspected the day before the test-firing. By myself and my father, personally."

He swallowed hard, his voice dropping to a hoarse whisper. "It was our responsibility to ensure everything was in proper working order. We should have spotted the issue, ma'am. But we didn't. And now, good men are dead because of it."

Madeleine felt a cold weight settling in the pit of her stomach. A human error. One that had cost lives and thrown the entire factory into chaos.

She looked at the young engineer, saw the anguish and self-recrimination etched into his features. He blamed himself, she realised. He now carried the weight of those deaths on his shoulders, a burden no one so young should have to bear.

"Stuart," she said softly, placing a hand on his arm. "Accidents happen, even to the most diligent among us. Your father knew that better than anyone."

But even as she spoke the words, they rang hollow in her ears. Because accident or not, the damage had been done. The factory's reputation was in tatters, the workers were in revolt, and their future hung in the balance.

How could she possibly hope to salvage the situation now? With the spectre of faulty workmanship hanging over them, who would trust in the safety of their engines? And who would be willing to risk their lives to work in a factory where such fatal mistakes could be made?

"But Mama?" Ellie spoke up beside her. "What if it wasn't an accident?"

Madeleine and Stuart both turned and stared at her.

"Mr Wainwright is far too clever to make a mistake like that," the girl explained. "He's the most brilliant engineer I've ever met." She looked at Stuart, her eyes shining with admiration. "Isn't it possible that someone could have tampered with the engine after your inspection, before the test?"

Stuart frowned, considering the idea. "It's unlikely, Miss Eleanor. Once they were finished, the engines were constantly in plain sight. No one would have been able to get near enough without drawing attention to themselves." He paused, his gaze lingering on the wreckage.

"Although," he continued slowly, "I suppose if someone were determined enough, they could have found a way. But they would have had to work during the night or in the very early morning, before the first shift arrived."

"Aha," Ellie exclaimed. "So there's a possibility?"

"Yes, but–"

"That settles it then. A saboteur is far more likely than you making a mistake."

"I wouldn't quite say that, Miss Eleanor."

While Ellie and Stuart nattered on, Madeleine remained silent. She gazed long and hard at the wreckage, as if the answer to this mystery could be read in those twisted piles of scrap.

Sabotage...

The very notion seemed too outrageous to entertain. Who would do such a thing? And why?

Madeleine shook her head, trying to dislodge the preposterous thought. No, it couldn't be.

Sabotage was the stuff of penny dreadfuls and lurid newspaper headlines, surely?

This factory was a place where honest, hardworking men toiled and laboured. She couldn't imagine any of them harbouring the kind of malice required to orchestrate such a heinous act. These were simple, decent folk – not the sort to engage in shadowy intrigue and malicious plots.

And yet, given the dire circumstances they found themselves in, could they afford to dismiss any possibility, no matter how far-fetched?

"Stuart," she said, turning to the young engineer, "I need you to continue your investigation. Leave no stone unturned. If there is the slightest chance that this was deliberate, then we must find out the truth."

"I'm afraid there's not much more I can learn from the wreckage, Mrs Fletcher. I've already gleaned everything it can tell me. There wasn't much left to begin with, and some of my findings are mere guesswork as it is."

Madeleine sighed. "I understand. So be it, then."

"I'm sorry I couldn't do more, ma'am," he said.

"On the contrary, Stuart. Your findings, and Ellie's theory, are both a step forward. Every piece of information brings us closer to discovering what really happened."

"That's true, I suppose."

"One thing though," Madeleine warned, her voice low and urgent. "What we've just discussed here... It must remain strictly between us. We can't allow this to spread, not until we know more. Do you understand?"

Stuart's eyes widened slightly, but then he nodded. "Of course, ma'am. I won't breathe a word of it to anyone."

Ellie, too, bobbed her head in agreement. "I won't tell a soul, Mama. I promise."

In the brief silence that followed, the three of them exchanged glances, sealing their shared secret.

"What would you like me to do with the wreckage, ma'am?" Stuart asked.

"Leave it here for now," Madeleine replied. "You never know what new insights might come to light."

"I'll pull a large canvas or some sheets over it," he said. "To keep it safe from prying eyes."

Madeleine murmured her consent and then left, with Ellie falling into step beside her. As the pair walked away from the storehouse, Madeleine's thoughts turned dark and fearful.

If Ellie was right, if there truly was a saboteur among them... The idea made her blood run cold. To think that someone within these walls, someone they trusted and worked alongside every day, could be capable of such wickedness. It was a chilling prospect, one that left her feeling vulnerable and afraid.

And what if the saboteur wasn't finished?

The terrifying thought sent her heart racing. What if these villains were even now plotting their next move, waiting for the perfect moment to strike again? The factory was already reeling from the explosion. It might not survive another blow.

She needed to talk to someone about this, to share her suspicions and fears. But who? Charlotte was too sensitive for such matters. Her cousin would be beside herself with worry and dread. No, she couldn't put dear Charlotte through that.

As they neared the infirmary, Madeleine came to a decision. She turned to Ellie, placing a hand on her daughter's shoulder.

"Ellie, I need you to stay here with Mrs Pemberton-Thorpe for a while. Help her tend to the injured and keep their spirits up."

Ellie frowned. "Where are you going, Mama?"

Madeleine managed a tight smile, trying to project a calm she didn't feel. "I need to pay a visit to a wise old friend. Someone who might be able to shed some light on our current predicament."

Ellie looked as if she wanted to protest, but something in Madeleine's expression must have convinced her of the gravity of the situation. She nodded, her jaw set with determination.

"I'll do my best here, Mama. You can count on me."

Madeleine pressed a quick kiss to Ellie's forehead, then turned and headed for the factory gates.

As she stepped out into the grimy, soot-stained streets, the acrid tang of chimney smoke assailed her nostrils. She paused for a moment, her hand resting on the rough brick wall beside her, as she tried to gather her thoughts and steady her nerves.

The task ahead loomed large in her mind, a daunting challenge that threatened to overwhelm her. But Madeleine knew she couldn't afford to falter – not when so much was at stake.

She straightened her back, as if she was preparing to face a physical foe. Her jaw tightened and a steely glint entered her eye. With a final, determined nod to herself, Madeleine set off down the street, her strides purposeful and unwavering.

She didn't know what answers she would find at the end of this journey, or what new dangers might lurk in the shadows. But one thing was certain: she wouldn't rest until she had uncovered the truth, no matter how ugly or terrible it might be.

I'll face this threat. And I'll overcome it.

And may God have mercy on anyone who stood in her way.

Chapter Twenty-Five

The hackney cab came to a halt before the imposing façade of Sir John's city residence. After paying the driver, Madeleine stepped down from the carriage, her boots clicking on the immaculately clean pavement. She turned to face the house, its elegant lines and impressive size a testament to the wealth and status of its owner.

If anyone could help her find clarity in this tangled mess, it was Sir John.

Madeleine took a deep breath, lifted her chin and ascended the stairs with a firm step. Standing before the imposing front door, she smoothed her skirts before grasping the ornate brass knocker and rapping it against the sturdy oak surface.

Moments later, the door swung open to reveal a crisply uniformed maid, her face a mask of polite enquiry.

"Good afternoon, ma'am," the girl said. "How may I assist you?"

Madeleine offered a small, apologetic smile. "I'm terribly sorry to arrive unannounced like this. I'm Mrs Madeleine Fletcher, a friend of Sir John's. I know I don't have an appointment, but

I was hoping he might be available to see me? It's a matter of some urgency."

To her surprise, the maid's face brightened with recognition. "Ah, Mrs Fletcher. Of course, please come in." She stepped aside, ushering Madeleine into the grand foyer. "Sir John has told us that you are to be admitted and brought to him immediately, no matter the hour or circumstance."

Madeleine blinked, pleasantly surprised by this unexpected revelation. "Oh, I see. That's very kind of him."

The maid smiled. "The master holds you in the highest regard, ma'am. He's made it quite clear that you are always welcome here."

She gestured toward the sweeping staircase. "If you'll follow me, I'll take you to him straight away."

As Madeleine trailed after the maid, her heart lifted a fraction. In the midst of all the chaos and uncertainty, it was a comfort to know that she still had allies – steadfast friends she could turn to in her hour of need.

And right now, she needed those more than ever.

The maid led Madeleine through the exquisitely decorated corridors of Sir John's residence, their footsteps muffled by the plush carpets underfoot. As they approached the study, the maid paused.

"Sir John is just inside, ma'am. I'll announce you."

The girl knocked and waited until Sir John replied with a brief "Come."

Then she opened the door and stepped into the room. "Mrs Fletcher to see you, Sir John."

"Madeleine, my dear!" Sir John's friendly voice filled the study. "What a delightful surprise. Please, come in."

Madeleine entered the room, a smile already forming on her lips at the fondness of her old friend's greeting. But as her gaze swept the study, her smile faltered and was replaced by a look of surprise and unease.

There, seated in one of the armchairs by the fireplace, was none other than Mr Dubois. The charming Frenchman rose to his feet, a polite smile on his handsome face. But Madeleine could see the discomfort in his eyes.

"Mrs Fletcher," he said, inclining his head in a slight bow. "What an unexpected pleasure."

Madeleine felt a surge of conflicting emotions – surprise, anger, and a traitorous flutter of something else she couldn't quite name. She forced her features into a mask of cool politeness, determined not to let her turbulent feelings show.

"Mr Dubois," she replied, her voice carefully neutral. "I didn't expect to find you here."

Sir John, ever the astute observer, quickly intervened. "Ah, forgive me, Madeleine. Mr Dubois and I were just discussing some matters related to my charitable endeavours. But I can send him away if you'd prefer to speak privately."

Madeleine hesitated for a moment, torn between her desire for Sir John's undivided attention and her reluctance to be in the same room with the man who had so thoroughly betrayed her trust. In the end, her pride won out.

"No, that won't be necessary," she said, sticking her chin out slightly. "Mr Dubois can stay. After all, *I* have nothing to hide."

The words hung in the air between them, a subtle yet unmistakable jab at the Frenchman's chequered past. Mr Dubois flinched almost imperceptibly, but he maintained his composure, his smile never wavering.

Sir John, sensing the tension, stepped forward and took her hands in his own. "My dear, you look troubled. Come, sit down and tell me what brings you here."

Madeleine allowed herself to be led to a chair, sinking into the plush upholstery with a sigh. She looked up at Sir John, an apology already forming on her lips.

"I'm so sorry for barging in on you like this, Sir John. I know how busy you must be. And here I am, interrupting your meeting with Mr Dubois."

But Sir John waved away her concerns with a gentle smile. "Nonsense, my dear. It was I who told you that you were always welcome to call on me, wasn't it? There's no need for formalities between old friends."

He settled into the chair beside her, his keen eyes searching her face. "Now, tell me what's troubling you. There's no use in hiding it. I can see something has you deeply worried."

Madeleine hesitated for a moment, glancing briefly at Mr Dubois. The Frenchman sat quietly, and when their eyes met, he hurriedly lowered his gaze.

"It's the factory, Sir John," she began after turning back to the squire. "I'm afraid we're in dire straits."

Her lips felt dry, while her fingers twisted in her lap as she gathered her thoughts. "The repairs from the explosion are going to cost a fortune, and we simply don't have the necessary funds."

"Can't you raise fresh capital?" Sir John asked. "Obtain a loan from the bank?"

"I fear no bank would touch us in our current state. And to make matters worse, our customers have started cancelling their orders. They've lost confidence in our ability to deliver."

She swallowed hard, the lump in her throat making it difficult to speak. "If this continues, we'll run out of money in two months."

The room fell silent, the weight of her words hanging heavy in the air. Sir John sat back in his chair, pressing his fingertips together in front of him. "This is dire news indeed, my dear."

Madeleine hesitated, glancing once more at Mr Dubois. The Frenchman sat motionless, his eyes fixed on her with an intensity that made her skin prickle.

"There's something else," she said quietly, her voice almost a whisper. "One of my engineers has been examining the wreckage of the engine that exploded. And he's found evidence of what appears to be poor workmanship."

Sir John's eyebrows shot up. "Poor workmanship? In your factory? But your standards have always been impeccable."

Madeleine nodded, her throat tight. "I know. Which is why Eleanor suggested another possibility." She paused, the words tasting bitter on her tongue. "Deliberate sabotage."

The room seemed to freeze, the silence broken only by the ticking of the clock on the mantelpiece. Sir John stared at her, looking bewildered. "Sabotage? But who would do such a thing?"

Madeleine shook her head, tears pricking at the corners of her eyes. "I don't know. I can't imagine anyone wishing harm on the factory or the workers. But the evidence–" She trailed off, her voice cracking.

Sir John leaned forward, placing a comforting hand on her arm. "My dear Madeleine, this is a shocking revelation. But I want you to know that you have my full support. We will get to the bottom of this, I promise you."

"Thank you, Sir John," she replied, a single tear sliding down her cheek. "I'm ashamed to admit it, but I don't know what to do anymore."

"Let's put our heads together then. Three are wiser than one," he said, his voice calm and reassuring. "Do you have any enemies? Anyone who might wish to see you fail?"

"No, not that I can think of. We've always tried to treat our workers fairly and maintain good relationships with our customers."

"What about that journalist fellow? The one who's been writing those dreadful articles about you."

"Charles Turner?" Madeleine's lips tightened as she spoke the name. "He's certainly been a thorn in my side. But would he really go so far as to sabotage the factory?"

To her surprise, it was Mr Dubois who spoke next. "I doubt it, Mrs Fletcher," he said. "Men like Turner, they are cowards at heart. They prefer to hide behind their printed words, stirring up trouble from a distance. It's safer – and more profitable."

"So what do you think, my young friend?" Sir John asked. "Who or what could be behind this catastrophe?"

"In situations like these," Mr Dubois began, "the question we must always ask ourselves is this: who benefits? Who would benefit from the demise of the Fletcher & Redhurst Steam Engine Works?"

"Absolutely no one," Madeleine exclaimed, her voice rising with emotion. "All the workers would lose their livelihoods. And everything that Benjamin and Ashton have built up over nearly two decades would be gone."

A small, knowing smile played at the corners of Mr Dubois' lips. "Ah, but Madame," he said gently, "you are an honest person. And so you think like honest people do. But in this case, you must open your mind... and think like a villain."

Madeleine stiffened, her eyes flashing with indignation. "I'm afraid I wouldn't know how to do that," she said coldly. "I have no experience in villainy. Unlike some individuals in this very room."

Sir John cleared his throat. "Madeleine, please. Mr Dubois is only trying to help."

"Mrs Fletcher is right to criticise me," Mr Dubois said, tilting his head slightly. "My past actions have given her every reason to doubt my character."

Madeleine blinked. She had expected his acknowledgment to give her a sense of triumph. But instead, it merely left her with a hollow feeling.

"But let us approach the question from a different angle," he continued. "What is likely to happen to your company in its present situation?"

Madeleine sighed, her shoulders slumping. "Unless some miracle happens, we will run out of money in a month or two."

"And then what happens?"

"We will have to cease trading, fire all the workers, and fold the company," she replied, her voice heavy with despair.

"And there are no alternatives?"

Madeleine shook her head sadly. "None that I can see at the moment, no."

"So your company is beyond hope?" Mr Dubois asked, fixing her with an intense gaze. "The ship will sink, so to speak. And you, as its captain, will go down with it?"

"That's a rather colourful way of putting it. But yes." An ironic grin came to her face. "Although it seems Ashton wants to spare me from drowning. He has offered to purchase my share of the company."

"Is that so?" Mr Dubois said, sounding intrigued. "Why would he do that, I wonder?"

"He claims it's for my own good," she replied, her voice tinged with bitterness. "He says he wants to relieve me of the stress and the burden, to give me a chance at a happier life again."

She laughed, a hollow, mirthless sound. "But secretly, I think he would be happy to be rid of me. Ever since I took over the reins after Benjamin died, Ashton has done nothing but complain and undermine my authority at every turn."

As the words left her mouth, Madeleine froze, her eyes widening with a sudden, chilling realisation. The pieces of the puzzle began to fall into place, forming a picture so twisted and dark that it left her breathless.

"You don't think that Ashton–" she whispered, her voice trembling with a mixture of fear and disbelief. "But that's impossible. He would never..."

She trailed off, unable to put words to the terrible suspicion that now gnawed at her insides. Could Ashton, her late husband's trusted partner, truly be capable of such treachery? The thought was so vile, so utterly betraying, that it made her feel sick to the stomach.

Mr Dubois leaned forward. "I must admit," he said quietly, "I never quite trusted Mr Redhurst. He has a mean and dishonest streak about him."

Madeleine's head snapped up. "Talk about the pot calling the kettle black," she retorted, her voice sharp as a whip.

Sir John cleared his throat, holding up a hand to forestall the impending argument. "Please, both of you. This is not the time for bickering. We must focus on the task at hand."

He turned to Madeleine, his eyes softening with compassion. "My dear, I know this is difficult to accept. But we must consider all possibilities. If there is even the slightest chance that Ashton is involved in this heinous plot, you must investigate it thoroughly."

Madeleine shook her head. "But how? How can we possibly prove such a thing?"

Sir John cast a sideways glance at Mr Dubois. "I believe," he said slowly, "that you and Mr Dubois should work together on this. Combine your knowledge and resources to uncover the truth, whatever it may be."

Madeleine recoiled as if she'd been slapped. "Work with him? Sir John, surely you can't be serious. I don't trust this man, not for a moment."

Mr Dubois flinched at her words, a flicker of hurt crossing his face. But he quickly composed himself.

"Mrs Fletcher," he said, his voice quiet and earnest, "I know I have given you every reason to doubt me. But I swear to you, upon my life and my honour, that my intentions in this matter are pure."

He hesitated, his eyes searching hers with an intensity that made her breath catch in her throat. "You are aware of how I feel about you," he said softly. "I could never betray those feelings, not for anything in this world."

Madeleine stared at him, her heart pounding with a dizzying mix of emotions. She wanted to believe him, wanted desperately to trust in the sincerity that shone so clearly in his eyes. But the wounds of his past betrayal were still raw, still aching with every beat of her heart.

Sir John, sensing her hesitation, rose to his feet and went to stand by the fireplace. "Madeleine, my dear," he said gently, "I understand this is not an easy decision. But please, consider your options. What other choice do you have?"

He glanced briefly at Mr Dubois, his expression hardening with resolve. "And let me make one thing perfectly clear. Should Mr Dubois ever betray your trust, ever cause you harm in any way, I will spend the rest of my days and every last penny of my fortune to ensure that he faces the full weight of justice."

Madeleine sat in silence for a long moment, her mind whirling with the enormity of the choice before her. She knew, deep in her heart, that Sir John was right. She had no other options, no other allies to turn to in this desperate hour.

With a heavy sigh, she nodded, her shoulders sagging with resignation. "Very well," she said. "I will work with Mr Dubois to uncover the truth. But mark my words," she added, turning towards the Frenchman with a fierceness in her eyes that visibly startled him. "If you betray me again, Monsieur, then there will be no place on this earth where you can hide from my wrath."

Mr Dubois met her gaze unflinchingly. "I understand," he said quietly. "And I accept those terms, with all my heart."

"Excellent," Sir John beamed. "Now, let's get to work."

Chapter Twenty-Six

"I believe our first step should be to speak with young Mr Wainwright," Mr Dubois said. "He may have insights that could prove valuable to our investigation."

Madeleine frowned. "And what exactly do you hope to achieve by that? Stuart has already told me everything he knows."

The Frenchman shrugged, a small smile playing at the corners of his lips. "Perhaps not much. But as you English say, we need to play it by ear, no?"

She sighed and glanced at the ornate clock on the mantelpiece. "Well, I'm afraid we won't be able to speak with him at the factory. Stuart will have gone home by now."

She paused as a thought occurred to her. "I suppose we could pay him a visit at his house. It would give me a chance to express my condolences to his family in person. After all, they've just lost their father and husband."

"A kind and thoughtful gesture, my dear," Sir John said. "I'm sure the Wainwrights would appreciate your presence in their time of grief."

But then Madeleine's eyes widened, a sudden realisation hitting her. "Oh, but wait! I can't just leave Ellie at the factory. She'll be wondering where I am."

"Not to worry, Madeleine," Sir John replied with a wave of the hand. "I can send my own carriage to take Eleanor home safely. It would be no trouble at all."

"That's very kind of you, Sir John. But I'm sure my coachman Bill is already waiting for us at the factory gates."

"Of course, how foolish of me," Sir John smiled. "In that case, I shall send word to the factory at once. To let your daughter know she is to ride home with your coachman. And then you and Mr Dubois can be on your way to the Wainwrights."

He rose from his seat, moving towards the bell pull. "I'll just ring for Perkins and have him dispatch a message immediately. No sense in wasting any more time."

As Sir John tugged on the bell pull, Madeleine turned to Mr Dubois, her expression serious. "I hope you know what you're doing, Monsieur. The Wainwrights are a family in mourning. We must tread carefully and respectfully."

Mr Dubois inclined his head, his eyes meeting hers with a solemn intensity. "I understand completely, Madame. And I assure you, I will handle this matter with the utmost delicacy and discretion."

Madeleine held his gaze for a long moment, searching for any hint of deception or insincerity. But she found only a steadfast determination and a glimmer of something else. Something that looked suspiciously like genuine concern.

With a sigh, she nodded, rising from her own seat. "Very well, then. Let's be off. The sooner we speak with Stuart, the sooner we'll be one step closer to uncovering the truth behind this dreadful business."

After bidding farewell to Sir John, the two of them were soon standing on the pavement outside the squire's residence, where the setting sun was already casting long shadows.

"Lady Fortune smiles on us," Mr Dubois grinned when he spotted a hackney that had just stopped to let out its passenger a few houses down the road. Moments later, they were inside the carriage and trundling along.

The journey to the Wainwright home was brief, and when they stepped out of the carriage, Madeleine took in the sight of the simple terraced house. It was a modest dwelling, nestled in a long line of identical looking homes.

To Madeleine's mind, it seemed like the sort of place where folks knew all their neighbours by name and were quick to lend a helping hand or a kind word.

Shortly after Mr Dubois had knocked, the door opened. It was Stuart and his eyebrows shot up in astonishment at finding his employer standing on his doorstep.

"Mrs Fletcher? Mr Dubois? What a surprise. Please, come in."

As they stepped into the narrow hallway, Madeleine could hear the chatter of voices coming from somewhere inside the house. Stuart led them through to the small dining room, where the Wainwright family was gathered around the supper table.

Mrs Wainwright, Stuart's recently widowed mother, looked up from her plate, her expression a mixture of surprise and curiosity. Also at the table were Stuart's eldest sister Daisy, and two younger siblings – a boy and a girl. To Madeleine's surprise, Robert was present as well, seated next to his fiancée Daisy.

"Mother," Stuart began, "this is Mrs Fletcher from the factory. And Mr Dubois, a business partner of hers."

Mrs Wainwright's eyes widened and she quickly rose from her chair, straightening her apron. "Mrs Fletcher, what an honour to have you in our home. And Mr Dubois, welcome."

"Mr Dubois is from Paris, Daisy," Robert said, trying to impress his fiancée. "That's in France."

Madeleine offered a warm smile, stepping forward. "I apologise for the intrusion at such a late hour, and during your supper no less. But I felt I had to come and offer my condolences in person. Your husband was an exemplary foreman, Mrs Wainwright. His dedication and hard work were truly admirable."

Mrs Wainwright's eyes glistened with unshed tears. "Thank you kindly, Mrs Fletcher. That means a great deal to us. My Jack always spoke highly of you and Mr Fletcher – Lord bless 'em and keep both their souls."

Madeleine nodded, her throat tightening with emotion. Pushing aside the memory of her own loss, she composed herself and turned to Stuart and Robert.

"I was hoping I might have a private word with you, Stuart. And you too, Robert. Mr Dubois and I have some important matters we wish to discuss."

"Why don't you take them into the front room, Stuart," Mrs Wainwright said. Turning to her esteemed guests with a shy smile, she added, "It's not much to look at, I'm afraid. But you'll be able to talk in peace there."

"Thank you, Mrs Wainwright," Madeleine replied. "But please, finish your supper first."

"Oh no," Mrs Wainwright insisted, swiftly taking away Stuart and Robert's plates. "I'll keep the boys' food nice and warm on the stove. They can finish their supper later. Business comes first."

With a grateful nod, Madeleine followed Stuart and Robert into the front room, Mr Dubois close behind. The modest parlour was simply furnished, with a well-worn sofa and a few mismatched armchairs arranged around a small fireplace. The mantlepiece was adorned with a handful of small family portraits and a vase containing fresh flowers, a touch of warmth in the otherwise plain room.

As they all took their seats, Robert turned to Mr Dubois with a friendly smile. "Mr Dubois, what a pleasant surprise to see you again, sir. When Mrs Fletcher told me that your role had come to an end, I was quite disappointed. It's wonderful to have you back with us."

Mr Dubois returned the young clerk's smile, his eyes crinkling at the corners. "Thank you, Mr Adams. It's a pleasure to be working with Mrs Fletcher once more. And of course, to see you again as well."

Madeleine watched the exchange with a small twinge of unease. Robert's open admiration for Mr Dubois was a stark reminder of the Frenchman's charm and the ease with which the man was able to win people over. She could only hope that this time, his intentions were as sincere as they appeared.

"Stuart, Robert," Mr Dubois began, his expression growing serious. "Mrs Fletcher and I have something important to share with you.

Something so vitally important that the very future of the factory may depend on it."

"Oh my," Robert said, shifting uncomfortably in his seat. "That sounds grim, sir."

Madeleine nodded, her hands clasped tightly in her lap. "We have reason to believe that the explosion at the factory was no accident, Robert. In fact, we suspect it may have been an act of sabotage."

"Sabotage? But by whom?" His eyes jumped anxiously between Mr Dubois, Madeleine and Stuart.

"So you're pursuing Miss Eleanor's idea more actively?" Stuart asked. "Have there been any new developments?"

"Not as such," Mr Dubois replied. "But we now think it may have been Mr Redhurst."

A stunned silence filled the room. Robert was the first to find his voice, his tone laced with disbelief. "Mr Redhurst? Why would he want to harm the factory? He owns half of it."

"We don't know his precise motives yet," Madeleine said. "But at the moment he's our most likely suspect."

"Now that you mention it," Robert said, "I do remember seeing Mr Redhurst at the factory very early on the morning of the explosion. I didn't think much of it then, because I just thought he wanted everything to be in perfect order, like we all did."

Madeleine's eyes widened. "I remember you telling me about that. And I also remember that he had smears of grime on his suit."

Making a short angry sound, Stuart clenched his hands into fists. "So he could have tampered with the engine. But why? What could he possibly gain from it?"

Mr Dubois sighed heavily. "That, my young friend, is what we must find out. But we must tread carefully. If Mr Redhurst is indeed behind this, he will stop at nothing to keep his secret safe. Or to accomplish his ultimate goal."

"Cor," Robert reacted. "Who would've imagined? Mr Redhurst of all people."

Just then, the door to the parlour opened and Mrs Wainwright came bustling in, carrying a tray with a steaming pot of tea and a plate of biscuits.

"Mr Redhurst?" she said while setting down her tray on the small table. "Funny you should mention him. My Jack, God rest his soul, he never did take to that man. Always said there was something off about him, something not quite right."

Pouring out four cups of tea, she shook her head. "And my Jack, he was a good judge of character, he was. He could sniff out a bad apple from a mile away."

Setting down the teapot, Mrs Wainwright turned to Madeleine, a warmth in her gaze. "But you, Mrs Fletcher? Nothing but praise my Jack had for you. Said you were a good'un, through and through. And I reckon he was right about that, too."

With a final, fond smile, Mrs Wainwright excused herself and left the four of them alone once more.

"So what do we do now?" Stuart asked as Robert began to pass around the cups and biscuits. "If Mr Redhurst really is behind all this, we can't just sit back and let him get away with it."

Mr Dubois sighed, stirring his tea thoughtfully. "I'm afraid that for now all we have are suspicions. We can't act on those alone, not without proof. It would be our word against his, and I fear we would come out the losers in that particular battle."

"But what if he tries something again?" Robert asked, his face pale. "What if more people get hurt?"

Madeleine reached out, placing a comforting hand on her young assistant's arm. "That's why we must be vigilant, Robert. Keep your eyes and ears open. If you notice anything unusual or suspicious, no matter how small, come to me or Mr Dubois immediately."

"You can count on us, Mrs Fletcher," Stuart said, his voice steady. "Thank you for confiding in us."

"Yes," Robert chimed in, his confidence growing again. "Hundreds of families depend on that factory. Including mine and Stuart's. We'll do whatever we can to help you."

Madeleine gave them both a grateful smile. "We'll get to the bottom of this, I assure you. For the sake of the factory, and for all those who lost their lives in the explosion. We cannot let this injustice stand."

And Ashton Redhurst will come to regret his vile deed.

Chapter Twenty-Seven

The hackney coach rattled and swayed as it carried Madeleine and Mr Dubois through the darkened streets. Sitting closely side by side on the worn leather seat, the silence between them was heavy, broken only by the clattering sound of the horse's hooves and the occasional creak of the carriage.

Madeleine sighed, her shoulders sagging with exhaustion. "I know it was the right thing to do, telling Stuart and Robert about our suspicions. But I can't help feeling like we've accomplished nothing tonight."

"Patience, Madame," Mr Dubois said. "These things take time. You must have faith in the process."

Madeleine felt a flicker of irritation at his calm demeanour. How could he be so unruffled when the future of her factory hung in the balance?

"Faith in the process?" she repeated, a hint of testiness creeping into her voice. "And what exactly is this process, Mr Dubois? Because from where I'm sitting, it feels like we're grasping at straws."

"I understand your frustration, Mrs Fletcher. But we must be methodical in our approach. Rushing in without a clear plan will only lead to disaster."

Madeleine's stomach chose that moment to growl loudly, reminding her that she had missed supper. She pressed a hand to her midsection, feeling the gnawing ache of hunger.

"Very well," she conceded wearily. "What do you suggest we do next, then?"

"You should go to the factory as usual in the morning. Deviating from your normal routine would only arouse suspicions. Mr Redhurst doesn't know yet that we suspect him. Which gives us a slight advantage over him."

Madeleine nodded, seeing the wisdom in his words. "And what will you be doing while I'm at the factory?"

"I will start digging into Mr Redhurst's life," he replied, his tone grim. "His past, his associates, his habits. Anything that might give us a clue as to his motives or his next move."

Madeleine felt a chill run down her spine at the thought of Ashton's duplicity. "I still can't quite believe it," she murmured, shaking her head. "Ashton, a villain. And to think Benjamin trusted that man."

"It's a hard lesson to learn, isn't it?" Mr Dubois said, his expression turning rueful. "You think you know someone, until they betray you."

Madeleine's head snapped round, her eyes flashing with a sudden surge of bitterness. "I suppose you're speaking from personal experience, then. As a fraud, you must have done your fair bit of betraying other people."

He flinched, but met her gaze steadily. "I won't deny that I've deceived people in my past, Mrs Fletcher. But I never enjoyed it. And I made it a point of honour to only ever steal from the rich. They at least wouldn't go hungry when they lost a large sum of money."

"How noble of you," Madeleine scoffed sarcastically. "A true Robin Hood, aren't you?"

Mr Dubois gazed out in front of him with a faraway look in his eyes. "After growing up in the orphanage, I vowed to become a wealthy man. I was determined to never again feel the sting of poverty, the gnawing hunger in my belly."

He shook his head, a bitter smile twisting his lips. "But I soon discovered that it was far easier, not to mention quicker, to become rich through dishonest means. My conscience, however... Now that was an altogether different matter."

Madeleine found herself wavering, a part of her drawn to the honesty and vulnerability he had shown. She searched his face for any hint of deception, but all she found was an unguarded sincerity that unsettled her.

She had to admit, if only to herself, that his story rang true. But her own wounded pride refused to fully absolve him.

And yet, a small voice whispered in the back of her mind, Sir John seemed willing to give Mr Dubois the benefit of the doubt. And Sir John was no fool. Perhaps, she mused, we all had our reasons for the choices we make and the things we do in life.

Leaving Mr Dubois to his own thoughts, she turned away from him and looked out the window, watching the gas lamps flicker past in a blur.

What other secrets lurked in this man's past?

Despite herself, she felt a shimmer of empathy for the orphaned boy he had once been, alone and adrift in a world that cared little for the poor and the forgotten.

But empathy was a dangerous thing, she reminded herself. And letting her guard down was a weakness, a mistake she needed to avoid at all cost.

She would work with him – to rescue the factory and to uncover the truth. But she would not let herself be fooled again. Her trust, and her heart, were not so easily won.

The carriage slowed to a halt outside her house, the horse snorting softly in the cool night air. Mr Dubois alighted first, turning to offer his hand to assist Madeleine. She hesitated for a moment before accepting, allowing him to help her down from the coach.

As they stood on the pavement while the driver waited for Mr Dubois to continue his own homeward journey, an awkward silence stretched between them.

"Perhaps we should meet again tomorrow, at Sir John's," Mr Dubois suggested. "Around lunchtime, so we can inform each other of our progress."

"Sounds like a sensible idea," Madeleine agreed. "I'll be there."

Mr Dubois inclined his head, a shadow of sadness passing over his face. Or was that merely a trick of the street light?

"Until tomorrow then, Mrs Fletcher."

"Good night, Mr Dubois," she replied, her tone cool but not indifferent, or so she hoped.

With a final nod, he turned and climbed back into the waiting hackney. Madeleine watched the carriage depart, a strange combination of emotions swirling in her chest.

Shaking her head, she sighed and made her way up the steps to her front door. Inside, the warm glow of candlelight and the familiar scent of home greeted her.

But before she could fully appreciate the moment of peace, hurried footsteps echoed from the living room. Ellie and Charlotte burst into the hallway, with a mixture of relief and worry on their faces. They rushed to Madeleine and pulled her into a fierce embrace.

"Oh, Maddie," Charlotte exclaimed, her voice trembling. "Thank heavens you're home safe. We've been beside ourselves with worry."

Ellie clung to her mother, burying her face in Madeleine's shoulder. "Mama, where have you been? When that note from Sir John arrived—"

Madeleine held her daughter close, stroking her hair soothingly. "I'm sorry, my darlings. I didn't mean to cause you such distress."

Charlotte pulled back as the worst of her anxiousness began to ebb away. "Ellie told me about the sabotage, Maddie. I can scarcely believe it. Who would do such a thing?"

Ellie lifted her head, her eyes wide and apologetic. "I know I promised not to tell anyone, Mama. But I couldn't keep it from Charlotte. She's family, after all."

Madeleine smiled softly, cupping her daughter's cheek. "It's fine, Ellie. I understand. And you're right, we shouldn't have secrets from each other. Not now, not ever."

"But Maddie," Charlotte said, "you still haven't told us where you've been. We've been imagining all sorts of terrible things."

"Let's go into the sitting room, shall we? I'll tell you everything. But first, I'm simply dying for a spot of tea and a bite to eat."

Charlotte sprang into action, ushering them towards the cosy sitting room. "Of course, of course. You must be famished. I'll have Mrs Dobbs bring us some tea and cakes. And something a bit more substantial for you, Maddie. You look like you could use a proper meal."

When Madeleine and Ellie settled into the comfortable armchairs, the warmth of the crackling fire soon chased away the chill of the night that still hung in Madeleine's clothes.

Here, in the company of her loved ones, she felt she could face anything. Even the darkest of truths and the most daunting of challenges.

Charlotte poked her head out into the hallway, calling out to the cook. "Mrs Dobbs? Could you please bring us some tea and cakes? And perhaps a plate of cold meats and cheeses for Mrs Fletcher?"

Madeleine leaned back in her chair, gathering her thoughts. She knew the news she was about to share would come as a shock to her daughter and cousin. But they simply had to know the truth.

"Let me begin by telling you that Mr Dubois has become involved again."

Charlotte's eyes widened. "Mr Dubois? But I thought–" She fell silent, not wanting to repeat the unpleasantness of Mr Dubois' betrayal and Madeleine's subsequent heartache.

"I know," Madeleine said. "But he's an aide to Sir John now. And the squire felt it was a good idea for the two of us to work together on this. Sir John believes Mr Dubois can be of great help in uncovering the truth."

At that moment, the door opened and Mrs Dobbs entered, carrying a large tray heaped with tea, cakes, bread, butter, cold meats, and cheese. The sturdy cook easily set her burden down on the table, the delicious aromas wafting through the room.

"Here you are, Mrs Fletcher," Mrs Dobbs said fondly. "A proper spread to get your strength back up."

Madeleine smiled gratefully, the sight of the food making her stomach grumble in anticipation. "Thank you, Mrs Dobbs. This looks wonderful."

After everyone had been served, the cook bustled out of the room and Madeleine turned her attention back to her daughter and cousin.

"Mr Dubois and I went to visit Stuart and his family this evening," she continued. "As it happened, my assistant Robert was there as well. Did I tell you he's engaged to Stuart's eldest sister?"

At the mention of Stuart's name, Ellie's face lit up, a faint blush colouring her cheeks. "You saw Mr Wainwright? How was he? And what were his family like? I bet they were just as lovely as he is."

"They're all good people," Madeleine replied, trying to hide the smile at her daughter's obvious infatuation.

She reached for a slice of bread and spread a generous amount of butter on it. Taking a bite, she savoured the comfort of simple yet honest food.

"We went to see Stuart because we had something important to tell him," she went on. "Something that's just as shocking as it is crucial to our investigation."

"What is it, Maddie?" Charlotte asked, pausing her cake eating. "What have you discovered?"

"Mr Dubois and I believe that Ashton Redhurst might be behind the sabotage at the factory."

Charlotte's hand flew to her mouth, her eyes wide with horror. "Ashton? But... but why? What could he possibly hope to achieve with such a terrible act?"

Ellie, however, seemed less surprised. She set her teacup down forcefully, the china clattering against the saucer. "I never much liked that man," she said with contempt. "He always seemed cold and calculating. Like he was constantly scheming something."

Madeleine nodded, a grim smile on her lips. "You're not the only one who has reservations about him, Ellie. But I never imagined he'd be capable of something like this."

"What will you do now, Maddie?" Charlotte asked. "What's your plan?"

"There's not much of a plan yet, I'm afraid," Madeleine sighed. "Mr Dubois and I are still trying to piece together the facts."

"Let me help with the investigation, Mama," Ellie said, sitting up straighter. "I can come with you to the factory in the morning. I want to do my part."

Madeleine shook her head. "Absolutely not, Ellie. It's far too dangerous. We don't know what Ashton's intentions are. Or what he might do if he feels threatened."

"But Mama," Ellie protested, a hint of desperation creeping into her voice. "The infirmary is closed now. Mrs Pemberton-Thorpe has sent the last of the patients home. I won't have a reason to be at the factory any more."

It wasn't hard for Madeleine to guess the true meaning behind those words.

"Ellie, my darling," she said softly, reaching out to take her daughter's hand. "I know how much you care for Mr Wainwright. And I understand how much you want to be near him. But this isn't a game. Innocent people have lost their lives. I couldn't bear it if anything happened to you."

Charlotte shivered, her face pale. "Your mother's right, duck. This is too dangerous. We can't risk putting you in harm's way."

Ellie's shoulders slumped, her eyes filling with tears. But she nodded, accepting her mother's decision. "I understand, Mama. I just... I feel so helpless. I want to do something."

Madeleine stood up, pulling her daughter into a tender embrace. "I know, my love. But for now, the best thing you can do is to stay safe. Stay here, with Charlotte."

She felt the girl taking a long and shivering breath.

"I love you, Ellie," she said. "More than anything in this world. Never forget that."

"I love you too, Mama," the girl replied, managing a watery smile. She let go, wiped at her tears and said, "You'd better eat now. Because you're going to need every ounce of your strength in the coming days."

"You may be right about that, my darling," Madeleine said as they both sat down again.

While Madeleine continued her late meal, Charlotte did her best to distract them with the latest gossip from the neighbourhood. Tales of scandalous affairs and unexpected engagements filled the room, providing a welcome respite from the heavy matters at hand.

After finishing off all the bread and a good portion of the meat and cheese, Madeleine even indulged in a piece of cake. With a satisfied sigh, she pushed her plate away and stood up.

"I think I'll go to bed now," she said, stifling a yawn. "I'm absolutely exhausted."

Although she suspected that sleep wouldn't come easily to her tonight. Her mind was too full of doubts and confusion, a restless whirlwind of thoughts that refused to be quieted.

And more than a few of those thoughts, she noticed, were about a certain Frenchman.

Chapter Twenty-Eight

The next morning dawned grey and dreary, a fitting reflection of Madeleine's mood as she stepped out of her house and towards the waiting carriage.

"Morning, ma'am," her coachman greeted while he held the door open for her.

"Morning, Bill. I don't like the look of those dark clouds today," she said, casting a weary glance at the sky. "Do you think we'll get rain?"

"Don't reckon we will, ma'am," he answered while she climbed into the carriage. "I can usually tell from the way my old Bess holds her ears. She has a sense for these things, she has."

"Clever horse," Madeleine smiled. "I wish her ears could predict what sort of day I'll be having at the factory today."

Bill closed the door and got up on his box seat. "If they could, you'd be the first to hear about it, ma'am." Then, with a few gentle noises, he spurred his trusted old mare into an easy trot.

Madeleine closed her tired eyes. She hadn't had much sleep last night, and she prayed for an uneventful day. Her thoughts began to drift while the carriage rattled through the streets, its motions lulling her into a light slumber. She didn't even realise she had dozed off until Bill's voice roused her.

"Seems the strike hasn't ended yet, ma'am," he said as the carriage drew to a halt outside the factory gates. "Shall I walk you to the door like yesterday?"

Madeleine peered out the window, bracing herself for another onslaught of hostility from the striking workers. But to her surprise, the crowd looked sullen and resigned rather than openly aggressive. They milled about, their postures slumped and their faces weary.

Letting out a relieved breath, she descended from the carriage. "No, I think I'll be fine on my own this morning, Bill. But I'll need you to drive me to Sir John's for a noon appointment."

"Of course, ma'am," Bill replied. "I'll come back for you at half past eleven then."

Passing through the factory gates, she scanned the sea of faces – searching for the one she dreaded the most: Charles Turner, the journalist who had hounded her mercilessly just the day before. But there was no sign of him, no trace of his mocking smile or his barbed questions.

As she drew nearer to the main building, she caught sight of a handful of workers who stood apart from the rest, their eyes dark with resentment. They glared at her as she walked past, their hostility palpable.

But Madeleine refused to be cowed. She lifted her chin, meeting their stares with a steady gaze of her own. She would not let them see her doubts. Not when so much depended on her strength and resilience.

Another day, another battle, she thought grimly.

When she entered the main building, the usual bustle and hum of activity was notably absent. Her footsteps echoed in the empty corridors, the stillness a stark reminder of the factory's current state.

Trying her best to ignore the eerie feeling, Madeleine made her way to the outer office that led to her own. She was half expecting to find the clerks sitting at their desks as she pushed the door open. But instead, she was greeted by a sight that made her pause.

The room was empty, every desk abandoned – save for one. There, hunched over a stack of papers, was Robert, his head bent low and his lips pursed as he pored over the documents.

"Robert? Where is everyone?"

The young clerk looked up, startled by her sudden appearance. "Oh, Mrs Fletcher. I didn't hear you come in."

He rose from his seat, straightening his jacket. "Mr Underwood sent the other clerks home, ma'am. Said there wasn't much for them to do, what with the factory being so quiet and all."

"I suppose that was a sensible decision on Mr Underwood's part," she conceded, shrugging off her coat. "But you're still here, I see."

"Mr Underwood wanted to send me home too," he grinned a bit sheepishly. "But I told him you'd be needing your assistant, strike or no strike."

"Thank you, Robert," she said softly, feeling a surge of warmth towards the young man. "I appreciate your being here."

Robert nodded, but then his expression turned serious. "Mrs Fletcher, there's something I need to tell you. About those accounting errors I found."

Madeleine's heart skipped a beat, alarmed by her assistant's ominous tone. "What about them?"

"Well, ma'am, after what you told Stuart and myself yesterday, about the sabotage and all... It got me thinking."

He hesitated, as if trying to find the right words. "What if those errors aren't mistakes at all? What if someone's been tampering with the books, just like they tampered with that engine?"

Madeleine stared at him, speechless, while she struggled to accept the implications of Robert's chilling suggestion. Somewhere in the back of her mind, she knew, she'd had the same idea. But it had been too dark, too far-reaching, for her to contemplate.

Until now.

"But who–" she started asking, just as the office door swung open with a bang. Ashton strode in, scowling even worse than usual.

Madeleine and Robert exchanged a brief, startled glance before she forced her face into a mask of neutral politeness. The last thing she needed was for Ashton to suspect they were onto him.

"Ashton," she greeted him, keeping her voice even. "Good morning."

She tried to look at him as she always had: as her business partner and her late husband's friend. But now, all she could see was a potential villain, a man who might have blood on his hands.

"Morning," Ashton grunted in response, his eyes sweeping over the empty desks before settling on Robert. The young clerk seemed to shrink under that dour gaze, his nervousness all too evident.

"What's this then?" Ashton sneered with disdain. "Holding down the fort all by yourself, Adams? Playing at being the big man, are you?"

Robert flushed, his hands twisting together in front of him. "N-no, sir. I just thought Mrs Fletcher might need some assistance, what with everything that's been going on."

Ashton snorted, his lip curling in a mocking smile. "Is that so? And here I thought you were just trying to make yourself look important."

Madeleine bristled at the insult to her young assistant, but she held her tongue. Engaging with Ashton's pettiness could only end in disaster.

Instead, she turned to face him, her expression strictly neutral. "Was there something you needed, Ashton?"

He fixed her with a hard stare, his eyes glinting with impatience. "I wanted to know if you've given any more thought to my offer."

Madeleine's throat felt dry all of a sudden, but she willed herself to remain calm. "I have, yes. But I'm afraid I need more time to consider it fully."

"More time?" he growled. "Madeleine, we don't have the luxury of time. The longer you dither, the worse our situation becomes."

For a moment, Madeleine was tempted to confront him, to lay bare her suspicions and watch his reaction. But something held her back, an urgent sense of caution that warned her to tread carefully.

"I understand your concern, Ashton. But this is not a decision I can make lightly. Surely you can appreciate that."

She paused, choosing her next words with care. Since a more direct approach was unwise, perhaps she could gauge his reaction to the news about the faulty valves.

"You know," she began in a deliberately casual tone, "I spoke with Stuart Wainwright yesterday. He's been examining the wreckage of the engine, trying to determine the cause of the explosion."

Ashton's eyes narrowed, his posture stiffening almost imperceptibly. "And?"

Madeleine frowned, feigning a look of naive confusion. "Well, he seems to think it was caused by some faulty valves. Apparently, they weren't secured properly during the assembly process."

She watched Ashton closely, searching for any flicker of guilt or unease. "You're the chief engineer around here. Do you think it could have been an oversight? Anybody can make a mistake, but–"

Ashton's face drained of colour, his skin taking on a sickly pallor. Just as quickly however, his features twisted into a mask of rage.

"An oversight?" he sputtered, his voice rising with each word. "Wainwright is a worthless excuse for an engineer, that's what. Letting something like that slip past his inspection..."

He slammed his fist down on the nearest desk, making Robert jump. "That's incompetence of the grossest level, and I won't have it. Not in my factory."

Madeleine felt her pulse pounding in her ears. She took a slow, deep breath, forcing the air into her lungs and holding it there for a moment before exhaling.

She couldn't let Ashton's outburst rattle her. Not when she was getting closer to catching him off guard. She had to continue playing her game.

"But young Mr Wainwright seems like such a capable engineer," she said innocently. "Always so meticulous and thorough. Couldn't there be some other explanation? One we haven't considered yet?"

She let the question hang in the air, watching as Ashton's face contorted with a mixture of anger and something else, something darker and more unsettling.

"Like what?" he snapped, his eyes boring into hers. "What are you suggesting, Madeleine?"

"Oh, I don't know," she shrugged. "It's just a thought, really. But could there be something more sinister at play? Could someone have made that mistake on purpose?"

Ashton turned an alarming shade of red, his jaw clenching so hard Madeleine thought he might crack a tooth.

"Don't be ridiculous," he growled, his voice low and menacing. "You're being hysterical, seeing shadows where there are none."

He turned abruptly, storming towards the door. "I have better things to do than listen to your wild speculations, Maddie. Good day."

Madeleine stood motionless in that large and empty office, while she listened to the echoes of his footsteps fading away down the corridor.

Ashton's reactions had been telling, she thought. But were they enough to prove his guilt? The man was known for his volatile temper, after all. What had this nerve-racking argument of theirs actually achieved?

Too little, she decided.

She sighed, rubbing her temples in a vain attempt to ease the tension that had been building up there. The truth seemed to slip through her fingers like sand, leaving her grasping at mere shreds and possibilities.

What she wouldn't give to have Sir John and Mr Dubois here now, to help her make sense of this tangled web. But she would have to wait until midday to see them and to hear their opinion on Ashton's behaviour.

A soft cough drew her attention, and she turned to see Robert still standing there, his face a picture of uncertainty. Her poor assistant looked as if he had just witnessed a street brawl, his posture tense while traces of fear lingered in his eyes.

"Robert," she said, trying to sound confident. "I need you to continue looking into those accounting errors. If there's something amiss with the books as well, we need to know about it."

The young clerk straightened up immediately, as a relieved smile washed away his unease. "Of course, Mrs Fletcher. I'll start by making a list of all the errors I've found so far, and then I'll keep digging."

He paused, a playful grin tugging at the corners of his mouth. "I'll be like a hound diving down a rabbit hole. Only instead of bunnies, I'll be chasing numbers."

Madeleine chuckled and shook her head at his boyish lovableness. "Meanwhile," she said, moving towards her office door, "I will be like a mole, burrowing into a mound of paperwork. Let's hope we both find what we're looking for."

With a final nod to her assistant, Madeleine stepped into her office and closed the door behind her. She settled down at her desk, eyeing the stack of papers that awaited her attention. It was going to be a long morning, she sighed.

But she reminded herself of Mr Dubois' advice: be patient and have faith in the process.

And so she picked up the first file and began to read, hoping that his morning would be more successful than hers.

Chapter Twenty-Nine

At half past eleven, Madeleine rose from her desk, stretching her back to ease the stiffness that hours of poring over paperwork had caused. She gathered her things and stepped out into the outer office, where Robert was still diligently at work.

"Robert," she said. "I'm off to a lunch appointment at Sir John's. I should be back later this afternoon."

The young clerk looked up from his papers, a smile brightening his face. "Very good, Mrs Fletcher. I hope your meeting goes well."

He paused, a slight blush creeping into his cheeks. "I'm actually seeing Daisy over lunchtime again today. But don't worry, I'll be back right after – to continue with my investigation."

Madeleine nodded, appreciating his dedication. "Thank you, Robert. Your work on this matter is invaluable."

Grinning, he gestured to the sheets of paper scattered across his desk. "I'm making so many notes, I think I might run out of ink soon," he joked with a twinkle in his eye.

"Oh my, we can't have that, can we?" she chuckled. "But I trust we still have an extra bottle or two lying around somewhere?"

"Oh yes, ma'am. We always keep the supply room well stocked. I'm sure I'll find more ink there when I need it."

"Good. Enjoy your afternoon with Daisy, Robert," she said as she moved towards the door. "You deserve a bit of happiness in all this chaos."

"Thank you, Mrs Fletcher. I hope your own afternoon proves to be pleasant as well."

Madeleine smiled, but inwardly she sighed. Despite the fine company she would be keeping, she had a feeling her afternoon would be considerably less enjoyable than Robert's.

Outside at the factory gates, she found Bill waiting patiently by his mare's side, just as they had arranged. The coachman tipped his hat in greeting and helped her climb into the carriage before taking his place at the reins.

Traffic was mercifully light, and soon enough, they reached the leafier neighbourhood where Sir John lived. When they arrived at the squire's house, Bill brought the carriage to a smooth stop and hopped down to assist Madeleine.

"Here we are, ma'am," he said, offering his hand to help her alight. "I take it you want me to wait for you?"

"Yes please, Bill. I'll ask the staff to provide you with something to eat and a hot drink. I don't want you going hungry on my account.

"Very considerate of you, ma'am," he said with a modest grin.

Madeleine stepped up to the front door, where the same maid as the previous day was already waiting to greet her.

"Good afternoon, Mrs Fletcher," the girl said with a quick curtsy. "Sir John is expecting you in the library. If you'll follow me, please?"

As they walked through the elegant hallways, Madeleine asked the maid, "If it's not too much trouble, could you ensure that my coachman outside is offered some refreshments? My appointment with Sir John may take a while."

"Of course, ma'am. I'll see to it right away."

Stopping at the closed doors to the library, the maid knocked before entering and announcing Madeleine's presence.

Sir John and Mr Dubois were already in the room, the Frenchman looking slightly out of breath and with a healthy flush on his cheeks.

"Madeleine, my dear," Sir John said, stepping forward to take her hands in his. "Even under these trying circumstances, it's always such a privilege to welcome you to my home."

"Thank you, Sir John. Your kindness never fails to warm one's heart. Mr Dubois," she nodded to the Frenchman, who returned the gesture with a slight bow.

"Mrs Fletcher, a pleasure as usual," he replied.

"Mr Dubois has only just arrived himself," Sir John said. "So I'm quite eager to hear what progress you both have made. Come, let's sit down."

Gesturing towards a set of armchairs in a corner of the library, he invited them to take a seat. "Mr Dubois, why don't you start by telling us what you've discovered so far?"

"As of yet, not much, I'm afraid," Mr Dubois admitted. "Ashton Redhurst seems to keep his affairs quite private. I did, however, discover that he is a member of Montgomery's. Which is a local gentlemen's club, I believe?"

"Montgomery's?" Sir John repeated, his eyebrows rising in recognition. "Why, I'm a member there myself. Although I must confess I don't frequent the establishment very often. All they ever seem to do is smoke cigars and play cards. Not exactly my cup of tea."

But then, his face grew thoughtful. "However, it might be prudent for me to drop in and ask around about Mr Redhurst. Discreetly, of course."

"That could prove useful, yes," Mr Dubois agreed.

"Worth a try anyway," Sir John said. "In fact, tell you what, old chap. Why don't you and I go there this afternoon? I can take you along as my guest."

"Splendid idea, Sir John," Mr Dubois replied. "There's no time like the present, as they say."

The squire then looked to Madeleine, an apologetic smile on his face. "I'm afraid though that you won't be able to accompany us. Montgomery's is a gentlemen-only establishment, you see. Women simply aren't allowed in. Personally, I find such policies rather short-sighted, but alas, tradition is a formidable force."

"I understand," she said, even though it disappointed her to be excluded. "I hope you and Mr Dubois will be able to gather some information during your visit."

"As do I," the squire replied. "And what about you, my dear? Have you found out anything new on your end?"

"As a matter of fact, I did have a rather interesting exchange with Ashton this morning."

She recounted the details of their discussion, describing how she had mentioned Stuart's findings about the faulty valves and suggested the possibility of sabotage.

"Ashton's reaction was... intense, to say the least," she said, frowning at the memory. "He turned red in the face, and he was quick to dismiss my concerns as wild speculation."

"Sounds like the mark of a guilty man to me," Sir John declared, his tone leaving no room for doubt. "An innocent person would have been concerned about the possibility of sabotage, not dismissive of it."

Mr Dubois, however, looked more pensive. "While I agree that Mr Redhurst's reaction is suspicious, I'm not certain it's sufficient proof of his involvement," he said, his words measured and careful. "A man with a temper like his might react similarly to any accusation, regardless of its truth."

"That's my concern as well," Madeleine said. "Ashton has always been prone to outbursts, especially when he feels his authority is being questioned."

She stood up and began pacing the room. "I want to believe we're on the right track, but we need more concrete evidence before we can confront Ashton directly."

Sir John hummed in agreement, his fingers drumming thoughtfully on the arm of his chair. "You're right, of course. We must be cautious in our approach, lest we reveal our hand too soon."

"There is one more thing I learned today," Madeleine said. "Something that my assistant brought to my attention."

She paused by the window and gazed outside. "Robert has been looking into some accounting errors he discovered in the factory's books. At first, we assumed they were simple mistakes, but now..."

Spinning around so she was facing the two men again, she delivered the hammer blow. "After the sabotage, Robert suggested that the books might have been tampered with, just like the engine. That someone has been deliberately manipulating our financial records."

"Good heavens," Sir John exclaimed, a look of shock and disbelief crossing his face. "If that's true, then your factory has become a nest of vipers, Madeleine."

He pursed his lips. "Which begs the question: is each one of those vipers trying to corrupt the company individually? Or have you got a conspiracy of villains on your hands, all working together?"

"But to what end?" Mr Dubois mused out loud. "What could be their purpose in all of this? Mr Redhurst doesn't strike me as the type to perform acts of random destruction simply for the thrill of it."

Tapping his chin thoughtfully, he continued, "And if he does indeed have accomplices, who are they? What do they stand to gain from the factory's downfall?"

Madeleine let out a frustrated grunt. "This is so bothersome. At every turn, all we ever seem to find are more questions, but hardly any answers."

She rested a hand on her chest, where a growing tightness was becoming more uncomfortable by the minute.

"I feel like we're grasping at shadows," she said. "As if we're trying to piece together a puzzle without knowing what the final picture is meant to look like."

Sir John nodded in sympathy. "I know it seems like an impossible task, but we mustn't lose heart, my friends."

He took his watch from his pocket and glanced at the time. "Perhaps what we need is a bit of sustenance to fortify us for the challenges ahead. The mind cannot function properly without decent nourishment."

Rising from his chair, he gestured towards the door. "Why don't we move to the dining room for a spot of lunch? A good meal and some friendly conversation might be just the thing to refresh our spirits and sharpen our wits."

The food was excellent, and both Sir John and Mr Dubois did their best to keep the mood light. But Madeleine found herself struggling to enjoy any of it. Her mind kept wandering round and round in endless circles.

Afterwards, Sir John and Mr Dubois prepared to depart for Montgomery's. But first, Sir John insisted on walking Madeleine to the door.

"Keep your chin up, my dear," he said softly. "We'll get to the bottom of this, one way or another."

"Thank you, Sir John. You're ever so generous with your support. How can I ever hope—"

"To repay me?" he said, finishing her question with a smile. "I've already told you: there's no need. Good friends help each other in times of trouble."

They paused while a footman opened the front door for her.

"Besides," Sir John continued, "it's clear there's a great injustice happening here. And that's one thing I can't abide. I've grown too old for that."

"Not old," Madeleine corrected him with a grin. "Wise is what you are, Sir John."

"You're much too kind, my dear. Goodbye for now."

She stepped outside and went over to her waiting coachman.

"Back to the factory, ma'am?" Bill asked.

Madeleine hesitated, a sudden impulse taking hold of her. "Actually, Bill, I'd like to go for a walk first. I noticed a rather lovely park on our way over here. Let's make a quick detour, and then we can head back to the factory."

"Certainly, ma'am. A bit of fresh air and greenery does wonders for clearing the head, my mother used to say."

At the park, a few nannies strolled along the winding paths, pushing prams and chatting amongst themselves. Nearby, a governess kept a watchful eye on her two young charges as they played on the lush grass, their laughter carrying on the gentle breeze.

Madeleine took in the tranquil scene and set off down the central pathway. She thought of her factory, the lifeblood of so many families. It was hard, she sighed inwardly, to accept that her decisions and her actions affected all those people.

But at the same time, it was a burden she was happy to bear, because she understood that it made her a small part of something much bigger and far more important than her own private cares and worries.

And then there was Ashton.

The man who was supposed to be her partner in this endeavour. Instead, he appeared to be relentlessly plotting her downfall, with his every move calculated to weaken her position and strengthen his own.

Madeleine felt a surge of anger rising within her, hot and bitter. It was so unfair, she thought, that one man's crazed ambition could threaten to destroy everything. Thousands of men, women and children depended on the factory. But Ashton Redhurst seemed perfectly willing to sacrifice all of that.

Simply because he couldn't bear the thought of sharing power with her.

It was more than unfair, she realised. It was outrageous. A disgraceful betrayal of everything she and Benjamin had believed in.

If Ashton truly was the evil genius behind all these wrongdoings, then she would stand up to him. She didn't know how, but she would find a way to stop him.

Chapter Thirty

With a brisk and powerful pace, Madeleine strode into the main building of the factory. That brief walk in the park had done the trick marvellously, she thought with a grin. Navigating the familiar corridors, her mind was racing ahead of her towards the office.

When she left for her lunch with Sir John and Mr Dubois, Robert had appeared to be making good progress with his investigation of the company's financial records. And now she was eager to hear if he had uncovered any new evidence of foul play.

"Robert," she said as she pushed open the door to the outer office. "Tell me you have good news for me."

But then she stopped short.

Her assistant was nowhere to be seen. His desk was empty, while his notes and the papers he had been looking at lay scattered across its surface.

Madeleine frowned. It wasn't like Robert to leave his work in such disarray.

"Mrs Fletcher?" a reedy voice asked.

From one of the other desks, Mr Underwood was staring at her with surprised and large, owl-like eyes. The senior accountant had been rifling through a stack of files, but now he sat there as if frozen in place.

"Mr Underwood? Have you seen Mr Adams? I was hoping to speak with him. About matters of some importance."

Madeleine knew that Robert had said he would be taking his fiancée Daisy out for lunch. But he should have been back by this hour. And what's more, his coat and hat still hung on the rack, she noticed as she looked round the room.

When she turned back to Mr Underwood, the accountant's face was pale. The sheets of paper he was holding betrayed the fact that his hands were trembling.

"Mr Adams?" he asked, quickly laying down the papers on the desk in front of him. "No, I haven't seen him anywhere, Mrs Fletcher. Why would I?"

He attempted a little laugh, but to Madeleine the effect seemed more like a pained grimace.

"I see," she replied with a raised eyebrow. "And what brings you to this part of the building, Mr Underwood? Don't you have your own office down the corridor?"

Mr Underwood shifted uncomfortably, his eyes darting around the room as if searching for an escape. "Oh, I was just... I needed to check on some documents. Thought they might be out here."

Madeleine narrowed her eyes. Mr Underwood had always seemed uncomfortable around her. She knew the man was in his late fifties and yet still a bachelor. Which had long ago led her to conclude that he was one of those gentlemen who were perpetually nervous and insecure with ladies.

But even for an odd duck like Mr Underwood, these reactions were undeniably strange.

Before she could press the senior accountant any further however, a commotion down the corridor drew her attention.

She heard angry voices and the sound of hurried footsteps growing louder.

Suddenly, the door of the outer office burst open, and a small group of agitated workers poured in. Madeleine immediately recognised Wilkes and Mason among them – the same men who had confronted her so aggressively on the first day of the strike, when emotions had run high.

Mr Underwood let out a frightened squeak and scurried behind Madeleine, clutching at her sleeve. "I didn't do it, I swear," he babbled, his voice high-pitched and panicky. "Tell them, Mrs Fletcher."

Madeleine turned to him, utterly confused. "Didn't do what, Mr Underwood? What are you talking about?"

But the accountant merely shrank back, his face turning an even more sickly shade of grey. He seemed to be on the verge of fainting, his entire body trembling like a leaf in a storm.

Then Wilkes stepped forward, his face grim. "Mrs Fletcher, we need to tell you something. It's about the coal house."

"The coal house? What about it?"

"We saw someone coming out of it earlier," Mason explained, his large hands clenched at his sides. "Thought maybe they were trying to steal coal. Seeing as times are hard for everyone."

"But when we went to check," Wilkes continued, "we found something else entirely. There was a fire, Mrs Fletcher. Someone had set the coal ablaze."

"A fire?" Madeleine gasped in shock. "Send for the fire brigade at once. If that blaze spreads–"

"We already stopped it, ma'am," Mason reassured her. "Scattered the burning coal and smothered the flames."

Letting out a long breath, Madeleine's tense shoulders slumped in relief. She looked at the men before her. There was anger and frustration in their eyes, but none of it was directed at her, she realised.

"Mr Wilkes, Mr Mason," she said with a steady voice. "I want to thank you for your quick thinking and your bravery. You may well have saved the factory from another disaster."

The two men exchanged a glance, and Wilkes nodded. "We just did what needed to be done, Mrs Fletcher. We may be on strike, but we don't want to see the factory ruined."

A sudden thought struck Madeleine. What Wilkes had just said presented her with an opportunity. If she played her cards right, then perhaps...

"So you still care about the company?" she asked softly.

"Of course we care, Mrs Fletcher. This factory's been good to us over the years. Your husband, God rest his soul, he always treated us fair. And you've been no different."

All the other men nodded in agreement, and Madeleine could feel the mood in the room beginning to shift in her favour.

"Gentlemen, there's something you should know." She looked at Wilkes and Mason. "This fire today, I don't believe it was an isolated incident."

She paused, letting her words sink in. "The explosion a few days ago? There's a chance that may have been deliberate as well."

The workers couldn't have looked more shocked if she had slapped them across the face with her glove.

"Deliberate?" Mason repeated, his voice trembling with barely contained rage. "You mean to say someone caused that explosion on purpose? Someone tried to destroy our bread and butter? And kill us all in the process?"

Madeleine nodded grimly. "I'm afraid that's a very real possibility."

The men erupted into a chorus of angry shouts, ready to storm out and teach that arsonist a lesson.

"Who's the scoundrel that did this?" Wilkes growled, slamming his fist into his palm. "Where's the blasted devil who'd risk all our necks?"

"I don't know," Madeleine admitted. "But I intend to find out. And I could use your help."

The workers fell silent, staring at her with a mix of surprise and confusion.

"Our help?" Mason asked. "How?"

Madeleine took a step forward. "By returning to work. By standing with me and showing whoever is behind this that we won't be cowed. That we're stronger together than they could ever imagine."

For a moment, the men seemed to hesitate, glancing at each other uncertainly.

But then Wilkes straightened his shoulders, a fierce grin spreading across his face. "You can count on us, Mrs Fletcher. We'll show this villain what we're made of."

A warm, grateful sensation coursed through Madeleine's veins. She had pulled it off.

"Thank you," she beamed. "From the bottom of my heart, I thank you all. There might not be a lot of work for you though. I'm told the explosion caused a considerable amount of damage."

And I haven't got the money to repair it, she added silently.

"Don't you worry about that, ma'am," Wilkes spoke up. "We've seen the state of the factory, and it's not near as bad as some would have you believe."

"That's right," Mason said. "With a bit of elbow grease, we should be able to get parts of this place up and running again within a week or two."

Madeleine could have leapt for joy. "That would be wonderful," she said. "Why, it's the best news I've had in days. Once again, thank you."

She reached out and shook hands with Wilkes and Mason, causing them both to blush.

"That's all right, ma'am," Mason said, sounding almost like a shy schoolboy. "It'll be our pleasure."

"And you let us know when you find out who's behind all this trouble, Mrs Fletcher," Wilkes added. "We'll want to have a word with him."

With a grin, he mimicked wringing somebody's neck. Behind her, Madeleine thought she heard a short whimper coming from Mr Underwood's throat.

"Right then, lads," Mason said, addressing the small group of men around him. "Let's be off. We've got work to do."

After the last of them had filed out of the office, Madeleine turned round to face Mr Underwood. The accountant was still staring at the door with terrified eyes. A fine sheen of sweat covered his grey and wrinkled skin.

"Mr Underwood," Madeleine said, startling him out of his trance. "What was that all about earlier?"

The senior accountant blinked rapidly a few times. "Mrs Fletcher?"

"You seemed rather confused. As if you weren't quite yourself."

"Oh, that. Well, you see–" he stammered. He took a handkerchief out of his pocket and used it to wipe his balding forehead.

"Please excuse me for a moment," he said as he edged around Madeleine and hurried towards the door. "I must step out to refresh myself."

Madeleine wanted to call after him, but he had already disappeared into the corridor.

Odd old man.

She shook her aching head and then began to rub her temples. There were still so many unanswered questions, so many mysteries to unravel. But at least she had regained the support of her workers. It was a small victory, but a vital one.

Just as she was about to go into her own office, the door burst open once again. Madeleine looked up, expecting to see another worker or perhaps Mr Underwood returning.

But instead, she was met by the sight of her daughter Ellie. The girl's face was flushed, her eyes burning with anger and hurt.

"Mother, how could you?" her daughter cried.

"Ellie, what's wrong? I don't know what you're talking about."

"Stuart has been sacked," Ellie replied, a single tear escaping down her cheek. "And it's your doing."

Chapter Thirty-One

"Sacked?" Madeleine repeated in disbelief. "What do you mean, Stuart has been sacked?"

"Don't pretend you don't know, Mother," Ellie bristled. "It was your decision, wasn't it?"

Madeleine shook her head, utterly bewildered. "Ellie, I assure you, I have no idea what you're talking about. I haven't sacked anyone."

"Then why did I find Mr Wainwright at home just now?" Ellie demanded. "I went to visit the family with a basket of fruit and a few other tasty treats."

Madeleine opened her mouth to speak, but Ellie raised her hand. "I know you told me I was to stay at home. But after you said how nice they all were, I wanted to give the Wainwrights a little token of our sympathy."

And perhaps try to get on the good side of Stuart's mother and sister, Madeleine grinned to herself.

"Besides," Ellie continued, "I didn't go alone. Charlotte came with me. In fact, she's still outside, waiting in the hackney we took to get here."

"It's fine, Ellie. You said Stuart was at home?"

"That's right. Imagine my surprise when Charlotte and I found him sitting at his mother's kitchen table. He told us he'd been dismissed."

"By whom?"

"By you, of course," Ellie replied impatiently, the accusation evident in her tone. "Stuart said Mr Redhurst came to see him at the factory. The man was in a righteous angry state apparently, and he dismissed Stuart on the spot. He claimed he did so with your blessing, Mother."

Madeleine stared at her daughter, shocked into silence. She hadn't authorised Stuart's dismissal. The topic hadn't even come up in the argument she'd had with Ashton earlier that day.

Although she remembered all too well how furious Ashton had become when she'd mentioned Stuart's findings about the faulty valves.

"Ellie," she said, calmly but firmly. "I promise you, I did not give Ashton permission to dismiss Stuart. It wasn't my decision."

Ellie's shoulders relaxed, some of the fight draining out of her. "So it had nothing to do with you, then?" she asked, her tone hopeful.

"Most certainly not," Madeleine replied. "Ashton acted on his own initiative. And I intend to find out why."

Madeleine's mind raced as she tried to make sense of the situation. Ashton had dismissed Stuart without her consent, and she needed to act fast to rectify the matter.

Thinking on her feet, she hurried over to her desk and grabbed a sheet of paper and a pen. She quickly wrote a message to Mr Dubois and Sir John, informing them of Stuart's dismissal – and of the arson attempt in the coal house.

Your advice is needed urgently on how to proceed, she concluded her note.

Folding the piece of paper in half, Madeleine wrote Sir John's address on the other side. Then she turned to Ellie, holding out the letter.

"You said Charlotte was waiting outside in a cab? Take this to Sir John's immediately. It's of the utmost importance."

"But Mama," her daughter protested. "What about Stuart? What are you going to do to help him?"

Madeleine sighed, her expression softening. "Ellie, I promise you, I will do everything in my power to make this right. But right now, I need you to trust me and deliver this message. Speed is of the essence."

She placed a gentle hand on her daughter's shoulder. "Besides, the factory is becoming too dangerous a place for you. I'd feel much better knowing you were safely away from here."

Ellie hesitated for a moment, her gaze searching her mother's face. Finally, she nodded, taking the letter from Madeleine's hand. "All right, I'll do as you ask. But please, don't let Stuart down."

"I won't, my darling. I promise."

With a quick embrace, Ellie hurried out of the office, leaving Madeleine alone with her thoughts.

The events of the day were taking their toll, and Madeleine felt a sudden, desperate need for a cup of tea. With no one else in the office, she realised she would have to make it herself.

She made her way over to the stove and poked at the fire to stoke up the flames. As the heat began to build, she rummaged through the cupboards, searching for the clerks' tea stash.

She was just reaching for what looked like a tin of tea leaves when a tentative knock sounded at the door.

"Hello?" a soft, feminine voice called out.

Turning around, Madeleine saw a young woman entering the outer office. It was Daisy, Robert's fiancée and Stuart's sister. Madeleine remembered her from the visit to the Wainwrights the evening before.

"Oh, Mrs Fletcher," Daisy said, recognising her. "I'm sorry to bother you, but I was wondering if Robert might be around?"

Madeleine shook her head, a slight frown creasing her brow. "I'm afraid not, Daisy. I haven't seen him since late this morning when I left for an appointment."

Daisy's face fell, confusion clouding her delicate features. "That's strange. We had arranged to go out for lunch today, but he never showed up. I waited and waited, but eventually, I had to give up."

She held up a small package, a hopeful smile on her lips. "I assumed he must have been too busy to get away, so I thought I'd bring him a packed lunch."

Madeleine's frown deepened. "It's the most bizarre thing, Daisy. I haven't seen Robert anywhere."

Just then, Mr Underwood returned, slipping into the office with the skittish air of a field mouse trying to avoid the fox's attention.

"Ah, Mr Underwood," Madeleine said. "You hadn't seen Robert either, had you?"

The man jumped slightly. He swallowed before replying, made all the more noticeable by the fact his Adam's apple stuck out from his thin neck.

"N-no, Mrs Fletcher. I can't say that I have. Not in a while at least."

Madeleine gestured towards the coat rack. "But look, his coat and hat are still here. He couldn't have gone far without them."

"Oh, no," Daisy said, turning pale in the face. "What if something's happened to him?"

Madeleine moved to the girl's side, placing a comforting hand on her arm. "Now, now, Daisy. Let's not jump to conclusions. I'm sure there's a perfectly reasonable explanation."

But Daisy seemed inconsolable, her hands trembling as she clutched the packed lunch. Madeleine could see how two such sensitive souls as Robert and Daisy would feel drawn to each other.

Taking a deep breath, Madeleine made a decision. It would be cruel to send the girl home in such a state.

"Daisy," she said gently. "Why don't we go to the police station together? We can file a missing person's report, just to be on the safe side."

Daisy looked up at her, tears shimmering in her eyes. "You'd do that for me, Mrs Fletcher?"

Madeleine smiled, giving the girl's arm a reassuring squeeze. "Of course, my dear. We'll get to the bottom of this, I promise."

More than an hour later however, Madeleine found herself escorting a distraught Daisy back to the Wainwright home.

Their visit to the police station had been far from productive, with the officer on duty dismissing their concerns as premature.

"Now, now, Miss," the policeman had said. "It's a bit early to be reporting your young man as missing. He's probably just off somewhere, enjoying a drink or two with his friends."

With a condescending smirk on his face, he had then added, "Or perhaps he's got another piece on the side, if you know what I mean."

Daisy had burst into tears at the crude insinuation, her shoulders shaking with sobs. Madeleine, appalled by the officer's lack of professionalism and empathy, had wrapped a protective arm around the girl and led her out of the station.

Now, as their carriage arrived at the modest Wainwright home, Madeleine's heart ached for the young woman at her side. Daisy's distress was undeniably plain to see, and Madeleine silently vowed to do everything in her power to find Robert and bring him back safely.

"Daisy," a worried Mrs Wainwright said as she opened the front door. "Where have you been, girl?"

Madeleine quickly explained about Robert's worrying absence. "So I thought I'd better bring Daisy home," she said after she had finished her brief account.

"Thank you ever so kindly, Mrs Fletcher," Daisy's mother replied. "Please, why don't you come in for a cuppa?" If she was bitter at

Madeleine about her son's dismissal, she wasn't showing it.

They were taken through to the small parlour, where Stuart sat nursing his own cup of tea. "Mrs Fletcher," he said, rising to his feet. "I didn't expect to see you here."

"Stuart, I'm glad I caught you," Madeleine smiled at him. "I want you to understand that your dismissal was not my decision."

"I knew it," Mrs Wainwright beamed. "I told you she was much too nice to do a thing like that, didn't I?"

Madeleine nodded at the compliment and then turned back to Stuart. "In fact, I didn't even know about it until my daughter came to tell me a short while ago."

"But Mr Redhurst said–"

"What he told you was a barefaced lie. Ashton Redhurst acted without my knowledge or consent, and I intend to rectify the situation here and now."

She sat down on the chair across from him and looked him straight in the eye. "Stuart, I want you to come back to the factory with me. I believe you're a brilliant engineer, and I won't stand for this injustice that has been done to you."

Blushing at her praise, the young man stared down at the table with a shy grin. "That's very kind of you to say, Mrs Fletcher." Then he lifted his gaze again and straightened up, looking an inch taller. "And yes, I'm more than happy to return to the factory with you."

"Splendid."

"Oh, this is so wonderful," Mrs Wainwright chirped. "Let me fetch tea and biscuits for everyone."

"No time, Mother," Stuart said, draining his own cup and standing up from his chair. "Mrs Fletcher and I need to be getting back to the factory."

"The sooner the better," Madeleine replied with a grateful smile. "I appreciate your offer, Mrs Wainwright," she told Stuart's mother. "But we can't afford to lose any more time, I'm afraid." She too rose to her feet, and moved towards the door.

"I understand, Mrs Fletcher. Thank you for giving my Stuart his job back."

"It never ought to have been taken from him in the first place, as far as I'm concerned," Madeleine assured her.

She and Stuart said their goodbyes to the two women, with Madeleine promising Daisy that she would send word if there was any news about Robert.

Then they stepped out into the street and started on their way back to the factory.

Where I shall have a stern word with Ashton Redhurst, Madeleine vowed.

Chapter Thirty-Two

Looking around for a carriage to hail, Madeleine quickly realised that none were to be found in this modest neighbourhood.

"It seems we'll have to go on foot," she said with a sigh. "I hope you don't mind a bit of a walk, Stuart."

The young engineer shook his head and smiled, "Not at all, Mrs Fletcher. A bit of fresh air and exercise never hurt anyone."

As they set off down the cobblestone street, it didn't take long before Madeleine found herself struggling to match Stuart's brisk pace. Her corset, so fashionable and ladylike, now felt like a vice squeezing around her ribs, constricting her breath with each step.

Trying to ignore the growing discomfort, she turned to Stuart. "There have been some developments at the factory since you left. And not all of them good, I'm afraid."

"More developments, ma'am?" He sounded concerned, but he didn't slow down his pace.

"There was an arson attempt, Stuart. Someone tried to set fire to the coal house."

The young man stopped dead in his tracks and stared at her. "An arson attempt? But how?

Could it have been an accident, perhaps? Sometimes coal can spontaneously combust if it's not stored properly."

Madeleine shook her head, her lips pressed into a thin line. "No, this was no accident. Some of the men saw someone hurrying out of the coal house just before the fire was discovered. That's how they were able to put it out in time."

Stuart let out a low whistle before they resumed walking again. "Thank goodness for that. If the fire had spread..."

"I know," Madeleine agreed, her voice tight. "It could have been catastrophic."

They walked in silence for a moment, each lost in their own thoughts. Then Stuart spoke again, his tone hesitant. "Do you think... Could Mr Redhurst be behind this as well?"

Madeleine nodded. "Yes, I do. It's too much of a coincidence, coming so soon after the explosion. He's becoming bolder, more reckless."

Stuart shook his head in disbelief. "I can't believe he would go this far. To deliberately put lives at risk, to destroy the very thing he claims to care about..."

"Hard to fathom, isn't it? But at least, there is some good news as well."

Stuart looked at her expectantly. "And what's that, ma'am?"

"The men have agreed to return to work. I managed to convince them to stand with me. And to show whoever is behind this that we won't be intimidated."

Stuart's face lit up with a bright grin. "This is why the factory needs you, Mrs Fletcher. You have a way of inspiring people, of making them believe in something bigger than themselves."

Madeleine blushed at the praise. "Do you believe so, Stuart?"

"The factory couldn't be in better hands, ma'am. The men respect you, and for good reason."

But then his smile faltered. "What about Robert though? Has there really been no sign of him?"

"None, I'm afraid. But I'm hoping he might have returned by the time we get back to the office."

She left the rest unsaid, not wanting to voice the darker possibilities that lurked at the edges of her mind. Robert was a good man, and a loyal assistant. The thought of something happening to him...

No, she told herself firmly. She couldn't think like that. They would find Robert, just as they would uncover the truth behind Ashton's treachery. They had to.

The factory gates loomed ahead, and Madeleine's breath came in short, sharp gasps, the exertion of their walk and the tightness of her corset taking their toll. Sweat beaded on her forehead, and she could feel the damp fabric of her dress clinging uncomfortably to her skin.

"Here we are," Stuart said cheerfully. But when he noticed her distress, his tone changed instantly into one of concern.

"Mrs Fletcher, are you quite well? Perhaps we should stop for a moment, to let you catch your breath. Or we could go to your office and I'll make you a cup of tea if you like."

"No, thank you, Stuart," she said, shaking her head. "There's no time for that now. We need to find Mr Redhurst. So I can give him a piece of my mind."

"As you wish, ma'am," he replied with a glimmer of admiration in his eyes. "Lead the way."

When they entered the main building however, they were faced with scenes of utter chaos. The factory floor had been turned into a vast, shimmering lake. Water, inches deep, covered every surface, lapping at the bases of machines and pooling in the corners.

And everywhere, workers were frantically wading through the flood, shouting to one another as they tried to salvage equipment and materials from the encroaching water.

"What in heaven's name?" Madeleine gasped, her eyes wide with shock.

Henry Mason came splashing towards them in a panic. "Mrs Fletcher! Thank the Almighty, you're back."

"Mr Mason, what happened this time?"

"It's the water tanks, ma'am. They've sprung a leak. Thousands of gallons, everywhere. We don't know what to do."

Another disaster. The third one in a row. Cursing Ashton Redhurst under her breath, she hitched up her skirts and waded into the water. "Show me," she told Mason.

Stuart followed close behind, his own trousers soon soaked to the knee, while Henry Mason led them to the water tanks.

Madeleine could feel the weight of her sodden dress beginning to drag at her, the fabric tangling around her legs and making it difficult to move. But she pressed on. This latest setback would not get the better of her.

When they reached the base of the water tanks, the source of the flood became clear. A jagged hole, easily a foot wide, had been torn into the main pipe. Water gushed forth from the ruptured metal in an unrelenting torrent, adding to the already considerable deluge.

"Stuart," Madeleine said. "I need you to find a way to stop this leak. See if you can patch it, or at least slow down the flow."

"Yes, ma'am."

"And be careful," she added. "We have to assume this is another act of sabotage."

If Ashton had done this, she thought, then the man was becoming unhinged. And Lord knows what more wickedness he was capable of.

"I'll do my best, Mrs Fletcher," Stuart replied. "But it won't be easy. The pressure behind that water is immense."

Madeleine laid a hand on his arm, her eyes meeting his with a fierce intensity. "I have every faith in you, Stuart. You're probably the best engineer I have right now. If anyone can find a way, it's you."

As Stuart set to work, Madeleine turned to survey the devastation around her. The factory was drowning before her very eyes. And the man who was supposed to be her partner in this venture was nowhere to be seen.

How convenient, she thought. *Where are you, Ashton?*

She could feel a deep, simmering rage building up within her, a fury born of betrayal and frustration. How much more could she take? How many more blows could she withstand before she broke?

Suppressing a muttered oath, she turned and waded back towards the middle of the factory floor. With her soaking wet dress clinging to her like sodden rags and with her damp hair sticking to her forehead, she now looked more like some monster from the deep, she guessed. But she didn't care.

"Mr Mason," she began shouting out her orders. "Make sure those crates are moved someplace dry."

They would salvage what they could, she decided, to minimise the damage as much as possible.

And then, when the immediate crisis was over, she would find Ashton. And heaven help him when she did.

"Mr Wilkes!"

"Aye, ma'am?"

"See if we have any sandbags. Use them to protect the machinery from the worst of the flood water."

She felt like a sea captain, standing on the deck of a storm-battered ship while trying to tame the elements. It felt oddly exhilarating, she realised with a small grin.

"Mrs Fletcher," a distant voice with a familiar French accent called out. Looking over her shoulder, she saw Mr Dubois hurrying towards her, his usually impeccable attire now dishevelled and soggy.

"Mr Dubois!" She beckoned him to come over. "Mind your step. The floor's treacherous."

"I came as soon as I read your note," he said, somewhat out of breath from his hasty journey.

"Your swift response is much appreciated. As you can see, we're in the middle of yet another crisis."

He nodded silently while his eyes drifted over the watery scene of destruction before him. "Sir John and I were still at Montgomery's when Miss Eleanor arrived with your note. She insisted on waiting for us to return. Quite a determined young lady."

"That she is, Mr Dubois. That she most certainly is." She grinned with pride, but then turned serious again. "Mr Mason, good work on those crates. When you're finished with them, I want you to identify and rescue the most valuable equipment first."

"Aye, ma'am."

"Are Ellie and Charlotte still at Sir John's?" she asked Mr Dubois next. "Please don't tell me they came back here with you?"

"Oh no, Madame. Sir John saw to it that your daughter and your cousin were returned safely to your home. I came alone."

"Good. And I'm glad you're here. We need all the help we can get." She turned back to the workers, her voice rising above the din. "Any luck with those sandbags, Mr Wilkes?"

"I'm afraid not, Mrs Fletcher."

"Too bad. Start bailing water. Every bucket counts."

Madeleine watched Wilkes and his group scuttle off, a fierce pride mingling with the worry in her heart. These were good men, she thought. Loyal and hardworking. They didn't deserve this.

"You can see what we're up against here, Mr Dubois," she sighed. "It just never seems to end."

"Another dirty trick of Mr Redhurst?"

"More than likely, don't you think?"

"He would be the most probable culprit, yes."

"When I get my hands on that scoundrel..." She shook her head, trying to concentrate on more urgent matters. "Did you and Sir John find out anything interesting at Montgomery's?"

"Yes, we did. Although I suspect you won't like it very much."

"What is it? Tell me."

"Apparently, Mr Redhurst has been seen dining and drinking with Charles Turner at the club, on several occasions. According to our source, the two of them were as thick as thieves."

"The journalist?" Shocked, Madeleine spun around to face Mr Dubois. But as she turned, her foot caught on something underneath the surface of the water, and she felt herself losing balance. Crying out in surprise, she tumbled backwards, landing in the water with a splash.

Immediately, Mr Dubois reached out his hand to help her up. "Allow me to assist you, Mrs Fletcher."

But she shrugged away his hand, anger and frustration boiling over at what she had just heard. She tried to get back to her feet on her own, but then exhaustion and the weight of her waterlogged dress caused her to stumble once more.

Hot, angry tears began to stream down her face. "Ashton and Turner," she said bitterly. "I should have known. I should have seen it."

Mr Dubois gently took hold of her arm, helping to steady her as he pulled her up. "You couldn't have known, Mrs Fletcher. Men like them, they are devious. They work in the shadows."

"All these men conspiring against me," she grumbled. She looked at Mr Dubois with a sudden, fierce intensity in her eyes. "Are you conspiring against me too? Is that what this is? Another ploy, another trick to make me lower my guard?"

"Madeleine, please–"

"How do I know you're not a part of this?" she hissed at him. "How do I know you're not working with them to destroy me?"

"I assure you, I would never–"

"Never what? Never lie to me? Never betray me?" She laughed, a harsh, bitter sound. "You already did that once, didn't you? Why should I believe you're not lying to me now?"

"You're upset, I know," he said calmly, trying to touch her arm in a soothing gesture. But on Madeleine it had the effect of a red rag on a raging bull.

Throwing herself at him in a fit of fury, she pummelled his chest with her fists. "You made me believe that you loved me. And you made me think that I–"

Undeterred, he grasped her arms to stop her from hitting him. "I do love you, Madeleine. I know I've wronged you in the past. And that I've given you every reason to doubt me. But please, you must believe me when I say that my feelings for you are true."

Tears came streaming down her cheeks and she pressed the side of her face against his chest. "I know your feelings are true. And that's what drives me mad."

"I– I don't understand," he stammered.

She took a step back, breaking off the embrace so she could look him straight in the eye.

"I wanted to be angry with you – for fooling me into trusting you and for nearly betraying me. But then I realised: it wasn't my pride that had been hurt. It was my heart. And do you know why?"

Underneath her hands resting on his chest, she could feel the rapid beat of his heart.

"Because I loved you too," she said.

The surprised look on his face made him appear so completely open and so utterly defenceless, that she thought she might kiss him there and then.

"Yes, I love you, you devilishly charming rascal," she repeated with a broad grin.

He pulled her into his arms, heedless of the water that still swirled around their feet. "I will never betray you again," he vowed. "I will stand by your side, always. Whether it's fighting against Ashton and Turner, or rebuilding this factory brick by brick, I will be there with you, every step of the way."

Keeping her close, he tenderly took her face into his hands, his lips enticingly close to hers. With his thumbs he brushed away the tears that still clung to her cheeks.

"I can't imagine my life without you in it," he spoke softly.

She turned her head slightly, pressing a kiss into the palm of his hand.

"And I can't imagine facing any of this without you by my side," she whispered. "Together, we're stronger than anything Ashton or anyone else can throw at us."

Suddenly, a warning shout from nearby shattered their moment of intimacy. They turned just in time to see a small crane, its supports weakened by the rising water, topple over with a resounding crash. The machine hit the floor, sending a huge splash of water in their direction.

Madeleine let out a raw, primal scream of frustration.

"If it's war Ashton wants," she growled, "then war he shall have. But we won't be fighting alone."

"What do you suggest we do?" Mr Dubois asked, wiping the water from his face.

"I'm calling a council of war. A meeting with the only people I can trust. You, Sir John, Stuart, Ellie, Charlotte. And Robert, if we can find him."

"I'll arrange it immediately," he replied with a grin. "And I think we should include Mrs Pemberton-Thorpe as well. The old warhorse won't want to miss a fight like this."

"Splendid idea."

"When would you like everyone to convene?"

"The sooner the better," she said resolutely. "Before Ashton gets a chance to strike again." Because at this rate, she thought, that madman might even be capable of destroying the factory by blowing it up.

"Very well," Mr Dubois said. "Leave it to me." After pressing a final kiss on her hands, he turned and hurried away.

Alone, Madeleine gazed at the scene before her: the factory floor awash with water while the men frantically tried to protect what they could.

She didn't know yet how to handle Ashton, or even how she would prove his guilt. But one thing was certain: he and his accomplices had to be stopped. Before it was too late.

Chapter Thirty-Three

The last traces of daylight had faded from the sky when Madeleine's carriage pulled up in front of Sir John's grand city residence. She alighted first, followed closely by Ellie and Charlotte, their skirts swishing as they made their way to the front door.

A smartly dressed footman greeted them with a bow. "Good evening, ladies. Sir John is expecting you in the library. If you'll follow me, please."

Trailing behind the servant through the peaceful house, the muffled sounds of rustling clothes and soft footsteps on the plush carpets only added to the urgency of their purpose.

As they entered the library, Madeleine was pleased to see that Mr Dubois and Mrs Pemberton-Thorpe were already present. The widow and the Frenchman stood talking to Sir John, while a generous spread of food and refreshments had been laid out on a side table.

"Madeleine, my dear," Sir John greeted, striding towards her with a fond smile. "Welcome, welcome. Miss Eleanor and Miss Kimble too of course. I took the liberty of providing a few tidbits," he said, gesturing at the food on offer. "So please, help yourselves."

Out of the corner of her eye, Madeleine could see her cousin scanning the table for cake. But Charlotte showed great restraint and went to greet Mr Dubois and Mrs Pemberton-Thorpe first with Ellie in tow.

"Thank you, Sir John," Madeleine said. "It seems there's no limit to your hospitality. I would have been more than willing to have this gathering at my home."

Sir John waved his hand dismissively. "Nonsense, my dear. As soon as Mr Dubois told me about your plans for a war council as you called it, I insisted on hosting it here. Wouldn't have wanted it any other way."

Mrs Pemberton-Thorpe, resplendent in a deep purple gown, detached herself from the others to join Madeleine and Sir John.

"Mrs Fletcher," the widow said with a warm and sympathetic tone. "Mr Dubois has explained everything to me. And I want you to know that you have my full support in this matter. As for that scoundrel Mr Redhurst, well, let's just say propriety and good manners forbid me to share the words I have for that man."

Madeleine clasped the older woman's hands gratefully. "Thank you, Mrs Pemberton-Thorpe. I'm honoured to have you on our side."

Just as Sir John was about to offer his guests some refreshments, a knock at the door announced Stuart Wainwright's arrival. The young engineer stepped into the library, looking slightly dishevelled from his hurried journey.

"Stuart, any news about Robert?" Madeleine asked him immediately. "Has your family heard from him?"

The young engineer shook his head, his expression grim. "I'm afraid not, Mrs Fletcher. Nobody has seen him since before lunchtime. It's as if he's vanished into thin air."

"Most troubling, his disappearance," Mr Dubois said.

"My sister Daisy is awfully worried," Stuart added, his voice heavy with concern. "She fears the worst, and I can't say I blame her."

"Where could he be?" Madeleine wondered aloud. Her mind was racing with possibilities, one more frightful than the other.

Sir John cleared his throat. "Forgive me for asking, but could this Robert chap possibly be the arsonist and the perpetrator of the flooding?"

Madeleine shook her head vehemently. "Impossible, Sir John. I've known Robert long enough to say with certainty that he's not capable of such things." She turned to Stuart, seeking his opinion. "What do you think, Stuart?"

"Robert wouldn't hurt a fly. He's one of the kindest, most gentle souls you could imagine."

"Were there any casualties from the arson or the flooding?" Mrs Pemberton-Thorpe asked. "Could Robert be among them?"

"Unlikely," Madeleine sighed with some relief. "This time, there were no casualties, thankfully."

"In that case," Mr Dubois said, "I can see only one other possible explanation: young Mr Adams has been taken against his will."

Madeleine was the first to break the stunned hush that fell over the room. "But why? Who would want to abduct Robert? He wasn't a threat to anyone."

Mr Dubois fixed her with a knowing look. "Your assistant was looking into some unusual accounting errors, wasn't he?"

Madeleine nodded slowly.

"Then perhaps," Mr Dubois continued, "Mr Adams came a little too close to the ugly truth."

Sir John raised his grey eyebrows. "Are you suggesting this accounting matter is linked to that blasted sabotage and the rest of it?"

"I believe it's safe to assume so, yes," Mr Dubois replied grimly.

"Sordid business this is turning out to be," the squire muttered. Shaking his head in disgust, he went over to the side table and picked off a few grapes.

Ellie had been listening from the sidelines, but now she spoke up. "If all these things are connected, then who else is involved in this scheme? Mr Redhurst couldn't possibly have done it all by himself, could he?"

"You raise an excellent point, Miss Eleanor," Mr Dubois said. "So far, we only know of one accomplice. As I already shared with your mother, Sir John and I have discovered that the journalist Mr Charles Turner is on rather friendly terms with Mr Redhurst."

"That would explain those slanderous newspaper articles he's been writing about Mrs Fletcher," Mrs Pemberton-Thorpe remarked, her eyes narrowing. "But how would Mr Redhurst have been able to tamper with the company books?"

"Mr Underwood," Madeleine blurted out. Suddenly, the pieces of the puzzle fell into place for her.

She recounted her senior accountant's oddly nervous behaviour earlier that day, the memory of his shifty eyes and trembling hands still fresh in her mind.

"Could he be Ashton's man on the inside?"

Stuart frowned, considering the possibility. "But Mr Underwood has never struck me as a particularly brave man. He's more the grey and stuffy old type, isn't he?"

"It doesn't take bravery to commit a crime, Mr Wainwright," Mr Dubois argued. "If anything, it's more a weakness of character that causes people to break the law."

"And one shouldn't underestimate the lure of money, or whatever else Mr Redhurst might have promised his henchmen," Mrs Pemberton-Thorpe added, her voice thick with disdain.

"The wicked are always prey to the temptations of power and greed," Sir John put in. "It's a sad truth of human nature, I'm afraid."

Brushing a few cake crumbs from her lips, Charlotte finally joined the conversation as well.

"So, we have Mr Redhurst, Mr Turner, and Mr Underwood as our likely suspects. What happens now? How do you intend to deal with these villains, Maddie?"

Madeleine sighed, her shoulders slumping. "Honestly, Charlotte, I don't know. We have no proof, only suspicions and deductions."

Mrs Pemberton-Thorpe leaned forward, her eyes focused on Madeleine. "What sort of outcome would you wish for, my dear?"

"I want the sabotage to stop," she replied without hesitation. "So that I can go back to running the company. I want to protect the livelihoods of the thousands of people who depend on the factory."

"And what needs to be done to make that happen?" the older woman pressed.

Madeleine's jaw tightened. "Ashton must be neutralised. He has to leave the company – for good."

Sir John hummed and nodded. "Why don't you simply offer to buy Redhurst's share then?"

"Knowing Ashton and his stubborn pride," Madeleine shook her head, "he would never agree to that."

"Not voluntarily, no," Mr Dubois agreed, his lips twisting into a wry smile.

"Besides," Madeleine added, "even if Ashton did agree, I haven't got the money."

Sir John and Mrs Pemberton-Thorpe exchanged a glance before turning back to Madeleine.

"We would gladly lend you the money, my dear," Sir John said, his tone gentle but firm.

"Absolutely," Mrs Pemberton-Thorpe nodded. "You can count on our financial backing. We would even pay for all the repairs that are needed."

Madeleine drew in a surprised breath, but then she shook her head. "No, I couldn't possibly accept. It's too much, really."

Sir John swiftly held up a hand however, silencing her protests. "If it makes you feel any better, it wouldn't just be a gift. It would be part loan, part investment. You would pay back the loan, of course, while the investment would give

Mrs Pemberton-Thorpe and myself a small stake in your company."

Ellie jumped back into the conversation. "That's the money side of things sorted," she declared enthusiastically. "Now how do we get Mr Redhurst to give up his share?"

"That's the whole problem, isn't it?" Madeleine sighed. "He'll never want to sell his share, not for all the tea in China."

"Then make him," Ellie said, her youthful brashness shining through. "Force his hand."

Charlotte, ever the sweet-natured voice of reason, shook her head. "You can't make anyone do something they don't want to, Ellie. It simply doesn't work that way."

"So pressure him," Ellie insisted, undeterred.

"Now then, duck," Charlotte cautioned. "We shouldn't resort to the same dirty tricks as these villains."

"There may be something to Ellie's idea though," Madeleine said. "Perhaps if we told Ashton that we know the truth – that he's the one who caused all the damage and destruction. And if we threatened to make that information public, then maybe he could be convinced to sell his share to me."

"To save his skin as well as his reputation," Mr Dubois mused, stroking his chin. "Yes, that might work on a man like Mr Redhurst."

"Perhaps we could even get a confession out of him," Madeleine added with a glimmer of hope in her voice.

"But how?" Stuart frowned. "I must say this all sounds very clever to me. But then again, as an engineer, I feel more knowledgeable about machinery than the inner workings of the human mind."

"Personally," Mrs Pemberton-Thorpe said, "I always prefer the direct approach. Confront the dastardly villain, lay out the facts, and then present your offer as his safest way out."

"Don't forget his accomplices," Sir John reminded them. "Charles Turner and this accountant fellow, whatsisname."

"I don't know what to do with them yet." Madeleine sighed. "It's all so maddeningly frustrating."

"Perhaps we ought to wait and continue our investigation first," Mr Dubois suggested. "Gather more incriminating facts and proof, before we move against Mr Redhurst."

"But we may not have that luxury," Madeleine replied. "Ashton has tried to ruin me three times already. His next attempt might be successful."

"And then there's Robert," Stuart said. "We don't know what happened to him. Any delay could prove disastrous for him as well."

A heavy silence fell over the room as the gravity of the situation sank in.

Waiting and looking for more facts was the prudent course of action, Madeleine knew. But on the other hand, time wasn't on their side. Ashton had proven himself to be a ruthless opponent, and there was no telling what he might do next.

She had to act, and she had to act now.

"We cannot afford to wait," she decided. "We're laying our trap tonight. We will lure Ashton, Turner, and Underwood to the factory and confront them."

She took a deep breath, her gaze sweeping over the faces of her friends. "I realise it's a huge gamble, but I feel we need to risk it – before I lose the factory, or poor Robert comes to harm."

One by one, the others nodded their agreement.

"But how will you get those three men to come to the factory in the middle of the night?" Charlotte asked.

"We could send each of them a forged note," Madeleine started thinking out loud. "Ashton and Mr Turner will each receive a message supposedly from Mr Underwood, urging them to meet him at the factory at midnight. And Mr Underwood will get a similar message, ostensibly from Ashton."

"Bold," Mr Dubois said. "But feasible."

"I admit it's not ideal, and my plan may very well fail miserably. But it's the only chance we have at the moment. As long as Ashton doesn't know we are on to him, we have an edge over him."

But it was a weak one at best, she realised all too well. And one that they would lose if they didn't succeed tonight.

"Well, my friends," Sir John spoke up. "It seems we have our work cut out for us. Let us prepare for tonight's confrontation and pray that fortune favours the bold."

"I'll produce those notes," Mr Dubois offered. "And then I will see to it that they are delivered as soon as possible."

"Splendid," the squire replied. "As for myself, I shall go to Montgomery's tonight and do my share there."

"Forgive me for saying so, Sir John," Mrs Pemberton-Thorpe bristled. "But this is hardly the time to be visiting your social club, don't you think?"

"Ah," the old squire said as a mischievous grin spread across his face. "But I'd be working hard to provide Mrs Fletcher with another arrow in her quiver."

Lowering his voice, he beckoned them to draw closer. "Let me explain..."

Chapter Thirty-Four

The factory lay silent and still, while an eerie quiet hung heavy in the cold, damp air. Creeping through the empty corridors, every step Madeleine took sounded to her as if it reverberated through the whole building.

Right behind her followed Mr Dubois, Stuart and Bill, all moving as one through the darkness without anyone speaking a single word.

As they navigated the deserted factory floor, Madeleine's eyes darted from shadow to shadow, half-expecting Ashton or one of his accomplices to leap out at any moment. Just thinking about her ruthless business partner sent a shiver down her spine, and she pulled her shawl tighter around her shoulders.

Despite Stuart's brave efforts to seal the ruptured water tanks earlier that day, evidence of the flooding remained. Puddles of varying sizes dotted the ground, their surfaces gleaming in the dim light that filtered through the high windows. The group skirted around them, their steps careful and deliberate.

As they drew closer to the number three storehouse, Madeleine could feel her pulse beating even faster. So much was riding on this confrontation tonight.

She knew there was a chance things might turn violent, given the level of destruction Ashton had already done. The thought made her heart pound and her palms grew damp.

For a moment, her mind drifted to Ellie. Bent on seeing justice done, her daughter had begged Madeleine to allow her to come along. It had taken the combined efforts of Charlotte and Mrs Pemberton-Thorpe to convince Ellie of the danger. And even then, the girl had only stopped her pleading with great reluctance.

But whatever happened tonight, Ellie would be safe. That knowledge was only a small comfort to Madeleine, but a comfort nonetheless.

She glanced over her shoulder at the three men accompanying her. Mr Dubois was right on her heels, and she could see the Frenchman giving her an encouraging smile.

Behind him was Stuart, who had volunteered to join their party. Madeleine had tried to dissuade him, as she was aware how devastated the young engineer's mother and sister would be if anything were to happen to him so soon after Jack Wainwright's tragic death.

But Stuart had insisted.

"I owe it to my father," he'd said.

At the rear of their little group, there was Bill. Good old Bill, she smiled to herself. His broad frame was a reassuring presence.

Madeleine was determined to stand up to Ashton on her own. But she knew that, physically at least, she was no match for him. So she felt a rush of gratitude now for the support and loyalty of these three men. With them by her side, she felt a little less alone – and a lot less vulnerable.

At last, they reached the storehouse doors. Mr Dubois stepped forward, his hand on the latch. He paused, turning to face the others.

"We should hide ourselves," he said. "Mr Wainwright, those sheets over the wreckage – they will provide adequate cover, no?"

Stuart nodded, moving quickly to rearrange the sheets into a makeshift hiding place. As they huddled together beneath the musty fabric, Madeleine could feel the heat of their bodies, as well as the tension in her own muscles.

The trap was set, she thought. All that remained was for Ashton to walk into it.

"Do you think they'll come?" Stuart whispered.

"I'm sure they will," Madeleine replied as quietly as she could. "I saw the messages Mr Dubois sent out: they had just the right combination of urgency and intrigue. Ashton won't be able to ignore it."

The words had barely left her mouth when they heard footsteps approaching the storehouse. Madeleine's breath caught in her throat, and Mr Dubois' hand found hers.

They waited, hardly daring to breathe, as the footsteps drew closer. Then, a voice cut through the silence – a voice Madeleine recognised instantly.

"Mr Redhurst?"

It was Mr Underwood, his tone jittery and nervous. A short, strained cough followed, as if the accountant was trying to clear his throat.

"Mr Redhurst, are you there?"

Slowly, Madeleine let out the breath she had been holding. The first of their guests had arrived. Now they simply had to wait for the other two – while praying that none of them would want to come snooping underneath those sheets over the wreckage.

The silence stretched on, broken only by the sound of Mr Underwood's nervous pacing. Madeleine's heart pounded in her ears, each minute feeling like an eternity.

After a while, the muscles in her legs began to hurt from squatting so close to the cold floor. But she tried to ignore the discomfort, and fought the urge to squirm.

Then, the sound of footsteps again, two sets this time. Madeleine's fingers tightened around Mr Dubois' hand.

"Underwood." Ashton's voice was a low growl, filled with irritation and suspicion. "What could possibly be so urgent that you wanted to meet us here tonight? Don't you know this is dangerous? The three of us can't be seen together like this."

Mr Underwood's reply was hesitant, confused. "But Mr Redhurst, I... I don't understand. It was you who sent me a message, requesting that I come to the factory."

There was a beat of silence, then a harsh bark of laughter from Ashton. "You must be mad, Underwood. Or senile."

Madeleine heard a snicker. *Turner, no doubt.*

"Or perhaps you've been drinking," Ashton continued menacingly. "Is that it?"

There was a scuffle of movement, and Mr Underwood let out a yelp of surprise. Madeleine risked a peek through a gap in the sheets, her eyes straining to make out the scene before her.

Ashton had grabbed the accountant by the lapels, pulling him close. "Let me smell your breath, Underwood," he snarled, his face inches from the other man's.

"No, no, Mr Redhurst. I never drink. Not a drop, I swear." Mr Underwood's voice was high and panicky, his words tumbling over each other in his haste to explain. "I abstain from all alcoholic beverages, you see."

Turner scoffed. "Teetotallers. Bunch of self-righteous prigs, if you ask me."

Ashton's laughter mingled with Turner's, the sound harsh and grating in the empty storehouse.

After a moment of uncomfortable silence, Mr Underwood cleared his throat and spoke again. "But seeing as we're all here, Mr Redhurst sir... How much longer do you think this endeavour of ours will need to go on?"

"As long as it takes," Ashton snapped angrily. "Until our dearest Mrs Fletcher finally comes to her senses and gives up her share of the factory."

"Stubborn one, isn't she?" Turner put in. "But then again, that's women for you, I suppose."

Ashton grunted his agreement. "Madeleine has proven far more headstrong than I anticipated. I thought she would have buckled after the first accident. But perhaps this flooding will finally break her."

A flash of anger surged in Madeleine's belly. She wanted to jump out of their hiding place to confront that despicable cad. But Mr Dubois held her back.

"Not yet," he whispered into her ear.

"I'll write another article about the incident," Turner said with malicious glee. "Turn the knife in the wound a bit."

Ashton made a sound of approval, then his tone turned critical, focusing on Mr

Underwood. "And what about you, Underwood? Your contributions so far have been rather tame. That's not how you'll earn that fat annual stipend I promised you."

"No, no, of course not, Mr Redhurst." The accountant's words came out in a rushed and desperate babble. "Please let me assure you of my unwavering commitment and dedication to our common cause."

"Your fancy talk is beginning to give me a headache, Underwood. I want action from you, not words."

"Yes, sir," Mr Underwood prattled on. "With that nosy Mr Adams out of the way, I'll have much more freedom to, um, to tinker with the books, as it were."

"I've heard enough," Madeleine shouted as she came bursting out from beneath the sheets. "This sinister circus ends here."

Mr Dubois, Stuart, and Bill emerged as well, spreading out behind her like a trio of vengeful guardian angels. The villains whirled around, shocked at being discovered.

"What the blazes–" Turner muttered. The journalist took a threatening step forward, but Ashton held him back.

In a heartbeat, Madeleine scanned her business partner's face for any clue to how he might react. And what she saw there made her doubt whether her gamble had succeeded.

Chapter Thirty-Five

"Quite the eccentric gathering this is turning out to be," Ashton mocked after quickly having regained his wits. "Tell me, Madeleine, what exactly were you and your merry band of friends doing hiding under there?"

Madeleine met his gaze steadily, and she stuck her chin out in defiance. "We sent those messages, Ashton. To lure you and your accomplices here tonight."

"How utterly devious of you, my dear," he replied sarcastically. "I'm almost impressed."

"It worked, didn't it?" she shot back. "I heard your confession, Ashton. I know the truth now."

His eyes narrowed and a calculating look came over his face. "Confession? I'm afraid I don't know what you're talking about."

"Don't play innocent with me, Ashton. You and your two lackeys here, you're behind all the recent troubles at the factory."

Ashton scoffed, waving a dismissive hand. "I made no such confession, Madeleine. All I said was that I thought you would have given up by now."

A pang of alarm briefly gripped her. She had come out of their hiding place too soon, driven by her rage. Cursing herself inwardly, she pressed on nonetheless. He wasn't going to get off the hook that easily.

"Then what about all this talk of your 'endeavour' and a 'common cause'? It's clear you three are conspiring against me."

Ashton's laughter was cruel and mocking. "You're grasping at straws, Madeleine. You haven't got a shred of evidence. It's your word against mine."

She bit her lip, knowing he was right. But she wouldn't give him the satisfaction of admitting that out loud.

It was then that Mr Dubois stepped forward, his eyes fixed on Ashton. "Tell me, Mr Redhurst, do you enjoy a good gamble?"

Ashton frowned, thrown off balance by the sudden change in topic. "What the devil has that got to do with anything?"

Mr Dubois smiled, even though there was no warmth in it. "Your sabotage has cost several lives, Mr Redhurst. That amounts to manslaughter, I believe. Are you willing to bet your neck that a judge would simply dismiss the case?"

Turner scoffed. "Don't listen to him, Redhurst. The frog's bluffing."

Madeleine's anxious gaze jumped from one man to the other, until it came to rest on Mr Underwood. The accountant's face had gone sickly pale, and he was fidgeting nervously with his cravat. Sweat beaded on his shiny forehead, and his eyes darted around the space like a cornered animal.

Sensing weakness, Madeleine pounced.

"And what about you, Mr Underwood? Do you feel confident that the court would spare you?"

"I'm merely an accountant," he stammered. "I didn't have anything to do with the explosion, or the fire, or the flooding."

Mr Dubois quickly picked up the thread. "Strictly speaking, that may be true, Mr Underwood. And for that reason alone you would probably escape the gallows."

He paused to allow the accountant a short breath before continuing. "Prison on the other hand, while not as final as a death sentence, is hardly a peaceful retreat. Especially for a delicate gentleman of advanced years."

Seeing the Frenchman's intention, Madeleine took over. "Think about it, Mr Underwood," she said. "Cold, damp cells. Meagre rations of revolting food. And I don't even dare to imagine what sort of people your fellow prisoners would be."

"It wasn't meant to go this far," the accountant cried out, throwing up his trembling hands as if to ward off her words. "We never intended to capture Mr Adams, I swear we didn't. But the fool started sticking his nose where it didn't belong, and then he overheard a conversation between myself and Mr Redhurst. We had no choice."

"Shut your mouth, Underwood," Ashton snarled. "Not another word, do you hear me?"

Ignoring Ashton's outburst, Madeleine rounded on Mr Underwood, her eyes boring into him. "So it's true then? You tampered with the books?"

"Yes," the accountant whimpered. "I falsified some of the records, in order to make the company appear less profitable than it really is."

Finally some truth, Madeleine sighed to herself.

"But why, Mr Underwood?" she asked. "Why would you do such a thing? After so many years of commendable service?"

The accountant's entire posture slumped, and he seemed to age at least a decade before Madeleine's eyes.

"I'm close to retirement, Mrs Fletcher. And Mr Redhurst, well, he promised me a generous annual stipend, in exchange for my help."

Ashton's face contorted with rage, and suddenly he lunged at the accountant, his hands closing around the man's throat. "You snivelling, cowardly traitor," he snarled while his fingers tightened their grip.

But before he could do any real harm, Bill sprung forward. And with his big strong hands, the coachman pulled the assailant away from the terrified Mr Underwood.

"Let go of me, you buffoon," Ashton seethed. But Bill didn't loosen his grip, and kept the writhing madman's arms pinned firmly behind his back.

Madeleine stepped closer to Mr Underwood. "I suggest you reconsider where your loyalties lie, Mr Underwood. Tell us everything, and help us to bring an end to Mr Redhurst's campaign of terror."

She paused and cast a sideways glance at Ashton before adding, "Unless, of course, you'd prefer for my coachman to release him?"

Mr Underwood's frightened eyes widened, and he shook his head frantically. "No, no, please! I'll cooperate, I swear. You'll find all of the original accounting records in my bedroom at home. And that's where we've locked up Mr Adams as well."

Robert! Madeleine's heart did a little somersault of happiness at hearing her assistant's name. Robert was safe, thank heavens.

"I'll tell you anything you wish to know, Mrs Fletcher," Mr Underwood continued in his frantically pleading tone. "But please, don't let that demon near me."

A triumphant smile spread across Madeleine's face as she turned to Ashton. "Your scheme has failed, Ashton. It's over."

"You must be so pleased with yourself," he replied with a bitter sneer.

"Pleased? No, not at all. Relieved, for sure. But how could I possibly be pleased after the pain and suffering you caused? And what for? Just so you could have the company to yourself?"

"It should have been mine after Benjamin died," he glared at her hatefully. "But instead, I ended up with you at the helm. And you're even more stubborn than your late husband. A bloody bulldog is what you are."

"I can see now why Benjamin made me promise never to let you have his share of the company. You're heartless, Ashton."

She shook her head, pity and disgust welling up inside her. "It's sad, really. Truly sad, what greed and ambition can do to a man."

Then she straightened her shoulders and looked him square in the eye. "But I'll show you that I'm the better person here. I'm willing to buy your share of the company. For the same price you were going to offer me."

"You must be joking," he laughed. "Why would I ever agree to that?"

"Because if you refuse," she replied coldly, "I'll make sure you face the full consequences of your actions. I have Mr Underwood's confession now, and I'm sure the authorities will be very interested to hear it."

She could see the hesitation in his eyes. Weighing his options, she guessed. His gaze flicked to Turner, as if seeking support there. But Madeleine cut him off before he could speak.

"Oh, don't think you can rely on your friend's poisoned pen to save you. Mr Dubois, would you care to explain?"

"Gladly," the Frenchman replied with a sly smile. "It would appear, Mr Redhurst, that Mrs Fletcher's dear friend and ally Sir John has become acquainted with the owner of Mr Turner's newspaper. The two gentlemen met at Montgomery's only recently."

Madeleine grinned mischievously. "And isn't it true, Mr Dubois, that Sir John was planning on inviting this new friend of his for a weekend of fowl shooting at his magnificent country estate?"

"Yes, that's what I heard as well," Mr Dubois replied, his eyes twinkling with amusement. "I think we can expect The Herald to start singing a very different tune about you in the near future, Mrs Fletcher."

Turning red in the face with indignation, the journalist muttered a grumbling protest under his breath.

"Don't worry, Mr Turner," Madeleine taunted. "I'm sure you'll find plenty of other fascinating topics to write about. Gardening perhaps? Local book clubs and knitting circles? Or if you want to put your vitriol to good use, you might consider becoming a theatre critic."

"Enough," Ashton suddenly snarled. "You win, Madeleine. I'll accept your offer."

Overjoyed, Madeleine felt like jumping up and down in sheer bliss. But she would show grace and dignity in victory, she decided.

"A wise choice, Ashton," she nodded calmly. "I'll have my solicitors draw up the necessary paperwork in the morning. And as of this moment, you are no longer welcome on these premises. Not ever."

She turned to Bill and Stuart. "Please escort Mr Redhurst and Mr Turner to the gates. See that they leave without further incident."

"My pleasure, ma'am," Stuart replied as he and Bill moved to flank the defeated villains.

"As for you, Mr Underwood," Madeleine said while Ashton and Turner were being marched towards the exit. "You will retire from the company. And you will do so immediately after we've liberated Mr Adams and when we have retrieved the original accounting records. Consider it a small price to pay for avoiding the shame and consequences of a public trial."

The accountant nodded meekly. Whatever malice may have possessed him before, Madeleine had yanked it out of him, roots and all.

"Of course, Mrs Fletcher. Whatever you say."

And with that, she realised with great relief, her nightmare was over. She had defeated Ashton, and saved the factory. Everything had been resolved.

She caught Mr Dubois' eye, and he smiled at her, silently congratulating her.

Well, nearly everything, she thought.

Following the Frenchman as he led Mr Underwood out of the storehouse, Madeleine knew there remained one other matter that was begging for a solution.

Chapter Thirty-Six

The drawing room at Sir John's residence was alive with chatter and laughter as the festive gathering hit its stride. Crystal glasses clinked, and the aroma of fine food mingled with the thrill of victory that hung in the air.

Standing by the fireplace, Robert found himself the centre of attention as he recounted his recent misadventure. His fiancée Daisy was right beside him, her hand resting reassuringly on his arm.

"So there I was," Robert said, "in the supply room, looking for a new ink bottle. Mine had run dry, you see, and I couldn't very well continue my work without it."

"I remember you telling me you were making tons of notes," Madeleine smiled.

"That's right, ma'am. I was. And just when I found a fresh bottle, I heard voices coming from the other room. It was Mr Redhurst and Mr Underwood. They must not have realised I was there."

He paused and blushed, by way of an apology. "I never meant to eavesdrop on them, but... Mr Redhurst, well, he was telling Mr Underwood off. Said he wasn't trying hard enough. And that the books needed to look a lot worse if they wanted to scare Mrs Fletcher into giving up the company."

A collective gasp rose from the listeners, followed by a chorus of disapproving tutting.

"I was so shocked," Robert continued, "I accidentally dropped the ink bottle. It shattered on the floor, and that's when they found me."

Daisy squeezed his arm. "You poor darling."

"Mr Redhurst was furious with me," Robert continued. "He said they had to lock me up. At Mr Underwood's house, of all places."

"Why there?" Ellie asked.

"Mr Redhurst said it was the safest solution," Robert shrugged. "Mr Underwood lives alone. Has a house all to himself, he has. On account of him never having married."

"I'm not surprised," Daisy sniffed. "What sane woman would want to marry a horrid little man like him?"

A ripple of laughter went through the group, breaking the tension.

"They never meant to hurt me," Robert assured his audience. "Although I must say, Mr Underwood's cooking left much to be desired."

"So what was their plan then?" Mrs Pemberton-Thorpe asked. "They couldn't keep you hidden away in Mr Underwood's bedroom forever, could they?"

"Heaven forbid, no." Robert shivered at the thought. "They told me they'd let me go as soon as Mrs Fletcher had signed over her share to Mr Redhurst."

"Well, I'm certainly glad it didn't come to that," Madeleine said. "And I'm even happier to have you back with us, Robert. Safe and sound."

"Hear, hear," Sir John said, raising his glass. "A toast to our dear Mrs Fletcher's triumph. And to the safe return of young Mr Adams."

The others raised their glasses as well, filling the room with heartfelt cheers and the sound of crystal clinking against crystal.

As she sipped her champagne, Madeleine felt a warmth that had nothing to do with the drink spreading through her chest. The storm had passed. The battle was won.

She cleared her throat, drawing the attention of the room. "I want to thank all of you," she began. "For your unwavering support and faith in me. Even when I doubted myself."

Her gaze settled on Charlotte, and she smiled warmly at her cousin. Charlotte returned the smile, her eyes shining with pride.

"And I would like to give a special thank you to Sir John and Mrs Pemberton-Thorpe." She turned to the squire and the widow. "Your financial backing means that the factory will be up and running again soon, securing the future for hundreds of workers and their families."

The room erupted in cheers once more, glasses raised high in a toast to Madeleine's words.

While Sir John's butler went round refilling everyone's glass, Madeleine gazed at her friends, glowing with gratitude.

She thought of Bill as well. Earlier that day, her loyal coachman had politely declined her invitation to the celebration.

"The squire's grand rooms are no place for the likes of me, ma'am," he'd said with his usual modesty.

Madeleine had understood. Instead, she had arranged for a lavish meal to be served to him in the servants' hall. She could picture him now, regaling Sir John's staff with tales of the night when his brave mistress had bested the evil Mr Redhurst.

The party began to break up into smaller groups, conversations buzzing in every corner. Madeleine made her way over to where Stuart stood with Mr Dubois and Ellie.

"Mama," Ellie exclaimed as she approached. "Mr Wainwright was just telling us about his ideas for the turbine project. They sounded ever so clever to me."

Madeleine smiled at her daughter's lovestruck enthusiasm. "I would very much like to hear those ideas, too. But perhaps some other time. Tonight is for celebration and," she glanced quickly at Mr Dubois, "friendship."

"Whenever you wish, Mrs Fletcher," the young engineer said.

"And I want you to know how terribly sorry I am that Mr Redhurst won't be facing formal justice for your father's death." She sighed. "Jack Wainwright was a good man who didn't deserve what Ashton did to him."

Stuart shook his head. "Watching Mr Redhurst dangle from the gallows wouldn't bring my father back, ma'am. But the man's been defeated and humiliated. And that's justice enough for me."

He smiled at her and said, "More importantly, the factory is safe now. In your capable hands, Mrs Fletcher, it has a bright future ahead."

"That's very kind of you, thank you."

Her eyes drifted off to Mr Dubois before quickly returning to Stuart and Ellie. "Would you excuse us for a moment, please? I was hoping to have a private word with Mr Dubois."

There was so much she wanted to say to him, so much that had been left unspoken in the whirlwind of recent events.

"Of course, Mama," Ellie said. Presenting Stuart with her most charming smile, she slipped her hand through the crook of the engineer's arm.

"Mr Wainwright," she twittered, "you simply must try some of these canapés Sir John's cook has prepared. They're absolutely divine."

Madeleine watched them leave with an amused grin twitching at the corner of her mouth. "I'll have to start keeping an eye on those two," she said.

"I believe you may be right," Mr Dubois chuckled.

"And what about you, Monsieur? What comes next?"

"To be frank, I don't know," he sighed. "I can't return to Paris or London. There are too many ghosts from my past lurking there."

"Why not stay in Sheffield then?" The words were out before she could stop them.

Mr Dubois looked at her for a heartbeat and then asked, "Do you think there might be... opportunities for me here?"

Madeleine felt a heat rising up from her shoulders to her cheeks. "We made a rather good team, you and I, didn't we?"

"We certainly did, Mrs Fletcher," he smiled. "I've enjoyed our liaison."

"Then why should we end it?"

She scrutinised his face for a reaction. But for once, he seemed genuinely dumbstruck.

"The factory could use a man of your talents," she continued. "Someone who knows a thing or two about money. And who has a way with words, both on the factory floor and in the boardroom. I'd like to offer you a position, Mr Dubois. To help me run things."

"You are... serious?"

"Quite serious. I can think of no one better suited."

He took her hand in his, and the touch sent a ripple of delight through her entire being.

"Then I accept," he said. "With gratitude and great pleasure."

They stood like that for a moment, gazing into each other's eyes while holding hands. But then she blushed and stared down at the floor.

"As for any other feelings between us," she said softly, "I must ask you to respect my wish to remain in mourning for my late husband. When Benjamin died, I vowed to wear the black for a year."

Mr Dubois brought her hand to his lips, and pressed a delicate kiss to her knuckles before letting go and taking a small step back.

"Of course, Mrs Fletcher. I understand completely. I will wait, for as long as it takes. For you, I would wait an eternity."

"Thank you," she whispered. Her voice was hoarse from emotion, as sadness and joy battled for control over her heart.

From across the room, Sir John caught Madeleine's eye. He was deep in conversation with Mrs Pemberton-Thorpe, but he paused and raised his glass to Madeleine in a silent salute.

The smile on his lips and the twinkle in his eyes told Madeleine that the squire had a fairly good idea about what she had been discussing with Mr Dubois. Raising her own glass in response, she nodded and returned the smile.

She would mourn her late husband for the remainder of the twelve months she had pledged.

And after that? Who knew what the future would bring?

Tonight however, she would savour this moment, surrounded by the warmth of true friendship and the glow of her hard-won victory.

Chapter Thirty-Seven

The sun shone brightly overhead as Madeleine walked through the cemetery gates, a vibrant wreath clutched in her hands. Attached to it was a deep purple ribbon that fluttered gently in the breeze, its rich hue a stark contrast to the pale grey of the headstones all around her.

As she made her way down the winding gravel paths, Madeleine marvelled at the peacefulness of her surroundings. Birds chirped merrily in the trees, and the sweet scent of flowers filled the air. It was almost as if nature was celebrating the beauty of life – a bittersweet reminder that even in a place so closely associated with death, the world continued to turn.

Madeleine passed by a hunched figure, and she caught a glimpse of the visitor's face. It was a woman, her eyes red and puffy from crying. The sight stirred a painful memory in Madeleine's heart, taking her back to that dark day when she had laid her beloved Benjamin to rest.

She remembered the despair that had engulfed her then, the feeling that her own life had ended along with his.

In those bleak moments, the only things that had kept her going were her love for their daughter Ellie – and the sense of duty she felt towards the factory Benjamin had entrusted to her care.

At the time, Madeleine had been convinced she would never again know happiness. The mere thought of joy had seemed like a betrayal of her husband's memory.

How wrong I was, she reflected with a soft smile.

As she approached Benjamin's grave, Madeleine's step lightened. She knelt down beside the headstone, arranging the colourful wreath with tender care.

"Hello, my love," she whispered, just as she did every time when she visited him. "I can hardly believe it's been a year since you left us."

Her fingers traced the engraved letters of his name, each groove a reminder of the life they had shared and the love that would always remain in her heart.

"I must admit, Benjamin, the past twelve months have been hard. Harder than I ever could have imagined."

She sighed, shaking her head. "And Ashton Redhurst certainly did his best to make them even more difficult. You were right not to trust him with the company, my darling. He's an awful, wicked man."

A note of triumph entered her voice as she continued. "But we dealt with him, Benjamin. He's gone now, and the factory is thriving like never before. Oh, I can't take all the credit for that. I've had some wonderfully smart and capable people helping me along the way."

As the words left her lips, Madeleine's thoughts drifted to Mr Dubois. A sigh escaped her, and a pang of guilt twisted in her chest.

Here she was, at her husband's graveside, thinking of another man with tenderness in her heart. She closed her eyes for a moment and tried to chase the sense of shame out of her mind.

"I vowed to mourn you for a full year, Benjamin. And now that time has passed. But I find myself uncertain about what comes next. Should I continue to grieve for you? Some have said I ought to move on with my life. Would you blame me if I did?"

Her hand rested on the cool stone, as if seeking comfort from its solid presence.

"I want you to know, my love, that whatever I do, whatever happens, my love for you will never fade. You will always hold a special place in my heart."

A gentle breeze whispered through the trees, but no answer came. Of course there wouldn't, Madeleine chided herself. How silly to think–

Suddenly, a flash of movement caught her eye. A small robin, its red breast vivid against the grey headstone, had landed on Benjamin's grave. It cocked its head, looking at Madeleine with bright, curious eyes.

For a brief moment, the two of them simply stared at each other. Then, with a cheerful twitter, the robin took wing, disappearing into the blue sky above.

Madeleine gazed after it, speechless. What an extraordinary thing. Was it merely a coincidence, a quirk of nature?

Or could it be something more, a sign of sorts?

Lost in her thoughts, she almost didn't hear the sound of approaching footsteps. Turning, she saw Charlotte making her way towards the grave, a bouquet of flowers in her hands.

"I thought I might find you here," her cousin said with a gentle smile. She knelt down beside Madeleine, laying the flowers on the grass.

"It felt right to bring these," Charlotte said. "To mark the anniversary."

Madeleine reached out and squeezed her cousin's hand. "Thank you, Charlotte. That's a very kind and considerate gesture."

Falling silent, they both gazed at the grave before them for a while.

"I still remember the day you met him for the first time," Charlotte mused. "He was smitten with you the moment he laid eyes on you."

"And I with him," Madeleine replied dreamily. But then she frowned and let out a long, sad sigh. "Little did I know that fate would rob him from me years later."

Charlotte turned to her with a compassionate expression on her sweet, round face. "Maddie, my duck. Don't you think you've done enough grieving? Time waits for no one, as they say."

Madeleine gave a short nod and looked down at her hands. "I know, Charlotte. But the thought of moving on feels... strange. Wrong, even."

Charlotte tilted her head, studying Madeleine's face. "Or could it be that you're merely afraid?"

Madeleine hesitated. "Possibly," she admitted. "But on the other hand, wouldn't it be disrespectful and unfair towards Benjamin if I–"

She trailed off, unable to finish the sentence. Standing here, by her husband's graveside, she couldn't bring herself to utter Mr Dubois' name. As if doing so would constitute some sort of awful moral sin.

"If you opened your heart to another man, you mean?" Charlotte finished for her. With kindness in her eyes, she placed a comforting hand on Madeleine's shoulder.

"Maddie, Benjamin loved you. During his lifetime, making you happy was his only true goal."

Her eyes softened, and she gave Madeleine a reassuring smile. "And if he could talk to you now, I'm sure he'd tell you to be happy again."

Tears welled up in Madeleine's eyes, a bittersweet mix of love and grief. Deep down, she knew Charlotte was right. Benjamin had always put her happiness first, even above his own.

"Thank you, Charlotte," she said. "Somehow you always seem able to say the right thing at the right time."

"I try," Charlotte replied. "And it's easier when you love and care for the person whom you're giving advice to."

Drying her tears, Madeleine rose to her feet. "I think I'll head home now. Would you like to come with me?"

Charlotte shook her head, a mischievous glint in her eye. "Actually, I heard there's a new cake shop in town. I thought I might stop by and give it a try."

Madeleine chuckled at her cousin's irrepressible love for all things sweet. She pulled Charlotte into a warm hug, feeling a surge of affection for this woman who had been her rock through so many difficult times.

"Enjoy your cake, my dearest Lottie," she said as they parted. "And thank you again, for everything."

With a final smile and a wave, Madeleine turned and made her way out of the cemetery. Perhaps, she thought, it was time to start living again.

Chapter Thirty-Eight

As soon as Madeleine arrived back home, she made her way straight to the living room. Throwing her hat on a nearby chair with a flourish, she strode over to the piano and pulled off the sheet that had kept it hidden during her long months of mourning.

Seeing the instrument again made her heart beat faster. Lovingly, she ran her fingers over the polished wood, before selecting her favourite music book and opening the keyboard cover. Then she settled herself on the bench, took a deep breath and began to play.

Soon, the room filled with the gentle strains of the melody, each note seeming to dance in the air as Madeleine's hands moved gracefully over the keys. It had been so long since she'd allowed herself this simple pleasure, and she found herself getting lost in the music.

Time seemed to melt away as she played, her worries and sorrows fading into the background. She'd almost forgotten how much joy this brought her, how the music could transport her to another world entirely.

So engrossed was she in her playing that she didn't even hear the doorbell chime. It wasn't until Mary, the maid, came knocking softly on the living room door that Madeleine looked up, startled.

"Pardon the interruption, ma'am," Mary said with a small curtsy. "But Mr Dubois is at the front door. He says he has some urgent paperwork for you."

Madeleine glanced at the clock, surprised to see how much time had passed. A slight flush crept into her cheeks, partly from the exertion of playing and partly from the thought of Mr Dubois waiting for her.

"You've been playing for nearly an hour, ma'am," Mary added with a smile. "It sounded very lovely, if I may say so."

"Thank you, Mary," Madeleine replied, rising from the bench. "Please show Mr Dubois in, and bring us some tea and refreshments."

After the maid had left, Madeleine took a moment to compose herself. She had just settled on the sofa when Mr Dubois entered the room, his handsome features lighting up with a smile at the sight of her.

"Mrs Fletcher," he said warmly, inclining his head in greeting. "I hope you'll forgive the intrusion."

"But of course," she replied, gesturing for him to take a seat. "Mary said you have some paperwork for me?"

He nodded, producing a slim folder from his briefcase. "I apologise for calling on you at home, but these papers require your immediate attention and signature. As you weren't at the office, I took the liberty of bringing them here."

"You did well," she replied, accepting the folder and scanning the contents. It was the final version of a contract regarding the new turbine project. She had read all the drafts and didn't see anything amiss with this copy.

"This all seems to be in order," she said, looking up at him. "Do you have a pen?"

Mr Dubois handed her his fountain pen, and she quickly signed the documents. Just as she gave them back, Mary entered with a tray of tea, biscuits and small sandwiches. The maid poured them each a cup of tea, and then quietly left the room.

"I couldn't help but notice the piano when I came in," Mr Dubois said after his first sip. "Do you play?"

Madeleine felt a sudden shyness come over her. "Oh, I dabble a bit," she replied modestly, her eyes lowered.

"Knowing you and your many talents, Madame," he smiled, "I'm sure you do far more than merely dabble."

She laughed softly, a faint blush colouring her cheeks. "You flatter me, Mr Dubois. But the truth is, I'm terribly out of practice. I haven't played in a year."

He took a slow sip of his tea, his gaze never leaving hers. "But now you are playing again?"

"Yes," she said, her voice filled with a quiet joy. "And enjoying it tremendously."

"I see," he murmured, setting his cup aside.

A brief silence fell between them, and Madeleine found herself hoping, praying, that he understood the meaning behind her words.

Just as she was beginning to wonder if she should drop another hint, he spoke again, his voice soft and earnest.

"Madeleine," he began, his eyes searching hers. "You know my feelings for you."

Her heart leapt in her chest. "I do," she whispered.

"And you once told me..." He hesitated, as if gathering his courage. "I admit it was during an emotionally tense moment for you, but... you said that you reciprocated those feelings."

"I did," she replied, her voice barely above a whisper. "And I still do."

A look of wonder and hope crossed his face. "In that case..." Clearing his throat, he adjusted his already impeccable cravat. "Madeleine... Will you marry me?"

"Yes, I will," she blurted out, feeling a rush of giddiness, like a thousand butterflies had been set free in her stomach.

They came together in a sweet embrace, murmuring tender words of love and devotion. As their lips drew closer, the promise of their first kiss hanging in the air, the sound of the door opening startled them apart.

"Mama, have you seen my yellow hat? The one with the– Oh." Ellie stopped short, her eyes widening. "Pardon me, I didn't know you had a visitor."

Madeleine and Mr Dubois exchanged a glance, both of them blushing like schoolchildren caught in a forbidden tryst.

"It's quite all right, Ellie," Madeleine said, quickly regaining her composure. "In fact, we have something wonderful to tell you. Mr Dubois and I are going to be married."

Ellie's face lit up with delight. "Oh, Mama, that's marvellous news." She paused, as a thought occurred to her. "We'll invite Mr Wainwright to the wedding, won't we?"

Madeleine laughed. "Of course we will, my darling."

Ellie's smile grew even brighter. "I must tell Phoebe at once," she exclaimed, already turning to leave.

"Phoebe?" Mr Dubois asked, a note of confusion in his voice.

"Mrs Pemberton-Thorpe's great-niece," Madeleine explained. "And Ellie's new best friend."

As Ellie's footsteps receded down the hall, Mr Dubois chuckled. "She seemed to take the news rather well."

"Of course she did," Madeleine replied with a knowing smile. "Ellie welcomes any excuse to see Stuart Wainwright."

Mr Dubois nodded, a thoughtful expression on his face. "There does seem to be something of a romantic nature blossoming between those two."

Madeleine waved a dismissive hand. "Oh, but Ellie is still much too young for love. She's barely eighteen."

"True," he agreed. "Time has a way of flying by however. In just a few short years, that adolescent girl will be a young lady. And then one fine day, Mr Wainwright will come calling on you, asking for your permission to court Miss Eleanor."

She reached for his hand, weaving her fingers through his. "Thank heavens I'll have you by my side when that time comes."

A mischievous glint entered her eye, and she tilted her face up to his. "Now, I believe there was that matter of a kiss?"

Mr Dubois needed no further invitation. With a tender smile, he drew her into his arms and caressed her lips with his own, sealing their love with a promise of forever.

The End

Continue reading...

You have just read Book 4 of The Victorian Orphans Trilogy. Other titles in this series include:

Book 1 - The Courtesan's Maid
Book 2 - The Ragged Slum Princess
Book 3 - An English Governess in Paris

Coming soon:
Book 5 - The Northern Girl's Peril

For more details, updates, and to claim your free book, please visit Hope's website:

www.hopedawson.com

Printed in Great Britain
by Amazon